MW00625032

A dark descent

Legends call it Xibalba—the Place of Fear. But some legends are true.

The discovery of a treasure in the Yucatan sets former Navy SEALs Dane Maddock and Bones Bonebrake on a search for the legendary Maya city of the dead, and into the path of deadly enemies. From ancient ruins to perilous jungles, Maddock and Bones must outwit the vicious Serpent Brotherhood, and find the fabled city before an old enemy unlocks its secrets and plunges the world into shadow. Can they survive the descent into Xibalba?

PRAISE FOR DAVID WOOD AND THE DANE MADDOCK ADVENTURES

"A page-turning yarn blending high action, Biblical speculation, ancient secrets, and nasty creatures. Indiana Jones better watch his back!" Jeremy Robinson, author of SecondWorld

"Dane and Bones.... Together they're unstoppable. Rip roaring action from start to finish. Wit and humor throughout. Just one question - how soon until the next one? Because I can't wait." Graham Brown, author of Shadows of the Midnight Sun

"What an adventure! A great read that provides lots of action, and thoughtful insight as well, into strange realms that are sometimes best left unexplored." Paul Kemprecos, author of Cool Blue Tomb and the NUMA Files

XIBALBA

A DANE MADDOCK ADVENTURE

DAVID WOOD

Xibalba, A Dane Maddock Adventure

Published by Adrenaline Press
www.adrenaline.press
Adrenaline Press is an imprint of Gryphonwood Press
www.gryphonwoodpress.com

Cover by Kent Holloway Book Cover Design

This book is a work of fiction. All events, locations, and characters depicted are products of the author's imagination or are used fictitiously.

ISBN-13: 978-1544284521
ISBN-10: 1544284527

BOOKS BY DAVID WOOD

The Dane Maddock Adventures
Dourado
Cibola
Quest
Icefall
Buccaneer
Atlantis
Ark
Xibalba
Solomon Key (forthcoming)

Dane and Bones Origins
Freedom
Hell Ship
Splashdown
Dead Ice
Liberty
Electra
Amber
Justice
Treasure of the Dead

Jade Ihara Adventures (with Sean Ellis)
Oracle
Changeling

Bones Bonebrake Adventures
Primitive
The Book of Bones

Jake Crowley Adventures (with Alan Baxter)
Blood Codex
Anubis Key (forthcoming)

PROLOGUE
March 19, 1517

It was unthinkable that the lush, fertile landscape could be so deadly, but Diego Alvarez de Castile knew that hell lay concealed beneath the green illusion of paradise.

It was their fifteenth day since the battle near the city the Spaniards had called *el Gran Cairo*—so-named for the towering pyramid-like structures which loomed above the stone houses—thirty-nine days since the expedition set out from Cuba to explore new lands and capture slaves to work the mines and fields of the new Spanish territory. The first meeting with the Indians had gone well. A small party of natives had rowed out to meet them and there had been an exchange of food and other gifts, but the next day, when the Spaniards had made landfall, the Indians had shown their true colors, attacking the landing party with arrows and stones.

Although the members of the expedition were not experienced fighters they had anticipated treachery and were armed with muskets and crossbows, and wore steel armor which offered greater protection than the cloth armor worn by the natives. They had held off the attackers long enough to regain the safety of their ships, taking three Indian captives, though at a cost of two Spaniards dead and several more wounded. Still, it had seemed like a victory, particularly when one of the captives began telling—or more precisely, pantomiming—tales of the magnificent riches in the interior. While the main expedition had continued along the coast of what they believed to be an island larger even than Cuba, Alvarez had taken a party of twenty-five able-bodied men to scout the interior and see for themselves if the stories were true.

Thus had begun the journey into hell.

A third of their group—nine men—had perished, lost to the perils of the jungle: wild beasts, venomous snakes and insects, fevers resulting from seemingly insignificant wounds. All who remained were suffering from lesser afflictions that would, if something did not change, eventually destroy them as well. The one danger they had anticipated and prepared for—attacks by hostile Indians—had not materialized, but then neither had they encountered any of the fabled riches. The significance of this was not lost on Alvarez.

He confronted their guide, the Indian hostage they had taken to calling Balthasar. "You tricked us," he raged, knowing that his wrath would be more comprehensible to the native than his actual words. He made a cutting gesture with his hand. "You led us into this wilderness to die. There is no gold. It was all a lie."

Balthasar quivered in fright, understanding only that the man intended him harm, and waved his arms to placate his captor. He pointed straight ahead, shaking his hand emphatically.

Just a little ways further.

He started in that direction, pulling Alvarez along with him.

"No." Alvarez shook himself free of the other man's grasp. "No more of your lies."

He raised his eyes, looking for the sun through the thick jungle foliage. The expedition had sailed west. If Alvarez turned north now, the small scouting party would reach the coast in a few days, and perhaps find their countrymen waiting. "We go this way."

Balthasar's face twisted into a mask of apprehension, and when the party started in this new direction, he resisted, moving only when Alvarez threatened to drag him along at the end of a rope.

They hacked through the thick vegetation, advancing only about fifty *pasos*—the length of a determined man's stride—before the deepening gloom signaled the approach of dusk. Alvarez set half his men to the task of establishing a camp, while the remainder continued blazing a trail in the waning light.

They barely coaxed a cooking fire to life when one of

the advance scouts hastened into the camp. "*Señor*, come quickly."

Alvarez could tell by the man's eagerness that whatever they had discovered portended well, so he took Balthasar's rope and pulled him along up the trail. They did not have far to go. Just fifty *pasas* from the edge of camp, the thick jungle seemed to both open up and fall away, sloping down into a lushly forested valley. A wide pool dominated the middle of the valley, sparkling in the setting sun, and close to it, a crumbling partly overgrown monolith that looked like it might have been the ruins of a *mezquita*—one of the pyramid temples where the Indians worshiped their heathen gods.

"*Cenote*," Balthasar whispered.

Alvarez knew the word. They had encountered other cenotes along the way; sinkholes that had filled up with water, like natural wells. The Indian seemed to revere them, casting small offerings into each one they passed, but something about this cenote inspired only terror in their hostage-guide. He began gesticulating wildly and whispering in his native tongue. "*Kukul'kan*."

"What are you trying to tell me?" Alvarez hissed, waving his hands. "What is it that frightens you?"

With an effort, Balthasar got himself under control, then he began making an undulating motion with his hand.

"Snake?" Alvarez copied the pantomime, cupping his hand like a striking viper.

It must have been the correct interpretation, for Balthasar next pointed to each of the Spaniards in turn, and then wiggled his fingers as if to simulate walking.

Walking snake, Alvarez thought. *Snake man, perhaps?*

Balthasar now pointed to the cenote, or perhaps to the ruined pyramid, and then to the ground behind him… *No*, Alvarez realized, *he's pointing to his own shadow.*

"*Valle de sombra*," whispered another of his men, who then proceeded to cross himself.

"Snake demons and a valley of shadow," Alvarez said. "He is trying to frighten us from the correct path with imaginary dangers, while leading us to ruin. Look for yourself. There are no fields. No cooking fires. No one has lived there in a hundred years. Perhaps there we will find the treasures we seek. Tomorrow, we will cross this place of shadow, and you will see."

Balthasar continued to chatter urgently, and the return to camp only made him more restive. He kept repeating the same phrases over and over again. "*Bo'oy. Kukul'kan.*" He pulled at the thick rope knotted around his neck, as if trying to drag Alvarez back down the jungle trail, quieting only when Alvarez threatened to beat him with a stick.

During the night, Balthasar used his teeth to tear open the veins in his wrists, spilling his lifeblood on the jungle floor.

The suicide cast a pall over the camp. Alvarez acted quickly to stifle the rising chorus of discontent and fear. "A trapped animal will tear its own flesh to escape a snare. This is no different."

"It is different," challenged Diaz, Alvarez's second-in-command. "He took his life rather than face the Valley of Shadow. And you would have us blindly go in."

"He took his life because his heathen gods demanded it," Alvarez countered. "We who serve the true God have nothing to fear. Do you not remember the words of the Psalm? '*Aunque ande en valle de sombra de muerte, no temeré mal alguno.*'"

"Are we to call you Fray Diego, now?" Diaz shot back. "You will lead us to ruin."

Yet Diaz's tone had lost some of its defiance. In quoting scripture, Alvarez had challenged his men to demonstrate that their faith was stronger than their superstitious fear. There would be no mutiny. But that did not mean the men were happy about it.

They struck camp quickly, leaving Balthasar's body where it lay, and started down into the valley. Their progress was slow at first, but it was not long before they encountered what appeared to be a road, paved with white stones, snaking through the forest. Although the jungle was encroaching on the path, enough of it remained clear to speed them along. By noon, they had reached the valley floor. The trees obscured the ruin, but the road seemed to lead in that direction, so Alvarez kept following it. Not long after, they reached the edge of the city.

At first, they saw only the foundation stones where houses had once stood, but further along, they found standing walls of stacked stone. Alvarez ventured into one of these, and found a large tree—an oak, he thought—rising up from the floor. From its size, he guess some thirty years or more had passed since the acorn first took root, but he sensed the house had been empty far longer than that. Nothing else remained of the people who had once inhabited it.

"This is a fool's errand," Diaz said when Alvarez came out. "The people who once lived here took everything with them when they abandoned this place. There is no treasure. There is nothing here."

"You are wrong, my friend," Alvarez insisted. "The Indians worship their gods by throwing golden baubles into the cenotes. They may have left, but they would not take back their offerings. Perhaps that is why Balthasar did not want us to come here, and even took his own life. He knew that we would plunder the riches given to his false gods. He must have feared their wrath."

This seemed to pique Diaz's interest. "And how would we recover this plunder?"

"One thing at a time. First we must find it. And we are close. I can—"

He was interrupted by a cry of alarm from further along the trail. He and Diaz hastened forward to discover one of the men on the ground in the throes of a seizure. The stricken man's face was scarlet under his beard, and his jaws were clenched, his teeth bared in a rictus. Spittle frothed from between them.

"What happened?" Alvarez demanded. "Was he bitten? A viper?"

Before anyone could answer, the man hissed out a final breath and then was still. The rest of the men began warily searching the vegetation, looking for the venomous serpent that had taken yet another of their number.

Suddenly, Diaz let out a howl of dismay and swatted at his own cheek. "Stung," he rasped.

Alvarez saw something fall from the other man's beard, not a wasp or spider, but simply a sliver of wood, a thorn, perhaps.

Diaz stared at the object for a moment, then went rigid and started to topple over. Alvarez reached out to catch him, and as he did, he heard a soft huffing sound. Something flashed past his face, missing him by less than a hand's width. Alvarez now realized what was happening.

"It's an attack!" he cried, wheeling in the direction from which the projectile had come. As Diaz collapsed, twitching on the forest floor, Alvarez unlimbered his crossbow and aimed it into the nearby thicket. Muskets were all but useless deep in the jungle; the pervasive moisture rendered powder and match wick too damp to ignite. Before he could loose the bolt however, there was a rustling in the leaves and Alvarez caught a glimpse of green scales, like the skin of a viper.

Snake-men! Balthasar's warning came back to Alvarez.

He heard more of the soft huffing noises, and the shouts of alarm became shrieks of pain. From the corner of his eye, Alvarez saw more of his men going down.

They were being wiped out, without even seeing the face of the enemy.

"Follow me," Alvarez called out, raising his sword and charging toward the thicket where he had glimpsed the scaly figure. He swung the Toledo steel blade before him, and as the vegetation fell away, he saw the creature again, all glistening scales, with a crest of bright plumage.

The snake-man was facing him, pointed teeth—like the teeth of a shark—bared in a fierce grin. The creature then hurled something at him.

Alvarez slashed at the object, deflecting it away from his head. His blade rang with the impact. The snake-man turned away, disappearing into the jungle again. Alvarez maintained his charge, hacking at the dense foliage to lay bare the white stone path.

All of a sudden, he found himself in a clearing—a plaza, paved with white stone that stretched a hundred paces to the base of the crumbling pyramid. The cenote formed the edge of the courtyard to his left. There was no sign of the snake-man.

Alvarez turned to rally his men, but to his dismay discovered that he was alone. He waited in silence, straining to hear the sound of footsteps or battle, or even the screams of the dying, but there was nothing. Not even a whisper.

But something *was* moving in the jungle behind him. Sinuous shapes, slithering through the vegetation, silently closing in on him.

He turned and ran, sprinting down the length of the plaza. If he could reach the *mezquita*, climb its flanks and perhaps even reach the summit, he would have the high ground, and his foes would lose the advantage of concealment. If there were not too many of them, there was a chance—a slim chance, but a chance nonetheless—of survival.

His armor grew heavier with every step until he was no longer running but shuffling across the pavement. Halfway to his goal, he paused and turned to see five of the snake-men advancing, hunched over like stalking beasts preparing to pounce. He steadied himself, taking careful aim with his crossbow. The snake-men continued forward, seemingly oblivious to the danger the weapon presented. He let the bolt fly, and one of the creatures let out a yelp as the quarrel struck home. Alvarez threw down the weapon, then turned away and resumed running, the brief respite giving him just enough energy to reach the base of the pyramid.

He clambered up onto its flanks, hauling himself up the crumbling exterior. He tore his helmet off and would have removed his breastplate as well if doing so would not have required precious seconds he did not have. Something cracked against the stone beside him, a hurled stone that bounced away. Alvarez kept going, his heart hammering, arms and thighs burning with the exertion.

A blocky stone structure had been erected at the apex of the pyramid, but time and neglect had taken a toll. The roof was gone and the upright columns that had once defined the entrance were broken or missing altogether, revealing an altar. The back wall still bore faint traces of the painted bas-relief that had once adorned it, a bestial face that might have been a lion or perhaps a wild dog, stylized in the grotesque fashion the Indians favored. In front of it stood a similarly weathered stone altar, and upon it, a small figurine, presumably the likeness of the same creature, resting on its haunches like a sphinx, a shallow cauldron between its front paws. The relic was about the size of a man's head, blacker than charcoal or shadow, but adorned with rings of gleaming gold.

Here at last the treasure he had sought. Despite the urgency of the moment, Alvarez advanced into the ruined temple and reached out to the relic.

It seemed to crumble at his touch, and for a moment, he feared that it was as illusory as the dreams of wealth that had drawn him into the emerald hell, but no... the blackness was just a fine layer of dust or perhaps ash. Beneath the black film, there was creamy green jade.

This prize was real.

He left it on the altar and turned to make his stand.

But the snake-men weren't there. He ventured out of the temple structure, looked down and located them. To his complete astonishment, they were kneeling, heads bowed as if in prayer.

Their passive, almost reverent posture, told him that he was in no immediate danger. Maybe the pyramid was sacred to them, forbidden ground, or maybe they were just going to wait him out. Either way, he could not remain atop the pyramid forever.

Yet, as he lingered there at the summit, his apprehension ebbed. They were not going to attack him, not here atop the pyramid, and not in the plaza below. He was certain of this, though he could not say why.

So certain was he that he returned to the altar and scooped up the jade idol with one hand. The relic would ensure safe passage through the jungle; the snake-men would revere him as the servant of their false god.

He emerged once more from the structure and began his descent. The creatures below remained motionless, but it was not until Alvarez neared the bottom of the pyramid that he saw why.

The snake-men had turned to stone.

Some part of him knew this could not be true. What he had taken for kneeling figures were actually ancient stone effigies, overgrown with dark moss. He even thought he remembered passing them during his mad dash across the courtyard.

But he also knew that these *were* the snake-men, the very same creatures that had attacked the party in the jungle. And he knew with equal certainty that they would not come back to life in order to menace him now.

There was no longer anything to fear. He knew exactly what he had to do next.

With the jade figurine still tucked under one arm, he headed across the courtyard and into the loving embrace of the dark forest.

CHAPTER 1

Miranda Bell rapped her knuckles against the molded plastic body of the dive light and worked the switch again. This time, the bulb lit up, shooting out a beam of white light. She worked the switch again, on and off several times, until she was satisfied that the problem had fixed itself, then slipped the pistol-shaped flashlight into a carrier on her hip.

The light, like the rest of the gear they'd rented from the dive shop in Tulum, was serviceable if somewhat antiquated. She had always used only the best equipment, sometimes field testing prototypes and cutting edge technologies unavailable to the public at large, but that had been in another life. Now she had to make do with whatever semi-obsolete, off-the-shelf equipment she could get her hands on.

She did a final head-to-toe check, then sat down at the edge of the cenote, letting her long legs dangle out over the azure water. She took a breath from the second-stage line of the regulator attached to the AL80 SCUBA bottle on her back to ensure the air was flowing, then turned and looked up at the anxious face of Charles Bell, her father.

"Don't run off," she quipped, before placing the mouthpiece between her teeth.

"Miranda," he pleaded. "Just wait. Half an hour. They'll be here."

Miranda fought the urge to roll her eyes. Her father was just being over-protective, which was, she supposed, his job as a father, but she had no intention of waiting for his so-called marine salvage experts to arrive. Knowing Bell, they were probably some over-priced tour guides who would probably shut them down and call in the local authorities when they realized what they had found.

Sometimes he could be so clueless about the way the

world worked.

What they had found, or at least what they thought they had found, was a previously undiscovered cenote, which was remarkable because the area around Tulum had been extensively explored and mapped, particularly here in the government designated archaeological preserve. The cenote was larger than some she had seen, and not as overgrown. They had stumbled across it during a hike through the forest, and at first believed they must be lost because it did not appear on the map. How this particular hole had gone unnoticed for so long was anyone's guess, but if it was truly uncharted, there was a good chance of finding artifacts of real value inside, which was all the more reason for her to make the dive now, without waiting for the *experts*.

"I'll be fine, Dad," she assured him, and then tapped the GoPro which rested just above the top of her mask. "It's recording, right?"

She knew it was and was only asking to distract him so he wouldn't delay her any longer. Bell held up his tablet computer, which displayed the live video signal from the digital camera. Because she was looking at him, the screen showed Bell holding up the tablet. Some deficiency of the technology prevented the image from repeating to infinity, but the effect was surreal nonetheless. The wi-fi signal from the digital camera would be lost once she was submerged, so Bell would have to wait until she returned to see the fruits of her exploratory dive.

Miranda nodded and then inserted the mouthpiece and scooted forward, dropping down into the water. The weight of her gear bore her down quickly, but only for a second or two, just enough for her to feel the pressure against her inner ear.

Below the surface, the white limestone seemed to glow a cool blue, like some kind of weird radioactive element. The water, only slightly brackish, was crystal clear but the hole was so deep that sunlight did not reach the bottom.

She popped her ears to equalize the pressure and switched on her dive light, probing the depths of the hole. Although the entrance at the surface was only about twenty-five feet in diameter, the cenote—which had, hundreds of thousands of years earlier, been a mostly dry cavern, hollowed out of the limestone karst by geological forces—broadened out in all directions. The overhanging ceiling blocked out most of the daylight, leaving the subsurface environment in a state of perpetual gloom, broken only by the cone of illumination cast by the light in her hand. Her bubbles were glittering silvery globes racing to pool on the stone ceiling above, while she continued at a more leisurely pace in the opposite direction.

The cenote did not have a flat bottom like a swimming pool or well, but undulated in a series of upright protrusions and deep crevices. It reminded Miranda of a gigantic molar. This impression was reinforced by a brownish silt layer that covered the rises, like an accumulation of plaque on a tooth. She knew better than to disturb the silt. Doing so would raise a cloud of the fine particles, effectively rendering her blind, but she nevertheless played her light over the surfaces, looking for any hint of something that might justify temporarily sacrificing visibility.

Something glinted from a shelf of rock off to her left. She swam toward it, her pulse quickening as she imagined carefully brushing away the sediment to reveal a priceless golden artifact.

Just one would be enough to put her father back on top of his game.

But even before she uncovered it, disappointment dashed her hope. An object lay there, an artifact made by human hands, but it wasn't made of precious metal and it wasn't from the Maya civilization. It was a beer bottle. The glint she had seen was from the gold foil around the neck. The label was still intact, and even through the silt she could make out the word: *Modelo.*

Not undiscovered after all, she thought miserably,

kicking back toward the center.

Still, a single piece of discarded trash did not mean the depths of the cenote had been completely plumbed. She swam in a wide circle, looking for a channel or crevasse that might take her deeper still.

After completing a full revolution around the irregular circumference, she moved toward the center and began another circuit, repeating the process in a concentric fashion until she had visually surveyed every square inch of the bottom of the cenote. She noted several deep crevasses, some that looked promising but ultimately yielded nothing of interest, not even more detritus of the modern world.

She checked her pressure and calculated that her air supply would hold out for at least another half-hour. She wasn't deep enough to worry about decompression stops, though given her actual time at depth, it would probably be a good idea to make a slow ascent. That still left her with plenty of time to explore, but she didn't really see the point. The cenote was, in every sense but the literal, a dry hole, and besides, her father was probably tearing his hair out. It was time to head back up.

Just for the hell of it, she decided to stretch out her ascent by swimming in a counter-clockwise corkscrew around the edge of the cavern. The change in perspective helped alleviated the boredom, but the results were no different.

She was almost back to the surface when something caught her eye, or more precisely, the lack of something. Hidden behind a tangle of roots from a tree that had infiltrated down through the ceiling, was a dark spot, like a shadow, into which the beam of her light disappeared completely. There was a void there, something she had missed during her initial descent. She swam closer and began pulling at the roots that blocked the way.

Her original assessment was correct; there was a passage behind the roots, a hollow space in the limestone big enough for her to swim into if she could clear the obstruction at the opening. She drew her knife and began sawing at the roots. They were as tough as cables but after a few minutes of dragging the blade back and forth, she succeeded in removing one. Rather than waste more time cutting, she simply pushed the others out of the way and wriggled through the resulting gap.

She knew that the safe course, the course of wisdom, would have been to simply mark the location of the passage for a future dive. That was what her father would have counseled. But her instincts told her the passage would be just another dead end. It made more sense to spend her remaining air to get a definitive answer than to raise her father's hopes only to have them dashed again.

Her instincts were wrong.

The passage meandered for about twenty yards before turning down and opening up into another spacious cavern.

Miranda's heartbeat quickened again as her light fell upon something that was most definitely not a naturally occurring geological feature. A large block of stone stood at almost the exact center of the cavern. Four feet wide and almost as long, relief images that were recognizable even to her relatively untrained eye as Mayan hieroglyphs adorned its length. She swam in close, keeping her gaze on the object so that the GoPro would capture every detail. There were more carvings on the sides, each a square glyph about eight inches across, no doubt some kind of religious myth or perhaps a historical record; her father would know.

She came around to the far side of the object and caught another glimmer of gold, only this time, it wasn't foil on an old beer bottle. It was the real thing.

The regulator fell from her mouth as she went slack-jawed.

Where the central glyph ought to have been, there was instead a recess in the stone, and inset within was a shiny yellow disk the size of a salad plate. The disk was adorned with a large central glyph of a four-legged creature—a dog, if Miranda was not mistaken—and several smaller images arrayed in a circle around the outside.

She replaced the mouthpiece then drew her knife again and carefully worked the point into the carved recess behind the disk. The golden artifact shifted and then popped free. Miranda brought her free hand around to catch it, but the water slowed her reflexes. The object sank to the bottom before she could grab ahold. It landed with a thud that she could feel vibrating through the water, and threw up a murky cloud of sediment that both marked and obscured the spot where it had hit.

Miranda breathed out an irritated curse, then kicked down into the cloud to retrieve the fallen disk. If it was solid gold, it would be a lot heavier than it looked, maybe too heavy for her to get all the way back to the surface, but she wasn't about to leave without making the attempt. She cautiously extended a hand into the silt cloud until she made contact with something solid. She curled her fingers around the object and tried to lift it.

To her complete astonishment, it came up with hardly any effort, as the murky water below her cleared, she saw why. The thing she was holding was not the golden disk, but a human skull.

She dropped it like it was a snake about to strike, and kicked away with a silent scream. As she shot up to the roof of the cavern her light played across the floor and in its beam she saw more skulls, at least two dozen of them, staring up at her with empty eye sockets.

She yelped again, her heart hammering in her chest.

Get a grip, Miranda, she told herself, taking a deep drag on her air supply to calm herself. *They're just skeletons. They can't hurt you. They've been dead for centuries.*

Except she was wrong about that, too. Most of the skulls lay with their disarticulated skeletons, their flesh and any garments long since decayed to nothing, but some still had ragged bits of decomposing tissue and clothing clinging to them. At least one of the corpses appeared to be wearing blue jeans and a button-up work shirt.

Miranda took another breath and decided it was time to go. This wasn't an archaeological site anymore—it was a crime scene.

But as she turned to look for the exit, she was confronted with not one, but several passages all evenly spaced around the circumference of the room. She couldn't tell which one she had come in through. She was having trouble counting them. There were at least ten, maybe as many as fifteen, all radiating out like the spokes of a wheel.

I am so screwed, she thought, but then shook her head. *No. You've got this Miranda. Think.*

Miranda took another deep breath… or tried to. The air didn't seem to want to come out of the tank. She grabbed the pressure gauge, but it only confirmed what she already knew. She was out of air.

Right the first time, she thought. *Definitely screwed.*

CHAPTER 2

As the old Toyota Land Cruiser rounded the bend, Maria Trujillo saw the old woman standing in the middle of the road and slammed on the brakes. The rutted track was slick from an earlier rain shower and the four-wheel drive vehicle slid forward several feet, but the old woman made no attempt to get out of the way.

The Toyota skidded to a halt and Maria pulled the emergency brake, left the vehicle to idle, and jumped out to make sure the woman was all right.

The old woman stared back at her with rheumy bloodshot eyes. She looked as if she was about to collapse from exhaustion or dehydration, or both, but she managed to summon up a grim, toothless smile. "*Curandera*," she said. "You came."

Maria was not in fact a *curandera*, a traditional healer, but a medical doctor, educated at the Medical College of Honduras and presently working for the Ministry of Health. Nevertheless, she had long since accepted that rural folk, particularly those of a certain age, were incapable of wrapping their heads around the idea that a woman could be a physician.

"*Si, Dona.*" She knew the woman's face, had treated her on numerous occasions previously, but in her role as a rural health care provider for the Honduran government, she had treated thousands of people. Keeping track of names in her head was simply impossible. "But why are you out here on the road?"

"I was looking for you," the woman replied, forlorn.

Maria sighed. "Well, I am here. Now, let's get you back home."

She took the woman's hand, guiding her around to the passenger side of the Land Cruiser. The old woman complied but remained agitated.

"Diego brought a curse upon us," she wailed.

Maria nodded patiently, helping the old woman up

and into the seat. She had no idea who Diego was, or what sort of curse he might have brought upon his fellow villagers. The likeliest explanation was that Diego had gotten drunk and done something foolish. Slept with someone else's wife, most likely. That kind of behavior often resulted in violence. In rural outposts like Opalaca, which wasn't a proper town but just a small community of less than two hundred souls in a cluster of houses and huts built along the side of the mountain road, it was still common for disagreements between neighbors to be settled with machetes.

That didn't explain why the old woman had ventured out from her home, despite knowing full well that it was Maria coming for her once-a-week visit, but Maria figured she would find out the details soon enough. The village was only a couple miles further up the road.

The woman continued to wag her head, and Maria realized she was weeping. "Diego brought the curse. Now we will all die."

Maria gave her a sidelong glance. "Why do you say that, *Dona*? What is this 'curse'?"

"*El Cadejo negro*," the old woman.

Maria had heard the term before. *El Cadejo* was a mythical phantom creature found in folklore throughout the region. It was said to resemble a dog with glowing red eyes. There was a white *el Cadejo*—sent by God to help travelers—and a black *el Cadejo*—sent by the Devil.

"Diego brought it among us. He is a *saqueador*."

Now Maria understood a little better. Diego was a relic hunter, or to use the old woman's preferred term, a looter. It was a common enough activity, particularly among young men with no other prospects for earning a living. He had probably found something in the rain forest, something which the old woman had linked to the superstition of *el Cadejo*. Something bad had probably happened in the village to coincide with that discovery, and the superstitious old woman had blamed the relic hunter.

Sounds like a job for a real curandero, Maria thought. Sometimes the only way to fight superstition was with more superstition. Maybe the mere fact of her presence would be enough to soothe jangled nerves.

As the first houses came into view, Maria saw that the old woman was not alone in her belief. Normally, the road would have been busy with children playing games and spinning tops on the ground, but there was not a single child in sight. A few older men and women stood at the doorway of their respective homes, like sentinels ready to turn away an intruder

"Where is this Diego, *Dona*?"

The old woman raised a withered hand and pointed up the road. Maria continued forward until the old woman's finger moved, pointing off to the side of the road. She wasn't pointing at a house, but at an open field dotted with wooden crosses.

"He'd dead?"

"*Si.*"

Maria frowned and pulled the Land Cruiser to the side of the road but did not shut if off. "How did he die?"

"The curse. It took him."

Maria considered turning the vehicle around and heading back to San Pedro Sula. If villagers had blamed Diego for some misfortune, it wasn't a stretch to believe they might have killed him in an effort to rid themselves of the imagined curse. "How, *Dona*?"

"The sickness. From the dog."

Maria breathed a little easier. "He was bitten by a sick dog?"

"Not bitten. It was not a real dog." She cupped her hands together. "A bowl, carved to look like a dog."

Maria had to struggle to keep her frustration in check. She was wasting her time talking about cursed relics and a dead grave robber. Then the old woman added, "But the curse did not die with Diego. Many more are sick."

That got Maria's attention. Diego could have fallen victim to any number of pathogens during his foray into the rain forest—an infection from a cut or scrape, accidental ingestion of a poisonous plant—and the only way to know for sure would be to exhume his remains, and absent a health crisis, she wasn't about to do that. But if there were others showing the same symptoms, then not only was there a potential crisis, but also other patients she could assess. And hopefully save.

But what kind of infectious disease could have acted so quickly? It had only been a week since her last visit, and nobody had been sick then.

"Show me."

The old woman led her to one of the houses, ominously marked with a black rag tied around a doorpost. A grim looking woman that might have been the older woman's daughter stood watch on the porch, and moved aside to allow Maria to enter, but conspicuously refused to follow. Maria decided to don gloves and a mask before going in, and was immediately glad that she had.

The smell was overpowering, the sour odor of sickness and unwashed bodies. Four patients, two male, two female, lay stretched out on the mats on the floor. One of them—a man, though it was difficult to tell for certain—appeared to be in the late stages of the illness. The only indication that he was even alive was his ragged, irregular breathing. Most of his hair was gone, and what little remained suggested that it had fallen out only recently. His cheeks were gaunt and hollow, but his mid-section appeared bloated, filled with gasses like a decaying corpse. His mouth was crusted with dried blood, as was his exposed skin, which looked like a map of scabs, drawn atop a scaly white rash.

The other patients exhibited similar physical symptoms, but to a less dramatic degree. The two women had most of their hair and only a few patches of the whitish rash on their cheeks and hands, but both were gripped with a racking cough that brought up flecks of blood. The second man's rash was more advanced, and odd welts, almost like slashing cuts, were erupting from the skin of his face and arms.

The skin rash suggested a fungal infection, but the other symptoms reminded her of influenza or possibly a hemorrhagic fever. Even more dramatic than their physical condition however, was their behavior. The three appeared to be in the grip of a major psychotic break.

The man was drawing on the dirt floor with his fingers, leaving wet marks, not letters but strange symbols that surrounded his sleeping mat. His forefinger was a bloody stump at the first knuckle, the symbols drawn in blood. One of the women had begun a similar art project, while the other was content to merely wave her hands in the air, lecturing in a mixture of Spanish and—if Maria heard correctly—Ch'orti', an old Mayan language still spoken in some of the rural villages.

Maria turned to the younger woman at the door. "How long have they been like this?"

The younger woman regarded her with grave expression. "Corazon and Mirasol began to cough three days ago. Ernesto four days. Raul six. He will die tomorrow. Sooner, maybe."

Six days. That meant Diego must have brought the so-called curse to the village *before* her last visit.

"Is anyone else sick?"

To Maria's chagrin, the woman nodded her head sadly. "*Si.*"

Maria's gut churned. "Where are the others?"

The woman gestured behind her. "Out there."

"I don't understand."

"The cough is not the beginning. First, they wander."

Suddenly, Maria's mouth was very dry. The woman was alone on the porch. The old lady who had brought Maria to the house was gone.

"First, they wander," the woman said again, "then they start coughing up blood and fall while walking on the road."

"How many?" Maria managed to croak.

The woman shrugged. "Twenty? Maybe more. We

don't find them all."

The news staggered Maria. Four sick people—five if Diego was included—might be explained by exposure to tainted water or food, or perhaps some exotic toxin on the artifact Diego had recovered, but this was beginning to look more like an infectious disease outbreak, and that was something that neither Maria, nor the Ministry of Health, was prepared to deal with. Nevertheless, there was only one thing to do.

"You must keep them here. All of them. Bring back as many of them as you can find," Maria told the woman as she stepped outside, starting for the Land Cruiser at a fast walk.

The woman chased after her, indignant. "Where are you going? They need medicine?"

"I don't have anything that can help them," she answered truthfully. "But I am only going to the nearest telephone. Then I will return."

She decided not to use the word quarantine. That would only frighten the woman. The truth was, until the disease—whatever it was—ran its course, none of them, not even Maria herself, could be allowed to leave.

Chances were, they were all dead already.

CHAPTER 3

Fighting back her panic, Miranda groped for the supply line for the small pony bottle attached to her main tank. The pony bottle was her emergency reserve—her "seatbelt," she called it, because like the seat belt in a car, it was something she used even though she truly believed she would never need it. And like a seat belt, she knew there was no guarantee it would save her life. The bottle held only a few minutes of air, and if she didn't choose a passage—and choose right on the first try—all it would do for her was prolong the experience of dying.

She let the regulator mouthpiece fall away, replacing it with the one from the "octopus" regulator attached to the pony bottle. This time, she did not indulge her desire for a deep, calming breath, but merely drew in enough to quiet the burn of excess carbon dioxide in her bloodstream.

Think, Miranda.

She closed her eyes, trying to remember exactly what the cavern had looked like when she had emerged from the passage.

The altar, she thought. The golden disk had been on the opposite site.

Miranda opened her eyes again and saw the settling cloud of silt at the base of the carved stone altar. She swam over it, positioning herself against the wall of the cavern, and turned around, trying to match what she now saw with what she remembered. When she thought she was correctly positioned, she turned to the wall and was confronted by three possibilities.

Her first impulse was to pick the center passage, but something about it looked wrong. It was narrower than the passage she remembered, barely wide enough to pass through without scraping her shoulders. She took another breath from the octopus and contemplated the remaining choices, searching her memory for other details about the passage that had brought her here.

She remembered that the passage had sloped down at the end, but unfortunately, so did both of these, the one to the left at a steeper angle. She swept both openings with her light, kicking herself for not leaving marks on the limestone walls or stringing a guide wire.

I screwed up, she told herself. *Rookie mistakes. I knew better.*

Her lungs started to burn again. She blew out the breath she had been holding and took another, deeper this time. There was no point in rationing her air now, and maybe a clear head would increase her chances of making the right choice.

Get over it. Make a choice. Trust your instincts. She almost laughed at the thought. Trusting her instincts had gotten her in this mess.

The light revealed nothing to uncomplicate her decision. She was wasting time and wasting air.

At least conserving battery life in the flashlight wasn't something she would have to worry about.

The answer came to her. Light!

She switched the dive light off and closed her eyes.

True darkness was a rare thing in the modern world. Even on the darkest night there was always some source of artificial illumination close by—light pollution from distant cities and street lamps, the faint glow of electronic devices in sleep mode. It was palpable, something that could be felt even blindfolded. True darkness, the kind of darkness that inspired absolute terror, was reserved for places like this. Underground. Underwater.

But not completely sealed off.

Miranda opened her eyes to the blackness and waited.

A faint blue glow was visible in the passage to the right. Daylight, filtering down through the entrance to the cenote, reflected by the dull white limestone and refracted through the water to reach her here.

The darkness wasn't absolute after all.

She triggered the light switch again and kicked forward into the passage, taking steady breaths from the pony bottle. It seemed to take forever, and for a few seconds, she almost thought she had misread the signs, chosen the wrong passage despite the glow of distant daylight, but then she rounded a bend and saw the roots partially barricading the mouth of the tunnel.

She wriggled through and saw the shimmering blue circle of light fifteen feet away and just a few feet above her head.

She disconnected her buoyancy compensator from the main line and attached the octopus to it, filling it up so there would be nothing dragging her down, and then kicked out for the center, but something held her fast. Her flipper was caught in the tangle of roots.

Miranda felt like screaming. She thrashed for a moment, trying to tear her foot loose, but then stopped herself. Maybe she didn't need the flipper to reach the surface, but then again, maybe she would.

She willed herself to a calm state once more and used her arms to propel herself backward, until the pressure on her ankle lessened. A slight twist of the foot was all it took to slip free, allowing her to kick herself away, shooting through the water like a torpedo.

As she neared the shimmering plane that marked the transition from one environment to another, the image of the surface world came clearly into view. She could see her father, leaning out over the edge, staring anxiously into the depths, even though he surely must have seen her.

Miranda broke through the surface and spit out the mouthpiece of the octopus, sucking in fresh air greedily, even though the pony bottle wasn't empty.

"Dad," she gasped. "I'm okay." She pushed the mask up onto her forehead and gasped down another breath. "You won't believe what I found."

His expression did not change, and as she gazed up at him, she could tell from the set of his jaw that he was not merely worried, but in pain. "That's great, honey," he said, his voice barely a whisper, as if merely speaking intensified his agony.

"Dad, what's wrong? Is it your lungs?"

Despite being a non-smoker and leading a healthy active life, Charles Bell had been diagnosed with chronic obstructive pulmonary disease, which was why Miranda, and not Bell himself, had made the dive into the cenote. She felt a pang of guilt at the thought that her solo dive and the fact that she had clearly pushed well beyond the limits of safety might have induced a stress-related flare-up.

He was breathing fast, breathing hard, but without difficulty. Whatever was causing him distress, it wasn't his COPD.

"Dad?"

Another face came into view, a man with a swarthy weathered complexion and the distinctive broad facial features of someone of Maya ancestry. "*Si, señorita,*" the man said, and then continued in broken English. "Come up out of there and show us what you found."

And then he pushed Charles Bell forward, just enough to show Miranda the knife pressed to her father's throat.

Miranda's blood froze in her veins. She took a deep breath, and raised her hands out of the water. Her buoyancy compensator kept her from sinking. "Hey, take it easy. Don't hurt him."

"Come out of there," the man said again, giving Bell an emphatic shake.

Miranda lowered her hands into the water and dog-paddled over to the rope ladder hanging down from the edge of the cenote. She held herself in place with one hand, and with the other reached down to remove her flippers. Her plan was to also draw the knife sheathed to her right calf, but before she could do this, the man with the knife leaned out to keep an eye on her. She decided to leave the knife where it was. With one thumb hooked around the ankle straps of the fins, she began pulling herself up the ladder.

When she cleared the edge, she saw that the man holding a knife at her father's throat was not alone. A second man stood behind them, a few paces away, machete held loosely in his right fist. Miranda was careful not to make eye contact with either man, or do anything else that might be interpreted as threatening behavior. That was the only way she and her father were going to survive this.

She raised her left foot to the next rung, settled all her weight onto that limb, and then stood up with an explosion of energy. As she straightened, she hurled the dive fins at the man with the machete.

The flippers looked like bat wings as they flew through the air. The man reacted, predictably, by slashing at the fins, knocking them out of the air with his blade. Even before he made contact though, Miranda landed in a crouch a few inches from the edge of the cenote, right beside her father.

The man holding Charles Bell also reacted predictably. Instead of threatening Bell, he focused on the immediate threat. He shoved his hostage away, and swiped his knife at Miranda.

But Miranda was already gone, twisting out of the way. As she came back up, she slipped out of her dive harness, gripped it with both hands, and then spun around like an Olympic hammer-thrower, gathering momentum. The empty 80-liter bottle whooshed through the air and slammed into the man's arm, knocking the knife away.

She struck again. The SCUBA tank arced around and slammed into the man's shoulder with enough force to topple him over the edge, into the cenote.

Miranda planted her foot and hurled the tank at the man with the machete. The projectile struck the raised blade, and although the man did not drop the weapon, the impact staggered him back.

He recovered and got the long knife back up again, but Miranda had her dive knife out and was stalking forward like a panther about to strike. Her fearless aggression must have been too much for the man. He turned and bolted toward the trees.

Miranda started after him, but halted after a few steps. She was barefoot, and if the man changed his mind and decided to take his chances in a knife fight, the reach of his machete would give him the advantage. Besides, she wasn't about to leave her father.

She turned back just as the other man hauled himself out of the cenote. He looked at Miranda and the blade in her hand, then past her at the retreating back of his accomplice, and then he too was running, fleeing the area down the same trail Miranda and Bell had used to reach the cenote.

Miranda sprang forward, trying to block his escape, but she was a half-second too slow. Yet, as he slipped past her, he stopped suddenly, rebounding as if he had just collided with a tree.

No, not a tree, Miranda saw, but something… someone rather, almost as unyielding. It was a man—a local she guessed, judging by his complexion, but he was just about the biggest Mexican she had ever seen. He stood well over six feet tall, with his long black hair pulled back in a ponytail. He wore dark gray cargo shorts and an open Hawaiian floral-print shirt over a black T-shirt, emblazoned with the message *"I'm not saying it was aliens…"* The tight fitting T-shirt accentuated a broad, muscled chest, and his powerful arms, clutching dive tanks, were as thick as Miranda's legs.

"Whoa, *amigo*," the big man quipped in a voice that was deep and sonorous. "*Donde esta el fuego?*"

His accent, not to mention his choice of words, told Miranda he wasn't a local after all, but an American. A second glance told her he was, in fact Native American.

The soaking wet would-be assailant popped back up and tried to slip around the big man, only to come face to face with another man. There was no mistaking the second fellow for a local. He had blond hair and eyes the color of a stormy sea. He stood about half a head shorter than the first man, but was built just as broadly.

The fleeing man turned and bolted away, crashing frantically through the vegetation beneath the trees.

Miranda advanced on the newcomers. "Why the hell didn't you grab him?"

The big man raised an eyebrow then turned to the shorter man. "Yeah, why the hell didn't you grab him?"

The fair-haired man ignored his companion's clearly disingenuous question and stepped forward. "Sorry about that. I guess our timing could have been a little better."

"I'll say." She put her hands on her hips, placing herself directly in their path. "You must be the so-called dive experts my father hired."

The big man's lips twitched into a smile. He cast a mock-accusatory stare at his friend. "Hired? You mean we're getting paid for this gig? You holding out on me, Maddock?"

The other man maintained his patient expression. "I think we got off on the wrong foot. I'm Dane Maddock. This buffoon is Bones." He gestured to a third person behind them on the trail. "And this is Angel."

Miranda's retort died on her lips. Angel, the third member of the party, was a strikingly beautiful Native American woman, tall and lean. She wore a white halter top that laid bare the chiseled shoulders and taut biceps of an athlete.

Miranda shook her head, trying to regain her composure. "That's great, Mr. Maddock—"

"Just 'Maddock' is fine."

"Mr. Maddock," she said again, emphatically. "Thanks for coming out, but as it happens, we don't need your help after all, so you might as well turn around and head back to the resort or whatever."

"Miranda!"

She flinched. Even though she was a grown woman in her early-thirties, her father's stern voice was as powerful now as it had been when she was just a little girl.

Bell stepped forward. "You'll have to forgive my

daughter, Mr. Maddock. She's very independent. Maybe a little too independent for her own good."

Miranda turned to her father. "Dad, we really don't need them. I've got this."

"I'm sure you do," Bell said. "But I asked these men to come here. It's not your decision."

She frowned and leaned in close, whispering. "Dad, I found something down there. Something…" She flicked her eyes meaningfully. "That we probably shouldn't talk about in front of strangers."

"They're not strangers," Bell replied with a paternal smile. "And they aren't just a couple guys I hired off the boat. They're Navy SEALs."

Miranda raised an eyebrow, then turned and cast a dubious eye at the two men. "Navy SEALs, huh? Sure you are."

CHAPTER 4

"We used to be SEALs," Maddock said quickly. Like most special operations veterans, he didn't talk much about his military service. It was a rule of thumb that if someone bragged about being a SEAL or Green Beret or something like that, they were probably lying. He was a little surprised that Charles Bell had been made aware of that detail about Bones and himself. It hadn't come up during their earlier conversation, which could only mean that Tam Broderick had told him.

"That was a long time ago," he continued. "We don't work for Uncle Sam anymore."

"They did teach us how to swim. Sometimes clothed," Bones said with a wink.

"You know I get funding from the U.S. government," Bell said, addressing the blonde woman whom Maddock assumed had to be his daughter, Miranda. "Well, they asked me to let Mr. Maddock and his team check in on us."

Bell looked to be in his late fifties, silver-gray hair trimmed in a crew cut. Miranda lean and athletic, had long blond hair, pulled back in a tight bun which was mostly hidden by the diving mask perched atop her head. The family resemblance was there in their faces, and both had the same startlingly blue eyes. Tam Broderick, who had put him in touch with Bell, had given Maddock their names, but not a whole lot more.

Miranda faced Maddock, one dubious eyebrow raised. "First you're a SEAL. Now you're some kind of government agent?"

Maddock shook his head. "It's not like that. I'm just repaying a favor."

"You just drop everything and run off to Mexico because you owed someone a favor?" Miranda persisted.

"More than one," Bones added.

"And whose fault is that?"

"Screw you, Maddock."

"We were in the neighborhood," Maddock went on, flashing a guilty look in Angel's direction. He was "in the neighborhood" on what was supposed to be a romantic vacation. Diving and treasure hunting wasn't just his job. It was something he loved doing, but all the same, the whole point of the trip to Cozumel had been to spend some time with the woman he was going to marry. Angel had, only half-jokingly, suggested that on their way back to the resort, they could stop at the Union, a sports club in Playa del Carmen, so she could do a little sparring.

"I wasn't," Bones grumbled. "I was on my way to Vegas. Sin City, baby. Right now, I should be hip deep in cheap booze and cheaper..." He glanced at Miranda. "Umm, buffets."

"Anyway," Maddock said, "we *can* help you out. As I told Dr. Bell, we're experienced divers and marine archaeologists. We know what we're doing, and we're happy to help." He paused a beat then added, "In whatever way we can."

"What was that we just walked in on?" Bones asked. "A little trouble with the locals?"

Miranda evidently wasn't satisfied with the explanation. "Why is the government so interested in what my father is doing?"

Maddock glanced over at Bell then shrugged. "You'll have to ask your father about that. I wasn't told much more than that. The person that sent us has her fingers in a lot pies, and seldom feels the need to explain herself."

"Typical," Miranda said.

It was an odd comment, but Maddock didn't press the issue.

"Tam's a tough nut," Bones put in. "But she's on the right side."

"Right side of what?" Miranda countered.

Bones just shrugged.

Miranda frowned, then turned to Angel. "And are you *just* an archaeologist, too?"

"Not even," Angel said, rolling her eyes. "I leave that to these two geniuses."

"She's a cage fighter," Bones said with what might have been mistaken for brotherly pride. Maddock knew his big friend was just trying to impress the other woman.

Miranda however was anything but impressed. Her face darkened in anger or maybe embarrassment. "If you don't want to tell me, fine, but you don't have to be an ass about it."

"Actually, he's not," Angel said. "I mean, he is, but in this case, he's telling the truth." She took a step forward, then reached out to cover Miranda's hand with her own. "Though I prefer 'mixed martial artist.' 'Cage fighter' sounds kind of trashy."

Miranda seemed a little startled by the gesture, but softened. "Seriously? You're an MMA fighter? You any good?"

Angel grinned. "I hold my own."

"I guess you don't get punched in the face very often."

"I try not to," Angel said. "Don't want to end up looking like this ogre." She playfully punched Bones in the shoulder.

Sensing that Miranda was finally going to let down her guard a little, Maddock attempt to steer the conversation back to a more immediate topic. "Seriously though, who was the guy we just ran into? You having some trouble?"

Miranda turned to her father again with a questioning look.

Bell looked uncertain. "Just some hoodlums who thought we had found something important."

"Did you?" Maddock pressed.

"We haven't really had a chance to talk about that yet," Miranda said. "Dad, there are bodies down there."

Bell nodded. "The Maya would sometimes throw sacrificial victims into cenotes."

"I thought they were called Mayans," Angel said.

"That's a common misconception," Bell said. "The people, their architecture, and so forth are called Maya. Mayan is the language they spoke."

Maddock nodded.

"Some of these bodies are a lot more recent," Miranda said. "Maybe just a year or two old."

"Maybe the local drug cartel is using it to dump bodies," Bones suggested. "Could be that's why someone wants to scare you off."

Bell appeared crestfallen. "A pity. But I suppose that would explain why this cenote isn't on the maps." He paused a beat. "Gentleman, I thank you for coming out here, and interrupting your vacations, but it would appear that I was a bit premature with my expectations. We'll have to turn this over to the authorities."

Maddock caught the look of hesitation from Miranda. She bit her lip then spoke again. "Dad, I found something else down there. A gold plate about this big." She held up her hands to indicate the diameter of the artifact she had left behind. "It was on a stone table…maybe it was an altar. I had to leave it behind, but I know exactly where it is."

The cloud over Bell lifted. "Were there glyphs on it? Describe it."

"I got video of it. But that's not my point. We can't tell the police about this place."

"My God, you're right."

Maddock looked from father to daughter, then glanced over at Bones, who just nodded. Clearly, his friend was thinking the same thing he was. "Dr. Bell, before you do anything potentially illegal, you really need to tell us what exactly it is you're looking for here."

Bell pursed his lips together, then answered in a low voice that was almost a whisper. "*Ciudad de Sombra.*"

"What does that mean?" Angel asked.

Bones answered first, his tone almost giddy with anticipation. "It means 'City of Shadow.'"

"And what is that supposed to mean?"

"I don't know, but it sounds awesome."

Maddock shook his head and looked back at the archaeologist. "Doesn't ring a... um, I'm not familiar with it."

Bell managed a smile. "*Ciudad de Sombra* guards the entrance to Xibalba."

Bones' grin broadened. "Told you."

CHAPTER 5

Isabella Beltran looked up from the computer screen as the door to her office opened. She felt an immediate surge of anger. Her orders were explicit and not open to interpretation; when she was working, she was not to be disturbed for any reason. When she saw the face of the man who had dared to breach the sanctity of her workspace, her anger quieted to something more like irritation.

"What do you want, *tio*?"

Hector Canul strode forward until he was standing right in front of her desk, and stared down at her with his customary supercilious contempt. "We have a problem, Isabella."

"I told you before. Your problems are not my problems."

"This time, they are. An American archaeologist has found *Cenote el Guia.*"

"So?"

She immediately regretted her dismissive tone. Canul was the brother of her deceased father though the two men could not have been more unalike. Hector had the dark skin and broad flat features common to Mexico's indigenous population, while Raul—and Isabella, herself—favored the Spanish blood in their mixed ancestry. Hector had immersed himself in his ethnic Maya heritage, while Isabella's father had opted to carve out a place for himself in one of Mexico's new dominant empires, the Gulf Cartel.

It was rare for the descendant of indigenous people to achieve any sort of stature within the drug cartels. The *narcos* typically saw the rural natives as a labor force to be enslaved but never respected, but Raul, perhaps because of his ambiguous physical appearance, had defied those expectations, rising through the ranks of the organization and even marrying the daughter of a senior cartel lieutenant. Yet, despite their differences, Raul had always been deferential to his brother's religious and cultural beliefs, even permitting Hector to train Isabella in the traditions of their people.

After Raul's death, Isabella mother had married Jesus Beltran, the number two man in the Gulf Cartel, but while Isabella had been obliged to take her step-father's name, she felt compelled to honor the choices her real father had made. And even though she had achieved a stature in the organization that her father never dared aspire to, not only supplanting her step-father, but taking control of the cartel's operations on the eastern Yucatan Peninsula, Uncle Hector was always welcome in her house.

"This isn't the first time someone has stumbled upon it," Isabella went on. "Why don't you just do what you usually do?"

"I sent two men," Canul said. "They failed."

"Send two more. Send five."

"It is not enough. There are more of them now. They have already dived on the cenote. It is only a matter of time before they find the bodies. They will contact the authorities, and that will be a problem for both of us."

Isabella frowned. Hector was not wrong. Unlike her late step-father and his predecessors, she favored good business practices over cruelty and violence, but sometimes it was necessary to deal harshly with enemies and turncoats in her own ranks. Disappearing them—not simply killing them, but making them vanish off the face of the earth—was one of the most effective ways to assert dominance and keep the wolves at bay. The uncharted cenote, known only to her uncle and a few others who followed the old ways, was the perfect place to make that happen, but if those bodies were found, everything she had built, everything she had fought for, would be undone. "What do you want me to do?"

"I can deal will the archaeologists, but the *federales* will investigate their disappearance. The search must not lead them to *Cenote el Guia.*"

"I will take care of the *federales.*"

Hector bowed his head. "Thank you."

Isabella expected her uncle to leave, but he remained where he was. "Is there something else?"

The man was silent for a long time as if weighing the importance of the matter. "It is probably just a coincidence."

"Say what you have to say, *tio.*"

"There are reports...rumors, really. Of a strange affliction. A fever that causes delirium and hemorrhaging."

"I have not heard these rumors."

"Not here. It is happening in northern Honduras, not far from the ruins of Copán." Hector paused a moment, then added. "It may be that *el Giua* has been found."

Isabella drew in a sharp breath. She had never really believed her uncle's stories, but the location was right, as were the symptoms he had described.

"The fever is spreading," Hector went on. "The villagers have begun calling it *El Cadejo Negro.* The Devil's black dog." He shrugged. "That may be just another coincidence."

"You don't believe that," Isabella said. She narrowed her eyes at him. "If someone has found *el Guia,* we must act quickly."

Hector, inexplicably, smiled.

"What?" Isabella asked. "You disagree?"

"Not at all. It pleases me that you said, 'We.'"

Maria drove only as far as the main highway, where she could get a signal on her mobile phone, and placed a call to the Ministry of Health.

Her boss at the ministry had responded exactly as she expected him to—moving from disbelief to denial to helplessness. Yes, he would declare a medical emergency, and have army troops enforce the quarantine, but there was little he could do for the afflicted. The government could barely afford to pay doctors like Maria the pittance they currently received; there certainly wasn't the money, resources or manpower available to combat an infectious disease outbreak. He would have to enlist resources from outside the poor Central American nation, and to do that, he would have to make his case directly to the president.

He spoke rapidly, repeating himself several times. Maria could tell he was trying to avoid the subject of her own health, and the likelihood that she had also been exposed to the pathogen. Truth be told, she was too, but there was cause for hope. She had not had direct contact with any of the infected—well, except for the old woman, and that had only been in passing.

Was skin to skin contact a vector? She had no idea.

Honduras had its share of tropical diseases—most mosquito-borne, like malaria and Zika—but this was something else. The first step toward battling it would be to get more information about how it was spreading, and the only way to do that was to return to the hot zone.

She cut short the call and turned the Land Cruiser around, heading back up the mountain road. As she neared the village, she encountered a man walking down the road toward her.

First, they wander.

She stopped in the middle of the road, fifty feet from the man. As he shambled closer, she donned a pair of gloves and a mask, and got out to meet him.

"*Curandera!*" the man called out, as if greeting an old friend.

"*Buenos tardes, señor.* What are you doing out here?"

The man's forehead creased in an uncertain frown. "I…" He shook his head as if unable to think of a reason. "I was looking for you. There is a sickness in the village."

Maria could tell he was grasping for an excuse to explain his behavior, and made a mental note of the symptom. A high fever could explain erratic behavior, but the man did not appear to be in the grip of delirium. His eyes were red as if irritated by some allergen, but otherwise he appeared to be in decent health. It was as if his body had decided to take him for a walk, and now his brain was trying to come up with a rationale for the compulsion.

But what kind of disease made people want to go for a walk?

"Yes," she said. "I know. That's why I am here. Will you take me to the village and show me where the sick people are?"

The man looked hesitant. "I really should…" He frowned again.

"Please. I just want to help."

He took another step as if the urge to keep moving was irresistible.

Maria decided to change tactics. "Tell me about *El Cadejo.*"

The man stopped again. "The dog?"

"Did you see it? Did Diego show you?"

"No. He hid it somewhere. Only a few men saw it. All dead now. I helped bury them."

She had held out hope that all of the infected might have received exposure from some toxin on the artifact Diego had discovered, but if the dog-shaped bowl was gone, it meant the affliction was being transmitted from person to person.

She needed to know more about how the disease progressed. "How long ago did they die? When did you bury them?"

"Diego died three days ago." He took another step. "I should go. I need to—" He broke off with a strangled sound and then was gripped by a coughing fit. The paroxysm lasted only a few seconds, but when the man straightened again, there was blood on his lips.

Three days, Maria thought. Was that how long it took for an exposed person to begin exhibiting the first symptom—compulsive movement—with bloody phlegm following almost immediately thereafter? She needed to know more.

The man immediately resumed walking and Maria

made no further effort to dissuade him. It would take him hours to reach the highway, if he did not collapse along the way. By that time, the army would have the road blocked to enforce the quarantine. She got back in the Land Cruiser and continued to the village. She found the house with the four patients who were showing advanced-stage symptoms, and began gathering as much data about them and the progression of the disease as she could. She took blood samples, even though there was no way to test them, and started IV fluid infusions for all but the sickest man—the one who was swollen like a bloated corpse and closest to death. More fluids weren't going to help him. When she palpated his organs, they felt mushy, as if partially liquefied. His breathing was erratic with long breathless episodes of apnea, followed by rapid, labored inhalations.

She doubted he could survive until nightfall.

After a while, more patients were brought in, all of them feverish and coughing blood, some babbling incoherently. At first, Maria ignored their ravings, but then she realized that all of them kept repeating the same phrases, or at least making the same incomprehensible sounds.

On an impulse, she took a closer look at the symbols scribbled on the floor by the other patients. They weren't identical, but the similarities were nonetheless astonishing. They also looked familiar, though she couldn't say where she had seen them before. As she attempted to sketch a rough facsimile of the symbols, it occurred to her that she was now doing the same thing as the infected.

The sickest man let out a long, rattling exhalation that seemed to go on forever, like a balloon deflating completely. His head lolled to the side and dark blood dribbled from his mouth and nose. Maria knew he was dead. She crossed herself, and then rose to check his vitals just to be sure but before she could, the woman standing guard on the porch called out to her.

"*Curandera,* someone is coming."

For a moment, Maria thought the woman meant more infected patients were being brought in, but then she heard the noise of helicopter rotors beating the air.

She ventured outside and saw, not one but several large dual rotor helicopters approaching from the south. Four of them had what appeared to be military-style Humvees dangling beneath them.

Evidently the president had not wasted any time mobilizing the army.

Within just a few minutes, the first of the helicopters—one that was not carrying a slung vehicle—settled on the road. Even before it was down, a squad of men—presumably soldiers—wearing full environment suits and carrying assault rifles jumped from a lowered cargo ramp in the rear of the aircraft. The helicopter took off quickly, making room for the next aircraft to perform a similar touch-and-go landing.

The Humvees came next. The vehicles were painted black, like the helicopters, with no markings. Maria watched, dumbfounded, as hazmat-suited soldiers climbed into the Humvees and drove off down the mountain road in both directions. When the road was clear, the helicopters began setting down, one in front of another, like a line of school buses. Their rotors continued to spin, hot exhaust pouring from their turbines. The rest of the soldiers, too many for Maria to count, fanned out through the village in small groups. One of the groups seemed to be heading straight for her.

She stepped forward to identify herself, but the soldiers brandished their rifles at her and she froze. A suited figure stepped out of the group, but it was only when the person was standing right in front of her that Maria saw it was a woman—a light-skinned woman with red hair.

"Are you in charge?" the woman asked. She spoke Spanish, but her accent marked her as from somewhere outside Honduras.

"I don't know if I'm in charge," Maria said, "but I am a doctor with the Ministry of Health. I called for the quarantine."

Behind the Perspex face shield, the woman's expression was unreadable. She nodded to the house behind Maria. "Are there infected inside?"

"Yes. One just died. Three more are in an advanced stage. The others are less advanced but still critical."

The woman turned away without acknowledging Maria, and addressed the soldiers. "We've got multiple subjects in here. Secure them for transport."

Maria gasped in surprise when she heard the woman speak in English. "Are you from the American CDC?" she asked haltingly in the same language.

"Something like that," the woman turned away as the soldiers pushed past Maria, moving into the house.

Further down the road, the soldiers were rounding up groups of villagers by the roadside even though they did not appear to be showing any signs of infection. Maria knew she ought to feel relieved by the swift and overwhelming response, but instead she was frightened, and not just because of the strange disease.

After a few minutes, a pair of soldiers emerged from the house, carrying one of the late-stage infected patients on a litter between them. The woman in the hazmat suit stopped them and after a quick assessment, signaled for them to continue. The soldiers took the patient to the helicopter and disappeared inside. One by one, the rest of the infected were brought out on litters, along with the body of the recently deceased man.

Maria approached the woman again. "Where are you taking them?"

The woman held up a hand to silence her, and Maria realized she was speaking to someone using a telephone or radio headset. Maria couldn't hear either side of the exchange, but after the last of the patients was transferred to the waiting helicopter, the woman called out to one of the soldiers. "We've got what we need. Clean it up."

CHAPTER 6

Xibalba was a name Maddock did recognize. It was the ancient Maya version of hell—the afterlife, land of the dead, etc. It wasn't a real place, and he had told Charles Bell as much.

"That may be true," Bell had replied with the same solemn tone. "But the City of Shadow *is* real. The golden plate Miranda found in the cenote proves it."

Maddock had not pressed for more information. The artifact was real enough. He'd seen it in the video footage from Miranda's GoPro. Whether it proved the existence of the City of Shadow or Xibalba or anything else was ultimately irrelevant. Tam Broderick had asked him to assist Bell, and right now, that meant helping the archaeologist recover the golden disk from the cenote, which was why he and Bones were now geared up and ready for a plunge into the depths. Unfortunately, Bell's daughter had insisted on joining them.

"I know exactly where it is," she had told them. "Honestly, you don't even need to go. Just loan me a tank and I'll bring it back inside of twenty minutes."

"Why do you need one of our tanks?" Bones asked. "Come to think of it, why didn't you bring it out on your first dive?"

"He's right," Maddock said. "Diving alone was foolish. You're lucky you made it back. Be grateful for that gift and don't push it."

"Fine," she snapped. "I'll let you tag along."

"You'll let—"

"I know where it is. The longer we're up here arguing about who goes, the more likely it is that those thugs will come back to finish what they started."

That was something that weighed heavily on Maddock's mind. He had only gotten a glimpse of one man of the pair that Bell and his daughter claimed had threatened them. The guy hadn't looked particularly threatening—he had been in full retreat mode *before* Maddock and this friends had shown up—but that didn't mean he wouldn't be back.

He turned to Bones. "Maybe one of us should stay topside. Just in case."

Angel broke in. "I think I can handle things for twenty minutes without a bodyguard."

"I didn't mean…" Maddock felt his cheeks go hot in embarrassment.

"Pretty sure you did, bro," Bones chimed in.

Maddock sighed. "I suppose I did at that." He moved closer. "Don't take any chances. If there's trouble…"

"I'll deal with it," she said, her voice brimming with confidence.

Lord save me from strong independent-minded women, though in truth, that was one of the things he loved about Angel Bonebrake.

He looked over at Miranda, who appeared to be holding back laughter, and shook his head. "We'll let *you* tag along," he told her, "but you're going to play by our rules. Gear up. Make sure you have three sources of light. And we're not going to rush. You cause a silt-out in those passages, and we'll be swimming blind. Once you show us where the entrance to the side passage is, Bones will take the lead and set a guide line."

Bones tilted his head toward his friend. "Maddock used to teach kindergarten. Can you tell?"

Miranda's smile twitched into a frown. She pulled on her dive harness, now outfitted with one of the tanks Maddock had carried in.

"Bones will take the lead," Maddock went on, "because anywhere his fat butt can fit, you and I will have no trouble getting through."

"I got it." Miranda snapped. Then she turned to the edge of the cenote and stepped forward, taking the plunge.

Bones raised his hands in a defeated gesture, then followed her into the pit.

Once he was in the water, head down and breathing

from his supply line, Maddock felt a little better. This was his element; he felt much more at home in the water and under it. There was something dream-like about the quiet solitude and weightlessness that both comforted and energized him. The crystal clear water of the cenote only enhanced the experience.

It was a pity they were going to have to rush the dive.

Miranda was about twenty feet away, waving her dive light to get his attention. She was floating beside a tangle of roots, which partially covered a shadowy opening in the cavern wall. Bones flashed a thumb's up, and swam over and began pulling at the roots. When he had cleared a space large enough for him to pass through, he pulled a double-arm length of monofilament from the reel attached to his harness, tied it off on one of the roots, and then wriggled through. Miranda seemed to take that as permission to follow, and before Maddock could reach the passage, she disappeared from view.

Maddock kicked over to the opening, took hold of the line and went in after her. He could see Miranda, silhouetted in the cone of illumination cast by her dive light. She was moving faster than he would have like, as evidenced by the fine motes of silt that now fogged the passage. It wasn't enough to jeopardize the dive, and he knew that Miranda was not solely to blame since Bones was setting the pace, but it nevertheless irritated him. Cave diving was generally considered the most dangerous recreation sport, as measured by the fatality rate among participants—arguably even more dangerous than high-altitude mountaineering or BASE jumping. There was no such thing as "too careful" when it came to cave diving, especially here where the surface was so deceptively close.

But maybe Bones was right; maybe he was too much of a mother hen.

He soon emerged from the passage into the cavern he had seen on Miranda's video. Bones had left the reel of monofilament at the mouth of the tunnel, with a couple bright green chemlights to increase its visibility.

Maddock took note of all the other passage openings around the circumference of the cavern. Twelve of them, all more or less evenly spaced like the numbers on a clock face. It was unlikely that they were all naturally occurring which suggested that the cenote had served some very important purpose in the ancient past. He regretted that there wasn't more time to carry out a comprehensive survey of the entire system, but the carpet of human remains on the floor below made that an impossibility. Once they had the disk in their possession and were safely away from the cenote, he would have to leave an anonymous tip with the Mexican authorities. Hopefully, once the police investigators were done, they would turn the site over to an archaeological team.

Bones and Miranda were just visible behind the carved stone altar in the center of the chamber. Maddock swam over to them to observe the recovery of the artifact. The disk had dropped into the bone pile, which he now saw was at least a couple layers deep. There were dozens of corpses in the cavern. Most were almost certainly sacrificial victims offered up by the ancient Maya, their bones slowly but surely dissolving away. But, as Miranda had told them, many of the skeletons were clearly recent additions.

The gold disk had landed atop the chest on an older skeleton, hitting with sufficient force to smash through the ribs, leaving what looked like a blast crater in the surrounding sediment layer. Bones was meticulously picking out the splinters of bone that covered the shiny yellow disk, careful not to stir up the silt again.

Maddock knew that if the disk was really made of gold it would be a lot heavier than it looked. He guessed it to be in the neighborhood of ten pounds, which didn't sound like much, and wouldn't have been if they could have walked out. Swimming with that much weight however was a little trickier, and simply trying to pick it up without causing a silt-out would be especially challenging.

Once the artifact was completely exposed, Bones produced a mesh dive bag and began working it under and around the heavy disk. Once it was safely inside the bag, he attached a small yellow lift balloon and used his octopus to inflate it. The lift bag swelled slowly and the line went taut, but the artifact remained where it was, as if anchored to the cavern floor, for several more seconds. Bones kept adding more air until the bag with the disk finally began to rise, then he drew it up effortlessly like a kid holding a helium balloon at a circus, and turned to give Maddock a thumb's up.

While Bones had been occupied with recovering the artifact, Maddock had been busy snapping pictures of the carved glyphs with the camera in his waterproof phone. The cavern had almost certainly been dry when the altar was put here, and given the local water table, that meant the ancient Maya had probably found a way to pump the water out, but evidently only long enough to set up the altar with the golden artifact. Why they had done that was a mystery that Maddock was keen to solve, especially if the answer was somehow related to Bell's search for the City of Shadow.

Maddock returned the signal, then gestured to the exit. They would go out in the same order they came in, with Maddock bringing up the rear and recovering the guideline as he went. Bones went through first, pushing the inflated lift bag ahead of him, and Miranda followed close behind—a little too close for Maddock's liking—kicking up silt in her eagerness. He rapped the hilt of his dive knife against his tank to get her attention, and then made a patting gesture.

Slow down.

Behind the glass of her mask, Miranda gave him a narrow-eyed glare of irritation, but the brief interruption gave Bones a little breathing room.

As Maddock pushed through the screen of roots at the end of the passage, he saw Bones rising up into the azure circle of daylight in the center of the cavern, with Miranda, once again, close on his heels. Maddock shook his head in irritation and was about to turn to untie the monofilament line when he saw Bones abruptly drop his left arm, his hand extended flat like the blade of a knife, slashing the water around him.

Maddock had no difficulty interpreting the message. *Stay back. Something's wrong.*

He let go of the still-tied safety line and kicked hard to catch up to Miranda. He snagged her harness, stopping her just a few feet shy of the opening, and hauled her back. As he did, he bled off some air from his buoyancy compensator to drag them both away from the surface.

Miranda however had other ideas. She twisted around, fixing him with another Medusa glare, and then kicked her legs hard, fighting the downward drag. One of her sweeping flippers struck his arm, breaking his grip, which not only caused her to jet away like a torpedo, but caused Maddock to sink like a stone.

He spat out his regulator, calling a warning into the water, but Miranda never looked back.

Miranda had no idea why Maddock had gone mental and attacked her. Maybe he had gotten his tanks mixed up and was breathing some exotic gas mixture. Maybe he had just panicked.

Or maybe he and his friends are going to try to steal the disk.

She doubted that was the case, but couldn't think of a better explanation to explain the former SEAL's outrageous behavior.

She broke the surface, and immediately kicked back, trying to put some distance between herself and Bones. The big Native American was grinning like a crazy man.

"What the hell?" she shouted.

But then she realized he wasn't grinning exactly. It was more of a grimace. Through his clenched teeth, he said. "We've got company."

It was like *déjà vu* all over again. A rough-looking local—not one of the pair she had run off earlier, but someone new—loomed above her and Bones. The only difference this time was that the man had a big Magnum revolver pointed down at them.

She had badly underestimated both the resolve and the resources of the local hoodlums.

"Stop wasting my time," the man shouted. He spoke English with only a slight accent. "Give me what you found, or we'll kill your friends."

With that ominous threat, the man drew back, but reappeared a moment later, gripping Angel's ponytail with one hand. The other held the muzzle of the pistol to Angel's jaw.

Miranda gasped involuntarily. Where was her father? Dead already?

Bones brought his hands out of the water. "Whoa. Slow your roll, homeboy. You got the pistol, so you keep the pesos. Does that seem fair?"

The man jabbed the pistol at Bones again. "The treasure you found. Bring it up."

"What this?" Bones poked a finger at the yellow lift bag. "I got a keg of beer on the other end of this. *Mucho cerveza, comprende?* The cenote's the perfect place to keep it cool."

Miranda gaped at him. Bones was a cool customer, she had to give him that, but his bravado was going to get them all killed.

Speaking of which, where was Maddock?

"I'm not going to tell you again!" The man shook Angel again.

"Good. 'Cause I'm tired of listening to you repeat yourself."

"What the hell are you doing?" Miranda hissed.

Bones threw her a sidelong glance and spoke through his teeth again. "What do you think I'm doing? I'm stalling."

He looked back up at the man with the gun pressed to Angel's neck. "Okay, you win. But this thing's heavy as hell. I'm not going to be able to pull it up the ladder. So either you let me come up there first, or you're going to have to pull it up."

The man shook his head, then shifted his aim, training the big pistol on Miranda. "You. Climb up with the rope."

"Do it," Bones said under his breath. "Play along. Buy us some time."

"For what?"

"Now!" shouted the gunman. "Move."

Miranda threw up her hands. "Okay. I'm moving."

She swam closer to Bones and gripped the mesh bag with the gold disk. She could feel its heaviness, its solidity. Getting out of the cenote with it wasn't going to be easy, but that gave her an idea.

As she paddled over to the rope ladder, she slid her hand up a few inches, letting her fingers curl around the spring-loaded locking bar of the carabiner that connected the mesh bag to the yellow balloon. She reached up, gripped one of the rungs, and pulled herself up, and as she did, she gave the carabiner a squeeze and a twist.

Suddenly, the lift bag was light as air in her hand.

"Crap!" she said, feigning frustration. "It slipped."

Bones was quick to catch on. "Sorry, dudes. We'll have to go back down for it. Might take a few minutes."

The gunman leaned forward, his face growing dark with rage. He stabbed the gun down at Miranda. "Are you kidding?" he hissed. "That was a big mistake."

Miranda saw his finger tightening on the trigger, and decided that he was probably right about that.

CHAPTER 7

Maddock plunged into the passage, swimming like the world's biggest bull shark was nipping at his flippers. While he didn't know for sure what had prompted Bones to wave him off, two things were certain: he couldn't surface, and he couldn't stay under indefinitely. That left him with only one viable option: Find another way out, and fast.

Air wasn't going to be a problem, or at least, not the most urgent one. He had at least an hour's worth of air in his main tank, which was plenty of time to explore the passages in the other cavern, but it was doubtful that his friends had that long.

He emerged into the cavern with the altar, and immediately turned to the right, and then turned again, plunging into the next passage. It was narrower than the other tunnel, and just a few yards in, it began sloping down. Maddock's first impulse was to stop and head back, but there wasn't enough room for him to turn around, so he kept going, praying the passage would eventually widen out enough for him to reverse course.

It didn't, and the slope remained constant, taking him deeper. Deeper underground was bad because it took him further from the people who needed his help, but deeper underwater was a lot worse because of the increasing risk of decompression sickness. He finally stopped, unbuckled his harness and shrugged out of it, letting it fall. He kicked forward a few more feet then rolled over and did a half-somersault that ended with him facing back up the passage.

Except now the passage was filled with an impenetrable cloud of sediment.

Maddock resisted the impulse to waste breath on a self-directed curse, and instead angled his body down and plunged headlong into the blinding murk. After a second or two, his groping hands encountered the rough stone floor of the passage. He swam forward, fighting back the almost overwhelming urge to freak the hell out.

His SCUBA gear was close by, right where he had dropped it, and he could hold his breath for a good two minutes.

Plenty of time.

His hand snagged something that wasn't unyielding stone. After a few seconds of patient probing, he realized that it was one of the supply hoses attached to his regulator, and after a few more seconds, he found the mouthpiece, bit down on it and took a much-needed breath. His sense of relief however was fleeting. He was no closer to helping his friends, and the clock was still ticking relentlessly forward.

He kicked forward, deeper into the gloom, one hand extended to the wall of the passage, the other dragging the SCUBA rig along with him. The silt cloud diminished a little and soon his field of view was clear again, but he waited until he was back in the main cavern to slip back into the harness.

One down. Ten more to go.

He shook his head. Trial and error wasn't going to cut it. There was no guarantee that any of the passages would lead him back to the surface. He couldn't afford any more dead ends or worse, risk getting lost in a submerged maze. If he couldn't find some way to reduce the uncertainty of his choices, he would have to take his chances with the front door.

Except, the passage back to the cenote didn't feel like a front door. If anything, it felt more like an afterthought; a way to drown the underground temple or crypt to hide its existence.

Twelve passages. One of them leading from the cenote. And eleven others leading God only knew where.

Maddock didn't know a great deal about Maya cosmology and traditions, but he knew their reputation as astronomers, and knew also that their architecture reflected their knowledge of the heavens.

He closed his eyes, trying to visualize the orientation

of the passage to the cenote.

North, he decided, though he was far from confident.

The side of the altar with the golden disk had been facing the opposite direction—south. Was south an important or sacred direction for the Maya?

Jade would know, he thought darkly. Jade Ihara, his ex-girlfriend, was a renowned archaeologist specializing in pre-Columbian cultures. In fact, Miranda Bell reminded him a lot of Jade, and in more ways than just that.

But Jade wasn't here, and regardless, it made sense that the main entrance to the cavern would be on the side facing the front of the altar.

Here goes nothing, he thought, kicking off the wall and swimming to the opposite side of the cavern.

There was a wide passage, sloping gently upward, directly opposite the front of the altar. Maddock thought it definitely felt more like a main entrance than the tunnel back to the cenote, but tried to temper his urgency with a little more caution than he had shown during his earlier explorations.

A hundred feet or so up the passage, the beam of his light hit a shimmery flat plane, like a mirror floating face down in the water. It was the surface.

He kicked furiously to reach it, and a few seconds later, was standing on an inclined ramp with his head and shoulders above water. He sniffed the air cautiously before taking his first full breath. It smelled faintly of mildew and damp, and he kept the mouthpiece ready, just in case he started to feel lightheaded.

A few more steps brought him fully onto dry stone. He slipped off his fins and left them on the ramp, and then decided to leave the rest of his SCUBA equipment there as well.

He clicked off his light and stared ahead into the darkness, searching for the glow of daylight, straining for a hint of a breeze or a whisper of sound.

Nothing.

He clicked on the light and started forward again in a jog, but after going only another fifty feet or so, hit a dead end. A pile of stones, most as big as beach balls, completely blocked the passage. It looked like a cave in.

Maddock played his light on the rocks, contemplating his choices. This felt like the original entrance to the cavern. It was likely that the outside world lay just beyond the collapsed section. Maybe he would only need to move a few of the stones to clear a space big enough to crawl through.

"Nothing ventured," he murmured, and scrambled up the rock pile. He chose one of the smaller stones to start with, gripping it with both hands and pulling it toward him. It moved with surprising ease, releasing a small avalanche of loose dirt and pebbles. He cleared another stone, widening the gap, and as he let the rock tumble down, he saw a glimmer of daylight.

He scooped away more of the dirt, widening the hole and savoring the rush of fresh air from the outside world, then froze when he caught the sound of voices on the wind.

"Crap! It slipped."

"Sorry, dudes. We'll have to go back down for it. Might take a few minutes."

The first voice was female, almost certainly Miranda, and the second belonged unquestionably to Bones, but both voices had a hollow quality, as if they were speaking from inside a bottle.

The next voice was unfamiliar, but clear as a bell. "Are you kidding? That was a big mistake."

The anger in the man's tone galvanized Maddock. He scrambled forward, squirming through the hole with no idea what would await him on the other side. The earthen barrier crumbled beneath him and he spilled out onto a gentle slope covered with green vegetation. As he tumbled down, Maddock found the hilt of his dive knife. He drew the blade and came up in a crouch, ready to engage any enemy.

But he was alone.

"It was an accident!" Miranda's protest sounded louder, but not by much. "I'll dive down and get it. Don't shoot."

Shoot? Maddock thought. *So they... whoever they are... have guns.*

He recalled the old line about bringing a knife to a gunfight, but it was that or nothing. The voices were coming from behind the hill, which was between him and the cenote, and explained why his exit had gone unnoticed. That would give him a slight advantage, but only if he acted immediately. He scrambled back up the hill, knife at the ready.

From the hilltop, Maddock had an unobstructed view of the cenote that was about fifty yards away. There were four men, all holding pistols, though only one of them looked like he was ready to use his. That man was standing at the edge of the cenote, gripping Angel's hair with one hand, but aiming a heavy caliber revolver down into the hole. Another figure—Charles Bell—lay prone on the ground, unmoving.

Maddock charged down the back slope at a full sprint, covering ten, fifteen, almost twenty yards before any of the men by the cenote noticed his approach. Two more bounding steps brought him to the halfway point even as gun barrels began rising and shifting toward him.

Crap!

He adjusted his grip on the knife, holding it in a hammer grip with his thumb resting on the back of the blade, and then without breaking stride, brought his arm around in an overhand motion and hurled the knife forward with all his might.

The blade shot forward, rotating slowly as it arced through the air. Maddock kept running, chasing after the knife. His target was the gunman holding Angel hostage. It was a risky choice. If his aim was off by even a degree, he might hit her instead of the bad guy, but of the four men, Angel's captor was the most immediate threat.

Maddock's aim was true, but as the knife reached the

end of its journey, rotating completely around so that its point was leading again, the man flinched. Instead of striking home, piercing the man's left eye socket, the point merely sliced a bloody furrow in the man's cheek as the knife sailed past.

Maddock kept running, acutely aware of the fact that he was now completely unarmed and facing four enemies with guns. The element of surprise was gone, but he still had one ace up his sleeve: he wasn't alone.

Angel reacted even faster than the gunman. She twisted around to face her captor, caught hold of his shoulders, and rammed her knee up into his solar plexus. The man curled over the point of impact like a worm on a fishhook, his gun and Angel's ponytail both falling from nerveless fingers. Still gripping him, she pivoted around, sling-shotting the man into one of his confederates, flattening both of them. And just like that, the odds were even.

Almost.

The men still had their guns.

As he reached the fray, Maddock saw Angel squaring off against one of the remaining gunmen. He also saw the man's pistol lining up for a center-mass shot.

There was nothing Maddock could do. The man was too far away, beyond Angel's reach, too. Maddock did the only thing he could think of, lowering his stance and tackling Angel to the ground.

In the instant that he did, something erupted out of the cenote. Maddock caught a glimpse of gold—Miranda's blond head—and both the gunman and Miranda went down in a tangle of limbs.

Maddock spotted the large-frame revolver lying where it had fallen and made a grab for it, but at the edge of his vision, he saw the remaining gunman line him up in the sights of his semi-automatic, and reversed course, twisting the other direction as the pistol discharged. A patch of ground near the discarded weapon—and right where Maddock had been just a millisecond earlier—erupted in a spray of dirt. The gun roared again, and again, and Maddock kept rolling, barely staying ahead of the bullets that stitched the ground in his wake.

Then the gun went silent. Maddock rolled a couple more times just in case, then scrambled to his feet in a fighting stance. Only there weren't any enemies left standing. Angel was kneeling over the man who had just tried to shoot Maddock, hammering him mercilessly with her fists, and Miranda was straddling the man that had tried to shoot Angel, pinning him down in a classic front-mount position.

Somebody taught her how to fight, Maddock thought, absently.

That left the two men that Angel had flattened during Maddock's initial charge. One of them—the guy with the big Magnum revolver—was down for the count, but the other man was struggling to rise. Maddock pounced, flattening the man with a two-handed hammer blow.

Another flash of movement from the cenote caught Maddock's attention. He whirled around, ready to meet this new threat, but it was just Bones, crouching over in a fighting stance and gripping his dive knife, ready for combat.

Maddock let out the breath he hadn't even realized he was holding, then grinned at his friend. "Perfect timing."

CHAPTER 8

As Bones and Maddock secured the four attackers with zip-ties and heavy tape, Miranda and Angel tended to Charles Bell. He had a one-inch gash in his right temple, courtesy of a savage pistol-whipping administered by the thug with the big gun. The blow had knocked him out cold, but he roused easily and reported none of the worrisome symptoms that would indicate a concussion. The wound was shallow but bloody. Fortunately, Angel knew a thing or two about wound care. She cleaned the laceration with bottled water and closed it with butterfly sutures from the first aid kit they had packed in.

Miranda glanced over at the row of captives, and pointed to one of them. "This is the guy that was running away when you showed up."

"His buddies made it here awfully fast," Maddock remarked.

Although they were only about ten miles from the coastal resort city of Tulum, the cenote was in a remote corner of the archaeological preserve, accessible only by primitive Jeep trails and a two-mile cross-country hike.

"What are we supposed to do with them?" Miranda asked.

Bones fixed one of the men—the one that had earlier menaced Angel and was presumably their leader—and nodded his head toward the cenote. "I say we just make 'em disappear."

Maddock knew that his friend wasn't seriously proposing cold-blooded murder, but their captives didn't know that. The local man went pale and shouted something into the strip of tape that covered his mouth.

"Not a bad idea," Maddock said, playing along, "but first, we should find out what they're doing here and who they're working for."

"What makes you think they're working for anyone?" Miranda countered. "Maybe they're just *banditos.*"

"*Banditos,*" Bones echoed, savoring the word. He reached out and yanked the tape away, unleashing a stream of curses from the captive, all in Spanish.

Bones glanced over at Angel. "You must have hit him pretty hard. He completely forgot how to *habla Ingles.*"

He pressed the tape back into place, then drew his knife and held the blade close to the writhing man's eye. "Now, let's try again, *bandito.* I'm going to take the tape off, and then you're going to tell us what you're doing here and who you're working for. *Comprende?*"

The man glowered at him for a moment, but then nodded.

Bones ripped the tape away again, eliciting another curse, but then the man spoke in English. "It's like she said." He nodded at Miranda. "We are bandits. We saw them diving for treasure in the cenote. The treasure belongs to us, not some gringos."

"How did you find us out here?" Miranda asked.

Maddock shot her a warning glance, hoping she would get the message. *Let Bones handle this.*

"Two gringos driving out in the forest? It wasn't hard to find you."

As the man spoke, Bones kept the knife in his view, testing the edge of the exposed blade with his thumb. Now he lowered the knife and picked up the big revolver the man had dropped. "This is a nice gun," he said.

He wasn't wrong. It was a Smith & Wesson Model 686, an L-Frame revolver with a six-inch barrel, chambered for .357 Magnum ammunition. It was a hefty gun, too, though in Bones' massive hands, it didn't look quite so intimidating.

"I think I'll keep it," Bones continued. "You don't mind, do you?"

The man said nothing.

"But what I can't figure is how a piece of crap hoodlum like you managed to get his hands on a piece like this. Makes me think you're more than just a…" He grinned. "*Bandito.* So, let's try again. Who are you working for?"

The man set his jaw, pursing his lips together to signal that he was done talking.

Bones regarded him for a few more seconds, then let his gaze drift to the other men. "All right, I didn't want to have to do this, but it looks like you're not giving me a choice. Maddock, I'm gonna need a quart of motor oil and four sticks about seven inches long. You know, twice the length of your...."

"Yeah, we get it," Maddock said quickly, cutting him off. He rose and headed over to where they had stacked their gear, pretending to look for the items.

"What are you going to do with those?" Miranda asked, feigning innocent curiosity. She knew exactly what Bones was doing, and didn't seem the least bit appalled by it.

Something about that bothered Maddock. He thought about how she had fearlessly and efficiently taken down one of their assailants, and decided there was more to Miranda Bell than was apparent at first glance.

"It's a trick I learned in the service," Bones replied with gleeful anticipation. "Guaranteed to make a man talk... unless he dies first. It's pretty ugly. The motor oil is the most important part. See, there's no way to get that stick in without it."

"In where?"

Before Bones could answer, another of the captives began squirming and shouting into his gag.

"Hold up, Maddock," Bones called out. "Let's hear what this joker has to say."

He gagged the first man again, then ripped the tape off the second man's mouth. "Okay, *amigo.* Start talking."

"They hire us to follow them," the man said, nodding at Bell and his daughter. His English was broken but passable. "Give us guns and money. Said to follow them. Ten thousand pesos if we take whatever they find."

"Who hired you? Cartel?"

The man shook his head. "No. Two men. I don't see them before. Rich guys. They try to hide it, but I see their fancy haircuts and girly fingernails."

"Mexicans? Gringos?"

"They don't sound like gringos, but…" The man shrugged. "They say just the old man and the girl. Didn't know they have company."

"Yeah, we like to screw up the best-laid plans of dirtbags and dipshits. You guys are the latter, in case you were wondering."

Maddock knelt next to Bones. "Come on, you've got to know more than that. How did these guys know to come to you?"

The man shook his head, helplessly. "I swear. I don't know."

"Anyone else coming? Got some friends waiting out there in the woods?"

The man shook his head.

Bones looked at Miranda. "What do you think? He telling the truth?"

Miranda considered the question with exaggerated gravity. "I don't know. Seems like there's only one way to really know for sure. Stick and motor oil."

"Please," the captive begged. Tears were streaming from his eyes and there was a faint smell of fresh urine in the air.

Bones silenced him with the tape strip then rose to his full height. "That's all he knows. Typical lightweight. No stamina. I say we strip 'em naked and stake 'em out." He winked at Miranda. "That's an old Cherokee trick."

"I don't think we'll need to go that far," Maddock said, no longer completely sure that his friend was still joking. "We've got their guns, and their phones and keys, too. It'll take 'em a while to get free, and they aren't going to be able to come after us or call for help. I'm more worried about the guys that hired them."

"Wait!" Angel called out. She strode forward until

she was standing right in front of the man who had earlier held her at gunpoint. She regarded him coldly for a moment, then with the swiftness and fury of a rattlesnake strike, lashed out with a low kick. The man's head snapped back, and he crumpled, unconscious. Angel turned to Maddock. "Sorry, just needed to get that out of my system."

Maddock grinned at her, then turned to Bell. "Someone's clearly after you. Any idea who it is?"

Bell shook his head, but his eyes were darting back and forth uncertainly. "Nobody knew we were coming here."

Maddock felt certain that Bell knew more than he was saying, but decided not to press the issue. "I've got an idea how we might be able to figure it out, but first we need to figure out what's so important about that disk." He glanced over at Bones. "Speaking of which...where is it?"

Miranda cringed a little. "I had to cut it loose."

"Good thing, too," Bones put in. "That was quick thinking."

Maddock knew his old friend well enough to recognize the compliment for what it was. Bones was doing what he always did, compulsively angling for a romantic liaison with a beautiful woman he'd only just met. At some point, he would even convince himself that it was true love, that she was "the one." It was a familiar pattern, except Maddock got the distinct feeling Miranda Bell would prove immune to Bones' charms. And that would drive the big Cherokee crazy.

"All right," Maddock said. "First we recover that disk. Then we figure out why it's so important. Maybe then we'll know why somebody thinks it's worth killing for."

CHAPTER 9

While assisting Charles Bell at the cenote—and saving his life—technically satisfied the terms of the favor they owed to Tam Broderick, there was never a question in Maddock's mind about parting company with the archaeologist and his daughter. Not while they remained in danger, and certainly not while the actual significance of the discovery in the cenote was still a mystery.

After leaving the cenote, they headed back to Tulum, but remained there just long enough to drop off their rental cars and pick up a new ride, a Chevrolet Tahoe with plenty of room for the five of them and all their gear. Then, they got back on the highway and headed south, away from the resorts on the coast where, or so Maddock hoped, Bell's as yet unidentified enemies would be looking for him. They booked a single room at a budget motel and, after checking to make sure that no one was observing them, headed inside where Bell immediately brought out the golden disk and Miranda brought out her mobile phone.

"No bars," she grumbled.

"Can't call your boyfriend?" Bones said, trying—and failing—to sound casual about his inquiry.

Miranda shot him one of her trademark withering glances, and turned her back on him.

"Smooth," Angel said, shaking her head.

Maddock took a seat at the table across from Bell. "So, tell me about the City of Shadow, and why that thing is so important."

Bell didn't look up but continued to study the disk, moving his fingers over the glyphs engraved on its surface like a blind man reading braille. "Like most other ancient cultures, the Maya believed in an afterlife in the underworld, which they called Xibalba."

"I'm familiar with it. It was their version of hell."

Bell inclined his head. "There are similarities, and

not just with the Biblical hell, but other ancient traditions. Egyptian, Greek, Hindu—all of them describe a place where the dead experienced horrifying torments. Xibalba means 'place of fear.' The best description of it is found in the *Popol Vuh*—"

"Pope of who?" Bones interjected.

Maddock shot him an irritated look, as did Miranda and Angel. Bones was always irreverent, but he seemed to be trying harder than usual, probably in a misguided effort to impress Miranda.

Bell took advantage of the interruption and went into full professor mode. "*Popol Vuh* translates to 'The Book of the People.' It's a collection of mytho-historical narratives of the Kiche Maya people of Western Guatemala. Oral histories, recorded and translated by an eighteenth century Dominican friar named Francisco Ximénez. Most of what we know about the beliefs and traditions of the Maya people, we owe to him and the *Popol Vuh*."

Bell paused several times as he spoke, taking rapid shallow breaths, as if simply talking was an ordeal. Maddock had noticed him wheezing and panting during the earlier hike from the cenote and suspected the man had a serious underlying health issue, but unless it put them all at risk, it was not his place to ask.

"That said, we know that Ximenez's own beliefs and the rules imposed by the Church clearly influenced his scholarly work. He said as much in the preamble. I suspect he may have emphasized the similarities between the Maya creation myth and the Genesis account.

"The book begins with the story of how the gods created men and animals. The first versions of humanity were flawed and the gods destroyed them with a flood of resin."

"Sounds familiar," Bones said, then caught himself. "Wait, what? Resin?"

Bell went on without missing a beat. "The account then turns to the exploits of Xbalanque and Hunahpu, the so-called 'Hero Twins.' They were the sons of Hun

Hunahpu, a god-figure who was defeated and sacrificed by the Lords of Xibalba in the Underworld. The twins were brought to the surface world by their mother. When they grew up, they were summoned to the Underworld by the Lords of Xibalba to play the ball game." He paused. "Are you familiar with the Mesoamerican ball game?"

Maddock nodded. "Sort of like a cross between basketball and soccer. Knock a ball through the hoop without using your hands or feet."

"And the losing team would get sacrificed to the gods," Bones added.

"Or sometimes the winning team," Bell said. "It was considered the highest honor. Every pre-Columbian culture had some version of it, and it's an important part of the myth. The twins travel to Xibalba, surviving various trials and murder attempts by the Lords of Death along the way, to ultimately defeat the Xibalbans and get their revenge."

Maddock nodded again. "Okay, that's the story. What's it got to do with that?" He pointed at the disk.

"The *Popol Vuh* is the primary source of information about Maya traditions, but it's not the only one. There are temple carvings and references in the three surviving codices—actual written accounts from before the arrival of the Spaniards. The one thing all the stories—written and oral—agree on is that Xibalba is a real place.

"Understand that even the most elaborate myths may contain seeds of truth. For all its fanciful aspects, the myth of the Hero Twins is basically describing a power struggle between rival societies—one that worships the Lords of Death, and one that worships the Sun and Moon. Strip away gods and magic, and the *Popol Vuh* is the story of Post-Classical Maya culture rising from the ashes of a great collapse.

"The Maya civilization existed, in one form or another, for three and a half millennia, so as you can imagine, their society underwent some dramatic evolution, and unfortunately, our knowledge is woefully incomplete. We know that the civilization reached its peak during the Classical period, from 250 BCE to 900 CE, but then abruptly collapsed, particularly in the south where entire cities were abandoned.

"You've probably heard people say that the Maya civilization vanished without a trace, or something to that effect. That's an exaggeration of course, but something unusual happened in the tenth century that undid a thousand years of progress. The Maya certainly didn't disappear though. Over the next five hundred years or so, they regrouped, particularly here in the Yucatan, and while they never regained the full glory of the classical days, they were doing quite well right up until the Spaniards came knocking.

"The *Popol Vuh* is generally thought to be a symbolic account of how one of those Post-Classical Maya cultures—the Kiche Maya—defeated rival societies, whom they subsequently vilified as demons. If that's true, the so-called Lords of Xibalba may have been the all-too-human rulers and priests of a rival society."

"But you think there's more to it than that," Maddock finished.

"I do. And this…" He patted the disk. "This is going to help me prove it."

"How?"

"This artifact is from the Classic Maya period. The Maya people comprised many different language groups. The dominant language was a form of Ch'olti—we call it Classic Maya. It was probably used throughout the Maya territory as a *lingua franca*, or possibly just by the educated class. We know a great deal about spoken Maya languages because of the work of Spanish scholars who recorded a phonetic alphabet, and because many of those languages are still spoken today, but the study of Maya written language is more problematic because there are only a few surviving examples, and not all of them are in the same language."

"Sort of like how English and Spanish use the same

alphabet?" Maddock said.

"Exactly. But thanks to some recent discoveries, we're making progress. And because this disk uses a Classic Maya form of written language, we know that it predates the rise of the Kiche Maya possibly by hundreds of years. It confirms that some aspects of the Hero Twins myth were known before the collapse."

Bell tapped the figure in the center of the artifact. "This is a representation of the Maya Lightning-Dog. We don't know the names of deities from the Classic period, but the iconography is ubiquitous across Mesoamerica. The Aztecs called him Xlotl. He was the god of lightning and storms, but is also associated with the cardinal directions. A guiding deity, and the escort for the souls of the dead, showing them the way to Mictlan, the Place of Shadows. In the *Popol Vuh*, the twins sacrifice a dog belonging to the Lords of Xibalba—"

"They killed a dog?" Bones interjected. "Not cool. You never kill the dog."

"Didn't the Cherokee eat dogs?" Maddock said, grinning.

Bones glared at him.

Bell smiled. "They brought it back to life to show their power over death itself, an action that ultimately enabled them to defeat the Lords of Xibalba. But I believe that myth, like all the others, is a symbolic description of real events. A real journey to Xibalba.

"The prominence of the dog icon tells me this disk is a map. A guidestone, pointing the way to what I call the City of Shadow."

"If it's not meant to be the literal afterlife," Maddock pressed, "then what is it?"

"Perhaps it refers to a rival civilization, unknown to history, which caused the collapse. We'll know for certain when we find it." Bell shrugged. "I can only translate part of it here; the rest is fairly complex. But I'm certain that we're on the right track."

"It still seems like a bit of a leap," Maddock said.

"I say we go for it," Bones said. "We've followed

fainter trails than this."

"True enough." Maddock said. "I can see why treasure hunters and tomb raiders might want to find this place, but why is Tam Broderick interested?"

Bell spread his hands in a gesture of ignorance. "You would have to ask her. I can only surmise that she is privy to some piece of vital classified information."

Maddock knew from experience that Tam would play her cards close to the vest, revealing only enough to get them started. She probably had what she thought were good reasons for secrecy, but it was aggravating nonetheless.

He nodded. "I guess we'll have to figure it out once we find the City of Shadow."

"Yes," Bell agreed. "Unfortunately, I'm not going to be able to finish deciphering the guidestone without some help."

"We need to go somewhere civilized," Miranda said. "Somewhere with cell reception and Internet."

Bell shook his head. "The kind of help we need isn't available online. There's only one person who can help us. Tony Griego at the National Institute of Anthropology and History. He's the definitive authority on translating Mayan glyphs and the site administrator at Chichén Itzá . It's just a couple hour's drive from here."

"Tomorrow," Maddock said. "Right now, we could all use some rest."

Bell conceded with a shrug and resumed inspecting the artifact, but Maddock suspected the older man was grateful for the respite.

He turned to Bones. "Flip you for first watch."

Bones dug out a peso coin and balanced it on his thumb. "Call it."

Angel cleared her throat. "Unless that's a three-sided coin, you're going to need to come up with a better system."

"Four-sided," Miranda added, stepping forward.

Maddock grimaced but tried to play it off. He turned

to Angel. "Well, I was hoping you'd keep me company for my watch."

Bones grinned at Miranda. "Tag team it? You know... wrestling?"

"You can keep dreaming," she replied, caustically. "And you," she pointed at Maddock, "should know better. Angel and I don't need supervision."

Maddock threw up his hands. "My bad. Everybody gets a shift. Do you want to make the schedule, or will you at least trust me to do that?"

Miranda shrugged. "Knock yourself out."

Bones chuckled, then threw himself down on one of the beds. "Just wake me up when it's my turn." He laced his hands behind his head and immediately began snoring.

Maddock nodded to Miranda. "You want first watch? Your dad might appreciate the help translating that disk."

Miranda nodded. "Sure. But I won't be much use to him. He's the expert. I just do the heavy lifting."

The admission caught Maddock by surprise. "I thought you were..."

"An archaeologist?" She shook her head. "Not me."

"It's not too late," Bell called out. He laughed, but broke off in a fit of wheezing.

Miranda gave a tight sad smile. "He should be home," she said in a low voice. "Teaching classes. Not out here in the middle of nowhere looking for lost cities. But try telling him that."

"Why isn't he?" asked Angel.

"Remember a couple years back how the world was supposed to end?"

"2012. The Maya apocalypse."

"Yeah. Didn't happen, right? Well, a couple years before that, Dad co-wrote a book with this New Age guru all about how the end of the Maya calendar wasn't going to be the literal end of the world, but the beginning of...well, a new age. The other guy made all the wacky claims. Dad was just supplying the scholarly stuff. The book deal was supposed to pay for his retirement. It sold pretty well for a couple months, right up until January 2013, then...pffft."

She made a little explosion with her fingers. "He tried to go back to teaching, but the university revoked his tenure. They called the book an embarrassment. Didn't want anything to do with him. And then, because it never rains, but it pours, he started having trouble breathing. COPD." She shook her head. "Can you believe that? He's not even a smoker. They say it was probably from years of breathing dust in the field. He's early stage III, so it could be worse. The meds help and he doesn't need to carry around an oxygen bottle yet, but he can't dig and dive like he used to."

"So why is he out here?" Angel asked. "Is it just about the money?"

Maddock was glad that Angel was there to ask the question. Miranda would probably have taken offense if he had asked it, but she seemed a lot more receptive to Angel.

"Not really. There are other ways to make money. I think what he really wants is a shot at redemption. Finding *Ciudad de Sombre* will be his legacy, but he can't do it alone. That's why I decided to take a leave of absence from my job and come help him."

"What do you do?"

Now Miranda hesitated, frowning, her gaze flickering from Angel to Maddock. "Well, the answer I'm supposed to give you is that I do consulting work for an international tech development company."

"You're a spook," Maddock said. "CIA?"

Miranda's mouth twitched a little, but she offered neither confirmation nor denial.

"Well that explains why you're so badass," he said, hoping she took it as a compliment. It explained a lot more, like maybe why Tam Broderick—a senior operations officer with the Agency—had taken an interest in Bell's activity.

Miranda now grinned, her gaze returning to Angel.

"It's just a job. I was always badass."

Angel's laughter was loud enough to prompt Bones to growl. "Stop yipping, you freaking coyote. People trying to sleep here."

"I guess you really don't need our help," Maddock admitted.

Miranda surprised him with a genuine smile. "No, it's cool. I'm glad you guys are here."

CHAPTER 10

The night proved uneventful, as did the two-hour drive into the Yucatan interior to the ancient Maya city of Chichén Itzá , located just a couple miles off the main highway on a cramped two-lane road which they shared with buses bringing tourists from Cancún. The ruins weren't visible from the road, which came to a dead end at a parking lot where crowds of visitors in hats and sunglasses and reeking of sunscreen were lined up and waiting for the site to open. Bell led them away from the groups and onto the grounds of a nearby resort hotel.

"Tony's main office is in Piste, a couple miles from here, but he keeps a suite here so he can be close to the site," Bell explained.

"Isn't there a museum or something?" Maddock said.

"Yes, but Tony's not directly involved with that. It's more of a gift shop anyway. Chichén Itzá is the second-most visited archaeological site in Mexico. Unfortunately, all these visitors touching the ruins and chipping off pieces of masonry for souvenirs have taken a toll, so the government is doing what it can to limit the impact. Most of the monuments are roped off. You can look but you can't touch."

"So no sightseeing?" Bones asked, sounding a little disappointed.

"I guess you're welcome to join the horde," Bell said with a forced smile. "But expect to be disappointed."

Bones shrugged. "We're here. Might as well check it off the list." He turned to Miranda. "How about it? Up for a walk?"

Maddock braced himself for the expected shoot-down, but Miranda surprised him by glancing over at Angel. "I'm up for it if the rest of you guys are."

Maddock shook his head. "We should probably stick together and keep a low profile, at least until we've got what we came here for."

"If Tony can help me make sense of the guidestone," Bell said, "you'll have a chance to see ruins that aren't on the tour route."

"Not yet anyway," Angel remarked.

Bell asked the receptionist at the front desk to ring Griego's suite, and after a short but enthusiastic exchange, they were shown to the anthropologist's room. Antonio Griego was a stocky man with salt-and-pepper hair and neatly trimmed beard. His naturally olive complexion was burnished to a deep bronze by hours spent under the Yucatan sun. Like many archaeologists Maddock had met, he looked more salt-of-the-earth than ivory-tower-academic-elite.

"Charles," he boomed in English. "You should have let me know you were coming."

"It was a spur of the moment thing," Bell explained before making introductions. Then he got to the point. "We came across some interesting inscriptions yesterday, and frankly, I'm a little stuck. Have you got a few minutes to take a look?"

"Something tells me that if you're stuck, this will take longer than a few minutes, but let's have a look and see."

Bell opened his laptop computer and showed Griego pictures, not only of the guidestone—as Bell had taken to calling the golden disk—but also several still images of the stone altar in the cenote, taken from Miranda's GoPro and Maddock's phone. The guidestone itself was safely tucked away in Maddock's daypack.

Griego flipped through them quickly, giving them only a cursory examination. "Interesting. Where did you find these?"

"I'm not quite ready to reveal that yet, but when I am, you'll be the first to know."

Griego chuckled. "I'm sure you wouldn't dream of breaking any of our laws, but I don't need to tell you that context is important when translating. Since you're not willing to share, I'll assume this is from a virgin site. Underwater, if I'm not mistaken. A cenote?"

Bell nodded.

"Here in the Yucatan?"

This time, Bell just gave a coy smile, which Griego answered with one of his own. "Well, this is a remarkable find. A written account of the journey to the Underworld from the Classical period. You probably already figured that much out."

"Yes. It's similar to the story of the Hero Twins, but there are differences." Bell leaned over the computer and clicked forward to a shot of the guidestone. "And it's obviously a much older version. This is where I'm getting stuck. I have an idea what some of the symbols mean, but there are variations with which I'm unfamiliar. More important, I don't know how they fit together. This disk tells a story, but I can't read the final chapter."

Griego leaned forward, until his face was just a few inches from the screen, and began scrutinizing the image. He spent several minutes like this, unmoving except for his eyes which were moving back and forth. Finally, he straightened. "I can see why you've hit a wall," he said, his tone evincing defeat.

Bell sagged a little, his disappointment palpable. If Griego was stumped, the search for the City of Shadow was over before it had begun. Bell extended a finger to one of the glyphs. "I know that's the symbol that indicates the cenote that is the entrance to the Underworld, but it feels like something is missing."

Griego's eyebrows came together, then rose as if inspiration had struck. "Maybe not." He stood up abruptly. "There's something you should see. Come with me. Bring your computer along."

Maddock and Bones exchanged a glance. Griego seemed trustworthy enough, but looks could be deceiving. Bell however, hurried after his colleague, leaving the rest of them with no alternative but to follow along. The Mexican archaeologist took them to a garage behind the main hotel building and gestured to a row of four-seat electric golf carts. "The resort lets me use these to access the site. We won't all fit in one though."

Bones spoke up almost before Griego had finished speaking. "I got this." He slid into the driver's seat of the second cart. "Ladies, your chariot awaits. Miranda, you want shotgun?"

Miranda rolled her eyes. "I'll ride with my dad."

Maddock shook his head and circled around to take the seat beside Bones, but held his tongue until they were loaded up—three to each cart, Angel riding with the two of them—and rolling at a brisk walking pace down the broad grassy path to the ruins.

"Dude, you're embarrassing yourself," he said, speaking in a low voice, even though there was little chance of being overheard by the occupants of the first cart.

"When has that ever stopped me?" Bones retorted with a grin. "Besides, the day I need your advice about women is the day I turn in *mi cojones.*"

"You've definitely got a lot more experience with what not to do. But believe me, you're not her type."

"What makes you say that?" Bones looked at him sidelong. "You think you're her type? Careful. Little sister might not like that much."

Angel leaned forward. "I think 'little sister' is Miranda Bell's type."

Maddock looked back at her. "So it wasn't just my imagination?"

"Nope. It's not the first time I've had to deal with it." She gave his shoulder a squeeze. "Don't worry, babe. You *are* my type. End of story."

Bones reacted as if he'd received an electric shock. "You mean she's into…" He trailed off, eyes widening and lips curling in a lascivious grin as the movie started playing in his head, but after just a moment, his smile fell and his head snapped around to look at Angel. He shuddered and looked away. "Gah. Bleach. Now."

He gripped the steering wheel and stared straight ahead in silence for a moment, but then said. "Maybe she just hasn't met the right guy, yet."

Angel let out a snort of disgust.

Further discussion on the topic was mercifully cut short as the Chichén Itzá complex came into view.

Bell had not been exaggerating the impact of tourism. The wide grassy areas separating the monumental buildings were crowded with visitors taking selfies, and vendors hawking hats and jaguar masks or playing pan flutes for spare change. The latter seemed to recognize Griego and mostly kept their distance, but one or two were bold enough to approach Maddock, waving their wares and shouting, "Five dollars, gringo?"

"It's like a frigging Renaissance faire," Bones grumbled. "Mexican style."

Maddock chuckled in agreement but, despite the obnoxious intrusion of commercialism, he could not help but think about the history of the place. The guidebooks he had read indicated that Chichén Itzá was one of the few Maya cities that had not collapsed at the end of the Classic period, but had been occupied from about 600 CE until the arrival of the Spaniards, nine centuries later.

The centerpiece of the site was, unquestionably, *El Castillo*—the Castle—which was the name the *conquistadores* had given to the seventy-nine-foot-tall pyramid Temple of Kukulkan. The pyramid was remarkable for reasons beyond the obvious. The staircases rising up the center of each side of the pyramid had exactly ninety-one steps—three hundred-sixty-four in total—which when combined with the platform at the top, meant a step for every day in the solar year. Additionally, the temple was oriented so that, on the equinoxes, the shadow from the northwest corner of the pyramid, cast on the north balustrade, gave the appearance of a snake wriggling down over the course of the afternoon, ending at the base where it met the head of Kukulkan, the feathered serpent god, just before sunset.

That was what the guidebooks said anyway. Maddock made a mental note to ask Griego if it was really true.

Their guide however turned south, away from El Castillo, and headed down a trail into the surrounding forest. For a few seconds, Maddock lost sight of the ruins, but then another ancient structure rose up directly ahead of them. The building looked a little like a pyramid that had been sliced off at the base; terraced stairways and steep sloping walls that rose to a broad platform, upon which had been built a cylindrical tower—unusual in in Maya architecture—topped with a crumbling dome.

Griego parked his cart directly in front of the building and got out. "This is *El Caracol*," he said. "The Snail, so-called because of the spiral ramp inside the tower. We are in the Casa Colorada group here. This was the heart of Chichen during the Terminal Classic Maya period. There are older structures in the Osario, but they are less well preserved."

"It looks kind of like the minaret of a mosque," Angel murmured.

"Or an astronomical observatory," Maddock said.

"Actually, you're both right. Astronomy was a major part of the Maya religion, and this place was both a temple and a way for them to observe the heavens. The windows in the dome were aligned with various astronomical events, the movement of Venus at certain points in the year and so forth. There are window slits in the tower that only permit the entrance of light for a few seconds only on the equinoxes, which enabled the priests to maintain an accurate calendar system. And I think it also holds the answer to your question."

He disconnected the rope barrier blocking their path and gestured for them to follow.

"I guess it's good to know the right people," Bones said, then lowered his voice so only Maddock could hear. "Do we trust this guy?"

"Bell seems to," Maddock replied. "But that's no reason not to stay on our toes. And somebody's bound to notice us climbing around a restricted area."

"Want me to stand here and look pissed off? That should keep people away."

"If not, your stench will do the trick," Angel said.

"Love you too, little sister."

"Maybe just until we're inside," Maddock said. "No sense in getting separated."

Maddock took Angel's hand and together they fell into step behind the others who were now ascending the steps of El Caracol. Bell struggled to keep up with Griego, his wheezing giving way to an alarming coughing fit as they neared the doorway leading to the tower. After a minute or two of rest, he indicated that he was ready to continue, and followed Griego through the rectangular entrance. Maddock signaled for Bones to catch up, and then he and Angel headed inside as well.

Inside the passage spiraled gently up to a two-tier platform where they were able to look out across the site. El Castillo and several other monuments were visible above the tree tops, but Griego was more interested in something inside the structure. He clicked on a penlight and shone it on the wall.

At first glance, it appeared to be rough undecorated stone, but as Griego traced his finger across one of the blocks, Maddock began to see the outline of a Mayan glyph, badly eroded by the passage of time. "Here is the same image," Griego said.

"A cenote," Bell said, nodding. "But the image on the guidestone almost certainly predates Chichén Itzá ."

"You're making an assumption, Charles. This isn't the symbol for a sacred well. You see these pockmarks here?" He tapped several spots around the edge of the brick. Maddock had trouble distinguishing the spots from the stains of time, but Bell evidently did not.

"The Milky Way! Of course."

"When the glyph for cenote—literally 'hole'— appears in conjunction with the Milky Way, it becomes *orificio que conduce al cielo.* The hole that leads into heaven."

Bones laughed as he joined them. "I knew a Catholic

schoolgirl who had one of..."

"Don't make me push you off this platform," Angel threatened, cutting him off.

"What's the significance of the Milky Way?" Maddock asked.

"From this window, at night, with no artificial light, the view of the Milky Way rising above El Castillo is spectacular. The Maya believed it was the mystic road that souls walked into the underworld."

"A road in the sky that leads underground," Bones said. "Sure. Why not?"

"So the hole leading to heaven is a doorway?" Maddock said.

"It could mean doorway or portal, but the word is most often translated as 'maw.'"

"Maw. Mouth."

Griego turned to Bell. "Show me the pictures again."

Bell opened his laptop and Griego flipped through the stills until he found the one with the glyph Bell had mistaken for 'cenote.' He tapped his finger on the adjoining carving. "When I see this, I'm certain of it."

"I have to confess," Bell said. "I have no idea what that is."

Griego shone his light at another section of the wall, and traced an image that was roughly the same. "It isn't a glyph. It's a constellation. Serpens."

Bones leaned down and scrutinized the image on the screen. "It looks like Humpty Dumpty to me. Got the big oval in the center and the stick arms and legs. Come to think of it, it looks like one of Angel's self-portraits."

She punched him in the shoulder, hard enough to make him wince. "Ow."

"I gotta agree with Bones," Maddock said. "I don't see a serpent."

"That's because it doesn't just represent a serpent. The central figure is Ophiuchus, the snake bearer. The horizontal line running through it is the serpent: Serpens Caput, representing the serpent's head, and Serpens Cauda, the serpent's tail."

Bell was also unconvinced. "The Greeks saw Ophiucus and Serpens in the stars, but that doesn't mean the Maya did."

"True," Griego admitted. "And our understanding of Classic Maya astrology is woefully incomplete, but some iconography is universal. Scorpio, just to name one example, is the same in both cultures."

"So what's the message here?" Maddock pressed. "Follow the stars?"

"If you connect the temples of old Chichén Itzá — walking the path as the ancient priests would have, starting to the south at *Edificio de las Monjas*—The Nunnery." He pointed to the back wall and then began moving his fingers, pointing out the general location of the unseen monuments. "The House of Dark Writing. El Caracol—here." He turned and pointed out the window to a pyramid they had passed on the way in. "The Tomb of the High Priest, there. And there…" He pointed to a spot to the northeast. Maddock couldn't see a temple there, but just a hollow with no trees. "The cenote. The serpent's maw. It's all connected. The new city, with El Castillo, the temple to Kukulkan, the feathered serpent, at its center, follows the same path leading to the other sacred cenote. The Maya believed that Kulkulkan went ahead of Chaac, the rain god, who lived at the bottom of the cenote. This symbolism appears over and over again in their architecture."

"Kukulkan," Bones echoed. "The Aztecs called him Quetzalcoatl, right? We know all about him."

"Kukulkan was the chief deity of the Post-Classic Yucatec Maya," Bell said. "The Kiche called him Q'uq'umatz. But the worship of the feathered serpent deity traces back to a much earlier tradition. In the Classic period, he was Waxaklahun Ubah Kan, the War Serpent." Bell sounded breathless, but not because of his disability. "They would have followed the same design in the placement of their holy cities. This is what the guidestone is trying to tell us. Follow the path of the serpent to find the City of Shadow."

Griego looked at him sharply. "*Ciudad de Sombre?* Is that what you seek? I would have thought you had learned your lesson by now, my friend. Please don't mention that I helped you. I have a reputation to protect."

"You don't believe Xibalba was connected with a real place?" Angel asked.

"Whether or not it was, searching for it panders to the sensational. You might as well search for Atlantis, or the Seven Cities of Cibola."

Bones coughed loudly and Maddock grinned. "Thanks for the help," he said. "We'll say we figured it out from watching the History Channel."

He let the matter of their goal drop while they made their way out of the tower, but when Bell paused for a rest, Maddock approached him. "So now we've got a map. What's the next step?"

"We have to find the start of the road. A sacred site that corresponds to the serpent's tail. I'll need Internet access to compare astronomical charts and Maya cities."

Maddock nodded. "I know a guy who might be able to help with that."

Bell nodded. "My instincts tell me we'll need to look to the south. The alignment of the guidestone in its original setting, and the serpent path here in the architecture all seem to follow that basic rule."

"How far south?"

"Honduras. The ancient Maya capital of Copán. It was a major city in the Classic period, and a major cultural capital. It's also almost exactly due south of here. If we can locate this glyph in the ruins there, we'll know we're on the right track."

"Maddock," Bones' voice had lost its usual sardonic edge, a sure sign that something was wrong. "Don't be obvious about it, but take a look at my eight o'clock."

Maddock made a show of stretching, as if trying to work out a kink in his neck, to hide a visual sweep of the area indicated. As he did, he glimpsed someone ducking into the woods about seventy-five yards up the trail leading back to El Castillo.

"He rabbited," Maddock said. "Did you get a look at him?"

Bones shook his head. "No."

Miranda now took note of their discussion. "What's up?"

"I think we attracted some unwanted attention."

Miranda evidently knew better than to question the assessment. "How do you want to play this?"

"I think it's time to take in a little culture." He turned to Griego and Bell. "Would you mind walking us through the route you just showed us?"

Bell started to protest. "I don't think that's really—"

Miranda cut him off. "Dad. We really need to do this." She took his hand and led him down the steps.

An uncomprehending Griego just shrugged and went ahead of them down a footpath. "I can show you the rest of the Casa Colorada group. The House of Dark Writing may be of interest to you in your search."

As the archaeologist launched into a comprehensive history of the site, Maddock lingered with Angel, ducking behind the south end of the observatory. A few seconds later, a lone figure came into view. He had the dark hair and complexion of a local, but wore nicer clothes and, more tellingly, wasn't carrying an armful of cheap souvenirs. Maddock drew Angel further along the side path, out of the man's view, and waited until he had passed before creeping forward slowly, just in case the man wasn't alone. There was no sign of other watchful eyes, and the man did not appear to have noticed that anyone was missing from the group he was following, but Maddock remained wary.

"He's following us, all right."

"You think he's just another hired gun?" Angel whispered.

"Hard to say. I guess we'll have to ask him. Wait here." He started forward, moving swiftly but stealthily, trying to stay directly behind the man to avoid detection.

Further up the trail, Bones was putting on a show,

gesturing wildly and talking loudly about the structure they were approaching—the Nunnery.

It wasn't an actual nunnery, and never had been, but that didn't stop Bones from making obscene jokes.

Maddock got within ten yards of his quarry before the man realized he was being stalked.

He whirled, a panicked look in his eyes, and then bolted.

Maddock made a grab for him, but the man slipped through his fingers, and charged off at an oblique angle, headed for the treeline.

"Crap!" Maddock snarled. He gave chase, even though he knew the effort would prove futile. There was little chance of catching the man before he reached the woods, and even less chance of finding him once he slipped into the dense jungle.

But just as the man reached the edge of the forest, he stopped abruptly and appeared to rise off the ground, as if attempting a backflip. The maneuver ended with him flat on his back and Angel standing over him, one foot pressing down on the man's throat.

She raised her eyes to Maddock as he drew near. "I love you, but you should know better than to tell me to wait."

"Noted," Maddock replied. He knelt beside Angel's struggling captive. "All right, friend," he said in Spanish. "Start talking. Why were you following us?"

"Following you? No, *señor*. You are mistake—"

Angel's foot pressed down harder, cutting off the denial.

"Let's try that again," Maddock said. "Why were you following us?"

The man emitted a strangled sound until Angel eased off a little. "I was only going to warn you."

"Warn us of what?"

The man's reply was a hoarse whisper that had nothing to do with Angel's boot on his neck. "*La Hermandad de la Serpiente*. They will never let you find *Ciudad de Sombre*."

CHAPTER 11

Isabella Beltran kept a firm grip on the saddle with her thighs, remaining perfectly erect as the stallion cut around the barrel, executed a three-quarter loop, and charged off again. She held the reins loosely, letting the animal do what it knew how to do, but ready to assert her authority if it needed a reminder. It did not.

Not anymore.

Early on, when she had first acquired him, she had been obliged to exert a much firmer hand, but now he not only knew who was in charge, but knew what he was supposed to do and did it without being goaded.

Animals seemed to learn that lesson so much better than humans.

They rounded the second barrel, but as the stallion started to gallop toward the next, she spotted Hector's car rolling down the drive. She thought about finishing the practice run; it was what the stallion would expect and she hated to interrupt him since it would only confuse him the next time they rode, but knew that her uncle would not have made a second in-person appearance in as many days if the matter were not important. She tugged on the reins, turning the horse toward the fence at a trot as Hector pulled to a stop on the other side and got out to meet her.

He had been in her thoughts a lot of late, and not just because of the risk of what might be revealed if the cenote became public knowledge. The possibility that *el Guia* and the curse which clung to it might be real had brought all of Hector's stories back to the surface, making her question the choices she had made.

She wanted her father, God rest his soul, to be proud of her, but had he wanted her to follow in his own footsteps, or her uncle's?

"I thought you were going to call me," she shouted. "Did you decide not to involve the *federales*?"

Hector looked pensive as he approached the fence. "The archaeologists managed to overpower the men I hired to deal with the situation."

Isabella reined the horse to a stop, but did not dismount. "Do you need me to arrange an intervention?"

He shook his head. "The damage is done. I have decided to try a different approach. That's not why I'm here."

"The other matter? Honduras? Did someone really find *el Guia*?"

Hector would not meet her gaze. "They're all gone."

"Gone?"

"Dead."

"What do you mean *all*? Everyone with the fever?"

"Everyone. The village is gone. Torched."

Isabella stiffened. "You need to get control of your people, uncle."

"It wasn't…" He hesitated. "The order did not come from me. I'm not certain what happened. There may be another player. Or… something else."

"But you have lost control of the situation," she snapped. She took a breath. "I'm sorry, Uncle, but you must realize how important it is to get this situation resolved."

"I do," he said. "I intend to take care of it personally."

"What do you need from me?"

"Right now, just a way to get there quickly and discreetly."

"Done." That was the simplest thing he could have asked for. The cartel's transportation network routinely moved both people and cargo—drugs, guns, cash—from Columbia to the Texas border and back again. "I will have Garcia make the arrangements."

Hector looked her in the eye. "And something else. If something happens to me…"

Isabella sucked in a breath. "Don't say that."

"*El Guia* must be recovered at any cost. You know this is true. And if I fall, you will have to finish this."

Isabella stared back at him for several long seconds. "Whatever you need, *Tio.*"

Maddock hauled the man to his feet, gripping him by his shirtfront. "*Hermandad de la Serpiente*? Serpent brothers? What the hell does that mean?"

The man quavered in fear, but said nothing coherent.

"Who are these serpent brothers?" Maddock pushed, giving the man a shake. "Are you one of them?"

The man shook his head, but Maddock couldn't tell if it was an answer or a plea for mercy.

The rest of the group was coming back up the path to join them. Griego looked dismayed, but did not intervene. Bones, however, moved in close, looming above the man. "Motor oil and wooden stakes," he said with gleeful menace. "I'll get him talking."

"They paid me to warn you," the man gasped. "That's all I know."

"Who paid you? Give me a name?"

"Nobody knows their names. They are the old one who guard *Ciudad de Sombre.*" The admission seemed to restore some of the man's courage. "They won't let you find it. They will kill you to protect the secret. I was sent to warn you."

"The City of Shadow," Maddock repeated. "You know about it?"

"*Si.* Everyone knows about it."

"Starting to seem that way," Bones muttered.

"Do you know where it is?"

The man shook his head again, emphatically, as if the question both frightened and offended him. "No one knows. The Shadow must remain hidden or the world will die."

"The mumbo jumbo is strong with this one," Bones said. "Let me handle this."

"You're not going to get anything from him," Miranda said. "He's just hired help. Like the guys that tried to rough us up back at the cenote."

Maddock was inclined to agree. "At least now we know who's behind it."

"Serpent Brothers?" Bones was dubious. "Sounds like the name of the world's worst boy band."

Maddock relaxed his grip, holding the man at arm's length. "Tell the Serpent Brothers that if they want us to stop looking, they're going to have to stop with the threats and vague warnings, and meet with us, face to face. Got it?"

The man just stared back at him, goggle-eyed. Maddock held onto him a moment longer, then let go. The man stumbled back a few steps, then took off running, plunging into the trees and vanishing.

Bones frowned and crossed his arms over his chest. "You sure that's a good idea, Maddock?"

Maddock thought about the man's dire warning— *the Shadow must remain hidden or the world will die*— and shook his head uncertainly. "I'm starting to wonder if any of this is a good idea."

Doug Simpson read the report again, hoping that he had missed something the first time, but the results remained what they were.

The problem wasn't the data. It was him. He was in over his head.

It had been foolish of him to think that he was up to a job like this, and indeed, when he had applied with the company, fresh out of the biotech program at UC Davis, he had not really expected to land the position. He was better suited to being a lab assistant, not head researcher, but the company was desperate for qualified personnel. The company was flush with cash, but nobody reputable wanted to work for them. There were rumors of unethical, even criminal behavior, but Simpson had ignored them. The scandals were yesterday's news. The biotech world was fickle that way; today's hero was tomorrow's goat, and who could tell what next week would bring?

As far as his own qualifications were

concerned…well, hell, research was all trial and error anyway, wasn't it? He could handle that.

Now people were going to die because he couldn't pull a miracle out of his ass.

The field team had brought back more than a dozen subjects. A sternly worded memo, straight from the boss's desk, had directed that they be referred to that way—not victims or patients, but *subjects*. All were presently in isolation, under Bio-Safety Level IV conditions, each one receiving a different treatment regimen to knock out the as yet unidentified infection that was killing them all.

Disgusted, he pushed away from his computer workstation, and was about to head out for a cigarette when the door to the lab opened and the boss walked in, accompanied by the red-haired *Latina* who had led the field team. Simpson didn't know her name; he wasn't even sure if she actually worked for the company, or had been brought in as an outside contractor.

He jumped to his feet. "Mr. Sca—"

The boss raised his hands, cutting him off. "Doug, you know how I feel about that. My dad was Mister."

Simpson gave a contrite nod. He was still having trouble getting used to the whole first-name basis policy. It just felt wrong, especially when addressing the head of the company, but the boss was insistent. Just as he insisted that the people in the isolation unit be referred to as *subjects.*

"Alex," Simpson amended. "What can I do for you, sir?"

"Sir?" Alex shook his head in feigned disgust. "That's really not much better." He did not introduce his female companion, but looked past Simpson, staring at the information displayed on the computer monitor. "How goes it?"

Simpson swallowed nervously. "Not good, I'm afraid. None of the therapies we've tried have had any effect. I mean, zip. Nada. We've lost three already, and two more are in bad shape. The others…" He shook his head.

"None of the conventional treatments are working?" Alex said, though he didn't sound at all disappointed. Simpson thought he actually sounded excited about the news. His face must have revealed his shock because Alex went on. "Don't forget our mission, Doug. We're innovators. The whole point is to develop a new therapy. It's good that this thing beats everything else we've got. If it didn't there wouldn't be any need for something new. And we would all be out of a job."

It was a rather cynical outlook, but Simpson understood. As terrible as this disease was, its resistance to the usual battery of drug treatments represented a singular opportunity in the highly-competitive biotech industry. The cure would be a silver bullet, effective not just for treating this disease, but potentially dozens more. And they would control the patent for it.

But only if he could find that cure.

"If we can't find something that works in the next forty-eight hours," Simpson replied, "we may be out of a job anyway. At least as far as this agent is concerned. The progression is like clockwork, and so far, we're looking at 100% mortality, though our sample size is admittedly very small. Aside from the obvious tragedy of that, it's going to pose a real problem with the research."

"What do you mean?"

"We're having difficulty culturing the agent outside of a living host. It evidently needs a very specific set of biological, chemical and physical conditions in which to propagate. Which means that when the last of the patients die, we won't have a way to test any of our therapies."

"What about lab animals? Rats? Monkeys?"

"The white mice seem to have a natural immunity. We suspect it has something to do with their naturally high metabolism. If that's the case, we'd be looking at the same limitation with most small animals. We might have better luck with a larger primate—a chimpanzee for instance, but we don't have any here."

"Get some. I don't care what it costs."

"It's not just a question of money. There are strict international rules governing the use of primates in research. Transparency is a big deal. We might be able to get a few through...um...unofficial channels, but that's a very high-risk solution."

"That sounds like an awful lot of trouble." Alex frowned and glanced over at the red-haired woman. "Do you think you can locate a few more human subjects?"

Something about the casual way he said it sent a chill down Simpson's spine.

"It shouldn't be a problem," the woman said. "But this is a waste of time. I told you. There is only one way to remove *maldición de la sombra*."

Alex smiled broadly, showing lots of teeth. Simpson imagined crocodiles smiling like that just before they chomped on their prey. "So you keep telling me. But I need results sooner, rather than later. You go find your lost...whatever it is. And Doug here will keep pursuing his line of research. Maybe we'll both get lucky."

"Maybe it's already burned itself out," Simpson said, nervously. "That would be lucky."

Alex turned to Simpson. "Don't be such a gloomy Gus, Doug. We didn't give the world death and disease. That was God's doing. We're just turning something bad into an opportunity." He leaned closer. "You find the cure for this, and we'll be the gods of a brave new world."

CHAPTER 12

Maddock leaned forward over the steering wheel, as if by getting closer to the windshield, he might have a better chance of seeing through the deluge. It was a futile effort. The tropical rainstorm, which had come seemingly out of nowhere, was dumping water by the bucketful. He could see the windshield wipers—twin black lines waving back and forth furiously in a losing battle with the rain—but everything else was a green-gray blur. He let his foot off the gas pedal, moved it to the brake pedal, and brought the rented SUV to a complete stop.

"Have you considered pulling off the road?" Angel asked from the passenger seat.

He shook his head. "Too much chance of getting stuck."

"Or swept away in a mudslide," Bones put in from the back seat. "God, this place is a hole. I can't believe we traded Cancún for this."

Maddock glanced in the rear-view mirror, curious to see what Bell's reaction would be. They were only in Honduras because the archaeologist had insisted that the ancient Maya city of Oxwitic—better known by the Spanish name, Copán—was the most likely location for "the tail of the serpent," the beginning of the road that would lead them to the City of Shadow.

Maddock wasn't so sure. While it was true that Copán had been one of the most important cities in the southern portion of the Classic Maya cultural area, Copán wasn't exactly a "lost" city. The site, located in western Honduras, near the border with Guatemala, had been thoroughly explored and cataloged by archaeologists, and it seemed very unlikely that they would simply happen upon something new. Additionally, it was well over four hundred miles away from the cenote where they had found the guidestone.

While that wasn't a lot in modern terms, it would have been a significant distance to the ancients.

But it was Bell's show, and they couldn't rule it out without first paying a visit.

"I thought you SEALs liked getting wet," Miranda said.

"That's a common misunderstanding," Bones said matter-of-factly. "It's not that we like *getting* wet. We just like it wet. I mean, except for Maddock. He—"

"Aren't you worried about another car plowing into us?" Angel interrupted.

"Not much chance of that. In rain like this, everybody stops." Maddock hoped that was true. They hadn't seen much traffic on the road to begin with. Honduras was one of the poorest countries in Latin America, and a recent *coup d'etat* had only made things worse. The road was in terrible shape, the pavement crumbling and riddled with pot holes that resembled mini-cenotes. Only a madman would risk driving the roads under such conditions.

Then again, it was Latin America, where insanity was a prerequisite for getting hired as a bus driver.

"It will probably slack off in a few minutes," he said, hopefully.

A buzzing sound signaled an incoming text message, which was a bit of a surprise since mobile coverage had been spotty at best since leaving the major city of San Pedro Sula more than three hours earlier. He took out his phone, but before he could check the message, Angel reached over and plucked it from his grasp.

"Hey!"

"No texting while driving," she said, with a good-natured grin.

"I wouldn't exactly call this driving," he replied, but she ignored him and checked the message.

"It's from Jimmy. He's says the Model 686 was purchased in Manassas, Virginia by a Samuel Jones."

Jimmy Letson was a reporter with the *Washington Post*, and a master of ferreting out information, particularly electronic records that weren't exactly freely available. Maddock had called him before leaving Chichén Itzá to have him explore some alternative theories about the location of the City of Shadow, but he had also asked his friend to run down the guns they had taken from the men who had tried to attack them at the cenote. It was a slim lead, but maybe it would help them identify the mastermind of the Serpent Brotherhood.

The Model 686, much to Bones' chagrin, was now buried at a randomly chosen spot in the Yucatan rainforest, along with the other guns. Because they were flying commercial, transporting guns across international borders, especially with no documentation to prove their ownership, was out of the question.

"Sam Jones?" Maddock said, a little disappointed. It sounded like an alias, which meant the guns were probably another dead end. "Ask him if he knows anything else."

Angel typed in the question, then read the reply which followed almost immediately. "He says, 'If I knew more I would tell you more.'"

"Good old Jimmy," Maddock said. "He's such a people person."

"It's because he spends all his time with computers," Bones said. "He lost all his people skills."

"You're one to talk about people skills," Miranda said with a snort.

"Oh, I've got skills," Bones averred. "Not people in general, though. Just with the babes."

Angel turned to look at him, one eyebrow raised. "Excuse me, but how many women have dumped you in the last few years?"

"No one dumps me," Bones said, his tone solemn and inscrutable. "I just move on with my life while they're catching up."

"Ass," Angel said.

"Seconded," Miranda put in.

The rain seemed to be slacking off, so Maddock put the car in gear and started forward. "Start looking for the turn-off," he said. "We should be close."

A few minutes later, they reached the spot where the GPS unit said they should turn south to reach the ruins, but the way was blocked by a large black SUV with a bar of emergency flashers on its roof and the words "POLICIA NACIONAL" emblazoned on the fenders.

"Uh, oh," Bones said. "Hope you brought extra cash for the bribes."

As Maddock brought the rental to a stop, nose-to-nose with the police vehicle, two men got out. Both wore black fatigues, replete with tactical vests, and carried assault rifles. The men looked more like soldiers than police officers. One of them approached while the other remained at a distance, his weapon at the low ready.

Maddock rolled down the window and addressed the man in Spanish. "Is there a problem, officer? We wanted to visit the Copán Ruins."

"The site is closed."

Maddock translated for Angel's benefit; everyone else in the group spoke Spanish, though Bones liked to say that he only knew enough to ask how to find beer, bathrooms, and brothels.

"Not according to TripAdvisor," Bones remarked. "Wonder why they didn't just put up a sign?"

"Do you know how long it will be closed?" Maddock asked. "We've come a long way just to see—"

"Indefinitely," the policeman said.

"Is it the rain?" Angel asked.

Maddock knew it wasn't but decided to ask anyway.

"Biological reasons," the policeman said, this time with a note of finality. "You have to leave, now."

Maddock offered a half-assed salute and put the car in gear, backing away.

"Biological my ass," Bones muttered. "They're hiding something. You think the Serpent Brotherhood figured out we were heading here?"

Maddock withheld comment until he had completed a three-point turn and was heading back down the rain-drenched highway. "I think we should find out." He tilted the mirror so he could look Bones in the eye. "You up for a little sneak and peek?"

"You know it, brother."

"Are you sure it's worth the trouble?" Miranda asked. "Coming here was always a long shot anyway. And what if that policeman was telling the truth? What if there some kind of contagion in there?"

Maddock tapped the brakes, stopping once more in the middle of the road, and turned to Angel. "You guys head back to the last town we passed. Santa Rita, I think it was called. Hang out for a while. Get some lunch. I'll try to call, but if we can't get a signal, you'll need to come back here to pick us up. Give us three hours."

"Copán Ruinas is closer," Bell pointed out, referring to the modern resort city on the edge of the archaeological site, just a couple miles further down the highway in the other direction.

Maddock shook his head. "That would mean driving past the watchdogs a couple more times, and I'd prefer not to remind them we were here."

"And if you're not here when we get back," Angel said, "how long should we wait?"

"Don't wait. Get away as fast as you can." He saw the concern in her eyes and offered what he hoped was an encouraging smile. "Don't worry. We'll be here."

He got out and found Bones already waiting for him. "You know, Maddock, if there really is something biological going on out here and you get me infected…" He shook his head. "All I can say is, I'd better get a hot nurse out of the deal."

Maddock chuckled. "No promises."

Once they were moving through the woods, Bones was strictly business. Neither man said a word; all communication between them was done with hand signals, though even those were mostly unnecessary.

The rain had turned the ground into soup, slowing them almost to a crawl, and the persistent drizzle sapped the heat from their bodies despite the tropical climate, but neither man complained. They had both been through a lot worse.

The ruins were only a couple hundred yards from the road, in a clearing on the valley floor where the ancient inhabitants of the region had first settled nearly three thousand years before. From the edge of the trees, Maddock could see several man-made structures. There were a few buildings, crumbling truncated pyramids, worn down by the passage of time, but nothing on the scale of what they had seen at Chichén Itzá . Copán's claim to fame was not its architecture but its art, specifically hundreds of stelae—carved stone monuments sculpted with relief figures and glyphs that told the history of the Maya city. The stelae at Copán were considered to be the best examples of pre-Columbian high-relief sculpture and unique among the Maya, who were known primarily for bas relief carvings, like the blocks on the altar in the cenote back in the Yucatan.

If there was a clue to the location of the City of Shadow, it was probably carved into one of the stelae, but examining them would have to wait. It wasn't just a matter of time, though that was certainly a factor. It would take days to properly examine all the stone markers. No, the problem was that somebody else had beaten them to it.

More than a dozen men in full military-style gear, armed with M16A2 rifles, were roaming the edge of the site. Maddock guessed they were policemen like the men blocking the road, but that didn't necessarily mean they were acting in an official capacity. In Honduras, as in much of the developing world, police and military troops were often available for rent to the highest bidder.

The real work, however, was going on inside the secure perimeter. Men and women—at least twenty, but possibly twice that many—were spread out across the grounds, examining and photographing every stelae, brick structure and interesting looking rock on the valley floor. They might have been archaeologists, conducting a comprehensive survey after closing the site to the public. In fact, that explanation made the most sense, except for one thing.

Maddock leaned close to Bones. "Are you not seeing what I'm not seeing?"

"If you mean hot nurses…"

"I mean HAZMAT suits. Whatever's going on here, it's not a disease outbreak or anything like that. Why circulate a bogus story about a biological hazard?"

"Think they'll tell us if we ask nicely?"

Maddock knew the question was rhetorical, but shook his head anyway. "Let's try to get closer."

They moved out, skirting the clearing on the south side of the site, furthest from the access road and the bulk of the armed men. The hike from the road had left both men covered in mud, natural camouflage which, in tandem with the persistent drizzle, hid their approach from the none-too-vigilant lookouts. Maddock and Bones low-crawled out to one of pyramids, scaling it to get a better view of what was going on.

The people conducting the survey looked like they might be college students. There was an even mixture of male and female, all wearing upscale casual attire that looked like it might have come from Urban Outfitters or Eddie Bauer. The group was racially diverse as well, which suggested they were not locals, but none of them were speaking loud enough for Maddock to determine nationality.

Maddock took out his phone, intending to snap a few pictures of the workers on the off chance that Jimmy Letson might be able to work some magic with facial recognition software, but before he could clear enough grime from his fingers to operate the touch screen, Bones hissed softly, warning him to freeze.

A small group—three men and a woman—had just exited a nearby structure. Two of the men were wearing dark polo shirts emblazoned with some kind of official logo—park employees, Maddock guessed. The other man was a hulking figure with buzz-cut blond hair and a bearing that advertised ex-military. The woman had the olive complexion of a Latin American, but with red hair and freckles. There seemed little doubt that she was the one in charge.

"I'm sorry," one of the park employees was saying in Spanish. "But there isn't anything else."

"Something you don't tell the tourists about?

"You have seen everything. There may be other structures in the forest, but we have used ground-penetrating radar to map the entire site. There are no buried structures. No tunnels or secret passages."

"What about stelae that have not been cataloged? Or artifacts that you've sold on the black market? Do you have photographs of them?"

The park employee appeared to take great offense at the accusation. "I would never get involved with criminals."

The woman cast a dubious glance his way. "I'm not interested in your illicit activities. I just need to know if anything has been found here that relates to the City of Shadow."

The man choked back laughter. "The City of Shadow? You might as well ask me about chupacabra or *el Cadejo.*"

The woman flicked her head in the direction of her large companion, and the latter struck like a bolt of lightning, burying his fist in the other man's gut.

Even as the flippant park worker went to his knees, doubling over and gasping, the woman whipped a pistol out from under her coat and aimed it at the forehead of the second Honduran.

The man's eyes went wide with terror. "You have to believe us. The City of Shadow is a myth. No one believes it. Just the *campesinos*, but they are superstitious fools."

The woman thumbed back the hammer of her weapon. "I believe it," she hissed. "Am I a fool?"

From his perch, some fifty feet away, Maddock detected the distinctive smell of urine in the damp air.

One of the park employees had just wet himself. With painstaking slowness, Maddock raised his phone, pointed it at the woman, and took her picture.

"Please," the man begged. "There is nothing here about the City of Shadow. If there was, I would tell you."

"But you have heard of it. Tell me what you know."

"Just the story. My grandmother told it. How the shadow of the death lords threatened to engulf the world, until the gods hid the city from mortal eyes."

"And Copán? It is the beginning of the Serpent Road that leads to the city?"

The man blinked at her in confusion. "The City of Shadow isn't a real place. That's all I know, I swear."

The woman nodded and then slowly eased the hammer down. The man sagged in relief, but instead of lowering the weapon, the woman swiped it sideways, striking him in the temple.

"What now?" asked Buzz-Cut.

The woman stared out across the site for several seconds before answering. "This was a waste of time. There's nothing here." She holstered the pistol, trading it for a walkie-talkie which she held up to her mouth. "Wrap it up," she said, switching to English. "We leave in ten minutes."

As the two walked away, Bones sidled up to Maddock. "Thinks she's a Serpent Sister?" he whispered.

"Don't know," Maddock admitted. "The Serpent Brothers seemed kind of low-rent compared to these guys. Whoever she is, she must have a lot of clout with the government to shut down the site at a moment's notice."

"Money talks. Especially foreign money. That big guy sounded American. Looks kind of like an ex-jarhead, too."

Maddock nodded. "Probably a private security contractor. No telling who holds the purse strings, or why are they suddenly interested in the City of Shadow."

"And right when we're looking for it. Coincidence much? You think someone found out we were coming here?" When Maddock didn't comment, Bones went on. "Wanna try grabbing one of these guys? Maybe get some answers?"

"We're outnumbered and outgunned. It's not worth the risk. Let's head back."

"These guys are gonna be gone soon. We'll have the place to ourselves and we've got plenty of time. Might as well have a look around, right?"

Bones wasn't wrong. The most of the people had already moved to the north end of the site where a long row of mud-splattered SUVs waited. Only a few stragglers remained, hurrying across the rain-soaked field to join their colleagues.

But Maddock shook his head. "You heard what they said. Bell got it wrong. There's nothing here that even remotely links to the City of Shadow. No glyphs. No secret passages or cenotes. Nothing to…"

He trailed off as something clicked in his mind.

"I know the sound of a Maddock epiphany when I hear one," Bones said. "Care to share?"

"Bell assumed that the Serpent Road described in the guidestone would connect Maya cities. But what if that's wrong?"

Bones made a "get on with it" gesture.

"That park employee said the gods 'hid the city from mortal eyes.' The Maya didn't built temples to the death gods, but they did worship them by offering sacrifices at symbolic entrances to the Underworld." He checked his phone—two bars.

Worth a try, he thought, and started composing a text message. There was little chance of being spotted or overheard now, and this couldn't wait.

"I still don't get it," Bones admitted. "If the spots on the glyph aren't cities or temples, what are they?"

Maddock grinned. "They're cenotes."

CHAPTER 13

"Cenotes!" Bell clapped his forehead. "Of course! That makes perfect sense. The cenote where we found the guidestone has to be one of the waypoints."

"But which one of the waypoints is it?" Miranda asked from the passenger seat across from Angel. Maddock and Bones, soaking wet and filthy, had climbed into the rear passenger area where the archaeologist was sitting.

"There's probably a marker just like it in each cenote along the route," Maddock said as he dug some mud out of his ear with a finger. It was an exercise in futility. He would need a long hot shower, maybe even two or three, to get the filth off and the chill out of his joints, but there wasn't time for that now.

After texting Jimmy, he'd called Angel and arranged for an early pick-up. There was no sign of police presence on the road. The group that had briefly shut down the archaeological site was long gone. By the time they'd reached the road, and long before Angel and the others arrived, he had the answer to Miranda's question, but he hesitated to pass that information along. The arrival of red-haired woman and her small army at Copán, less than a day after Bell's decision to travel there, troubled him. The most likely explanation was that Antonio Griego had given up the information, probably under duress, but it seemed prudent to speak only in general terms.

"There are eleven marks on the glyph that seem to correspond to main stars in the Serpens constellation. Jimmy compared the alignment of the constellation with the location of known cenotes, using the one we already know about as a variable and assuming the same north-south alignment but at different scales. That gave us a number of possibilities, most of them in the Yucatan."

"Wonderful." Miranda's tone was thick with

sarcasm. "Right back where we started."

"I don't believe that all the waypoints will be in the Yucatan," Bell said, though he had lost some of his earlier confidence. "The Maya influence during the Classic period was strongest in the southern regions of their empire. The *Popol Vuh*, our primary source of information about the Underworld, originated with the Kiche of western Guatemala."

"We don't need to actually visit all the waypoints. Jimmy has ranked the results in order of probability based on the number of matches to known cenotes or unexplored areas." That little bit of extra legwork would cost Maddock a couple bottles of Wild Turkey, but if there was one lesson Maddock had learned over the years, it was that he could count on Jimmy for results, which made the information cheap at the price. "The latter makes a lot of sense because, obviously if the City of Shadow had already been discovered, we wouldn't be having this conversation." He didn't add that Bell was correct. The most likely location for the lost city, according to Jimmy's simulation, was not in the Yucatan, but in northern Guatemala.

"That's the good news," he continued. "The bad news is that some of these locations are pretty remote."

"Remoter than this?" Miranda said. "Let me get this straight. You want us to traipse all over creation looking for a lost city that we're not even certain actually exists?"

"Miranda," Bell murmured. "This is what I do. And the city is real."

"She's right though," Maddock said. "There's a better way. I've contacted Tam Broderick and asked for some logistic support. She's sending someone to meet us at Palacios Airport. It's not too far from here."

That was only partially true. While the Palacios airfield looked close on the map, it could only be reached via a rugged mountain road, which given the rainy conditions, took several hours and put the off-road capabilities of their rental vehicle to the test. There were closer airports, but Maddock had chosen this one in hopes that its remoteness would help conceal their departure from the Serpent Brothers or whomever it was the red-haired woman was working for.

Hector Canul paused in the doorway, letting his eyes adjust to the low light inside the cantina and taking a moment to survey the room. Hours of chasing rumors across the remote Honduran interior had brought him here. The tables were empty and there were only a few people at the bar, their backs turned to him. He studied them, trying to guess which of them was the man he sought. The fellow at the end of the bar seemed like the outlier. He was hunched over his drink, a posture that was both defensive and pathetic.

Hector advanced and took a seat at the bar, keeping one empty stool between himself and the other man. He made eye contact with the bartender, nodded, then leaned over to the other patron. "Join me for a drink, friend?"

The man rolled his head sideways, gazing back warily, and shrugged.

Hector turned back to the bartender. "Two of whatever my friend is having."

Two streaked glasses containing clear liquor were delivered. Hector lifted his, sniffed the contents. It smelled sweet, like rum.

"*Guaro*," the other man said, wrapping his hand around his glass.

"Your name is *Guaro*?"

"No. The drink is *guaro*. Sugar cane liquor." The man's speech was slurred. "My name is Rodrigo."

"I am Hector. What shall we drink to, friend Rodrigo? Home?"

Rodrigo ducked as if the word had stung him, and Hector knew right then that he had found the right man. "I have no home. Not anymore."

"What happened?"

"The curse. *El Cadejo Negro*. First it made people sick. Then the spacemen came. They killed everyone.

Burned the village."

"Spacemen?" Hector repeated.

"Don't believe him," the bartender said, dismissively. "He's a drunkard, telling stories so that people like you will take pity and buy him drinks."

Hector turned to the bartender. "Is any of it true?"

The bartender inclined his head in a gesture of compromise. "There was a fire up in the mountains. I heard it was bad. But there is no curse. No spacemen."

Hector nodded then turned back to Rodrigo. He shifted over to the empty stool, getting closer, and patted the drunk man on the shoulder. "It's okay, friend. I believe you. Tell me more. How did you know that they were men from another planet?"

Rodrigo shook his head. "Not men from another planet. Men in space suits. Soldiers. They came in helicopters. When I saw them in the sky, I hid in the forest."

"Why did you hide? What were you afraid of?"

Rodrigo's earlier wariness returned. "Who are you? You aren't from here. Why do you want to know about this?"

Hector leaned closer. "I buy things, Rodrigo. Expensive things that men like you find in the jungle. You know what I'm talking about, I think."

Rodrigo looked like he had just gone stone-cold sober. "No. I'm sorry. I can't help you."

"Maybe I can help you." Hector placed a hand flat on the bar. Protruding from beneath it was the corner of a banknote—Honduran *lempira*—marked with the number *1,000*. "Tell me about *el Cadejo*."

Rodrigo eyed the money suspiciously. At the current exchange rate, it was worth almost nine hundred pesos, or about forty American dollars, which would keep Rodrigo in *guaro* for a while. "I don't know anything about that."

Hector pulled his hand back, sliding the note out of the other man's reach.

"Diego found it," Rodrigo blurted. "A little jade

figure of a dog, covered in black dust. That's what he said. I never saw it. Everyone who did…" He shook his head. "The curse."

Hector withdrew his hand but he allowed the 1,000 lempira note to remain where it was on the bar. Rodrigo's hand snaked out and snatched it as if afraid that it might evaporate.

Hector produced another banknote, displaying it in similar fashion to the first. "Where did Diego find this black dog?"

"I don't know. We are…we were competitors. I know where he might have hidden it, but…" He shook his head.

"But what?"

Rodrigo eyed the second bill. "You don't have enough money to make me ever go near that thing."

"Are you certain? I have a great deal of money, friend."

Rodrigo shook his head, but it was an uncertain gesture.

Hector left the second bill on the bar in front of Rodrigo. He downed his drink in a gulp and slammed the glass down on the bar, laying another currency note atop the empty. "Think it over," he said, patting Rodrigo on the shoulder. "I'll be around, but not for long."

He exited the cantina without looking back, pausing once more at the door to shade his eyes from the relative brightness outside. The rain clouds were finally burning off, and now the air was thick with humidity.

He wasn't looking forward at all to what he would have to do next.

Rodrigo was another dead end. The man was too terrified of the curse—and rightly so—to be enticed by dreams of avarice. No, there was only one way to find the artifact the superstitious Hondurans had taken to calling *el Cadejo Negro*, and end the curse before it could spread to the outside world.

As he stood there outside the cantina, a big SUV rolled past. The vehicle was the same make and model as the one he had almost rented in San Pedro Sula, and much too expensive to belong to a local. As it drove past, he got a look at the occupants.

Gringos.

He watched the vehicle until it turned at an intersection and disappeared from view, and then continued on his way.

The helicopter was waiting for them when they reached the airfield.

"Red Cross," Miranda observed, noting the aircraft's white exterior and the distinctive emblem of the international relief agency on the fuselage. "Typical."

Maddock considered asking her to explain the remark, but remembered the woman's earlier revelation about working in the intelligence community. She was probably accustomed to using non-governmental organizations as cover for operations in far-flung corners of the planet.

He didn't know if the aircraft—an Airbus H135—was actually from the Red Cross's fleet or had simply been painted to look that way, but the pilot who got out to greet them was most definitely not a part of that organization.

"Well look what cat puked up," Bones said, grinning. "Does Dear Leader know you borrowed the helicopter?"

Kasey Kim, Korean by heritage but in every other way a 100% Southern California girl, shot Bones the bird, then turned to Maddock, acknowledging him with a nod. "Heard you needed a lift."

"You heard right," Maddock replied. "Got room for five plus our gear?"

Kasey gave the rest of the group a quick visual inspection. It might have been Maddock's imagination, but he thought he detected a look of recognition when her gaze fell on Miranda. He wondered if the two had crossed paths at some point in the past.

Kasey was an operations officer with the Central Intelligence Agency, assigned to Tam Broderick's special task force—codenamed: Myrmidons. Maddock and Bones had briefly worked in an official capacity with the Myrmidons and continued to trade favors with Tam, which usually proved mutually beneficial. The fact that Kasey had been able to reach the rural airport only a few hours after Maddock's call told him that Tam was more interested in Bell's research than she was letting on.

He wondered what else he wasn't being told.

But if Kasey and Miranda did know each other, neither felt the need to acknowledge it openly.

"Depends on what kind of gear you're talking about," Kasey finally said, crossing her arms over her chest. "Weight's an issue. We might have to leave Bones behind."

Bones gave a forced and abrupt laugh, and then glared at her with feigned indignation.

"SCUBA stuff and some climbing equipment," Maddock said. "Tents and sleeping bags."

"Guns?"

"Just two machetes."

"Wow. You're a couple of real Boy Scouts." Kasey shrugged. "Yeah, all right. Shouldn't be a problem. And I might be able to help you in the firepower department. Same destination you gave Tam?"

"Yes."

"Where exactly are we going?" Miranda asked. "You never told us."

"Guatemala. Up north near the border with Mexico in the rain forest."

"I said 'exactly,'" Miranda said through clenched teeth. "You can't expect us to just follow blindly."

"Miranda," Bell snapped. "They're helping us."

"That doesn't mean we have to just meekly…"

"It's okay," Maddock said, quickly, trying to head off an argument. "It's really in the middle of nowhere, but I can give you the GPS coordinates." He took out his phone and brought up the text message Jimmy Letson had sent with the exact coordinates that were the most likely location of the City of Shadow. He thought the mere appearance of cooperation might be enough to mollify her, but Miranda was intent on getting the precise location. She took out her own phone and began meticulously entering the coordinates as he read them off.

Kasey began tapping her fingers against her biceps impatiently. "Can we get this show on the road? I'd like to be in and out before dark."

Without waiting for an answer, she headed back to the helicopter, climbed in.

"You heard her," Maddock said as the aircraft's twin Turbomeca Arrius 2B2 turboshaft engines began spinning up. "All aboard."

He jogged back to the rear of the SUV to collect their gear. Bones joined him.

"You don't trust her?" he said, speaking in a low whisper.

"Short answer, no. But I don't distrust her, either. Let's just say I'm being extra cautious."

Bones gave a nod of approval.

Ten minutes later, they were in the air, cruising at 130 knots above the lush green landscape below.

"Welcome to Guatemala," Kasey announced a few minutes later, her clipped California up-talk accent coming through loud and clear over the headsets they all wore. "We're cleared for a flyover only. I'll be able to touch down for a few minutes for a hot unload, but then I'll have to leave you and head on to Belize City to refuel. I'll be back to pick you up in twelve hours, but you'll probably want to keep a low profile and avoid interacting with the local authorities."

"Hopefully, no authorities where we're going," Maddock said into his lip mic.

For the next hour or so, conversation was kept to a minimum as they were all treated to a low altitude flyover above forests, lakes and sprawling coffee plantations. Only Miranda Bell seemed unimpressed with the view; she kept checking her phone, almost compulsively, even though reception was spotty at best.

Her expression reflected her growing frustration.

"Having trouble posting to Snapchat?" Bones asked.

She shot him another one of her trademark withering glances. "We're off course."

Maddock shook his head. "I don't think so."

"I *do* think so." Miranda held up her phone to display the map. "We should be heading almost due north, but we're going north-northwest."

"Are you sure?" Maddock took the phone and made a show of examining it. "No. We're on course," he said. "You just entered the wrong coordinates."

"Like hell I did," Miranda snapped.

"You'll have to forgive my daughter, Mr. Maddock," Bell interjected. "She can be a bit…"

"Anal retentive?" Bones finished.

"I'm not," Miranda said. "I just don't like it when people are careless. I'm not careless. I entered the coordinates exactly as you read them, so if a mistake was made, it was yours."

Maddock shrugged. "Well, this longitude is off. It's supposed to be eighty-five degrees, fifty-five minutes, west. You've got eighty-five, fifty-nine. Maybe you misheard me. Five and nine sort of sound the same."

"Not to me," Miranda growled, but took the phone back and corrected the input without further question.

Maddock smiled inwardly. Miranda had not heard him wrong. He had intentionally given her the wrong coordinates. The difference was minuscule: only about five miles separated their actual destination from the point he had given her. He was surprised she had caught on, since they were only a few degrees off the erroneous heading. But if Miranda was, whether actively or unknowingly, working with the people who had somehow beaten them to Copán, sending their rivals five miles off course in the dense rain forest just might buy Maddock and the others the time they needed to find the City of Shadow.

CHAPTER 14

The rotor wash stirred the treetops, like a gigantic invisible hand ruffling the nap of a sprawling green rug. The whirlwind revealed a narrow gap in the vegetation, not wide enough to land the helicopter, but just enough to expose the jungle floor, twenty or thirty feet below.

"That's as close as I can get you," Kasey called out.

Bones leaned close to Miranda. "I'll go first so I can catch you."

She ignored him, but instead of disdain, her face wore a look of concern. "My father is in no shape to be jumping out of helicopters."

"We won't be jumping," Maddock explained. "I rig a line and we'll rappel down."

Miranda's expression indicated that she regarded this solution as little better, but instead of arguing with Maddock, she turned to her father. "Maybe you should sit this one out, Dad. I'll get video of everything."

Bell patted her arm. "Miranda, you worry too much. I'm not going to turn back, not when I'm this close."

"Rappelling is ninety-nine percent mental," Maddock said, trying to reassure both of them. "I'll rig two lines so one of us can go down side by side with you."

Bell just nodded.

Maddock rigged a pair of releasable abseils with 100-foot lines, while Bones got the bags with all their equipment prepped for descent. They both worked quickly, knowing that Kasey wouldn't be able to hold position for long. Bones went down first, after which Maddock lowered the gear down to him. Maddock then gave a quick refresher course on technique for the benefit of everyone that remained. Angel had done some climbing and rappelling with him, but it was a perishable skill. Miranda listened patiently, then volunteered to guide her father down. Not surprisingly, she knew her way around the ropes.

Eight minutes after arriving at the designated coordinates, they were all on the ground. Maddock pulled the ropes from their anchor aboard the hovering helicopter, and as they fell in coils around him, the aircraft banked away and disappeared over the forest canopy.

Maddock and Bones went to work with the machetes, clearing a landing zone for the helicopter, while Angel and Miranda set up their base camp. Kasey would return in twelve hours, which meant that, regardless of whether they found the City of Shadow, they would be spending a night in the bush, and because tropical rainstorms could strike without warning, shelter was an immediate priority, though given the extreme humidity, Maddock wasn't sure they would notice a difference. After just a few minutes of hacking away at the vegetation, he was drenched.

While the others were occupied with their respective tasks, Bell started poking around at the perimeter of the clearing, looking for anything that might indicate a Maya presence in the remote jungle, but it was Bones who discovered their first lead when the blade of his machete rang against solid stone, concealed under a dense covering of vines. He scraped away the undergrowth to reveal a stelae, carved with distinctive Mayan glyphs and topped with a full-relief sculpture of a style similar to what they had glimpsed at Copán.

"That's the lightning dog," Bell exclaimed. "Just like the image on the guidestone. Miranda, get video of this."

As she moved in to record the discovery with her GoPro, Bell turned to Maddock. "You were right. The City of Shadow is here."

"It's an encouraging sign," Maddock admitted, trying to temper his own enthusiasm.

Bell positioned himself so that he was facing the stone effigy. "This marker would have stood beside the ancient Maya road." He pointed to the jungle behind it. "That's where we need to look."

They went to work, clearing the free-standing monument and then pushing the trail in the indicated direction. It was slow-going, and exhausting work, but neither of the two former-SEALs was going to admit to fatigue, ringing the figurative bell to call it quits. After an hour however, Maddock was feeling a little light-headed, a sure sign of dehydration, so he swallowed his pride and called for a water break.

Angel stepped forward with a water bottle, but instead of handing it to him, she pointed at the machete. "Trade you."

As if that was her cue, Miranda approached Bones, one hand extended, palm up. "Hand it over, big guy."

"What? I don't get water?"

"Get it from Maddock."

"He backwashes. If I'm going to swap spit with someone, I'd rather it was you." Bones gave her a lewd wink.

Miranda shook her head. "And here I thought you SEALs were willing to drink each other's piss."

Without missing a beat, Bones turned to Maddock. "We've done that, right?"

"Stop!" Angel cried out with a shudder. "Not another word."

She grabbed Maddock's machete and went to work, hacking at the underbrush, while Bones just laughed.

The mood turned serious again when Miranda took a step forward and abruptly plunged forward. Her right leg, from the knee down, had disappeared into a hole covered by foliage. She caught herself and withdrew her leg, which was soaked from a complete immersion.

"You've got to be kidding me," she spat, throwing down her machete.

Bell however, was excited by the mishap. He hastened forward and began clearing away the area around the hole, which turned out to be considerably larger than it first appeared, stretching several yards in either direction before curving away into the forest, out of sight. Yet, despite the fact that it was clearly a pool of water, the surface remained obscured beneath a blanket of floating vegetation, and the limbs of trees growing at its edge reached out to form a canopy that shrouded the area in ominous shadow.

"A cenote?" Maddock asked.

Bell shook his head. "Not exactly. Cenotes are naturally occurring pools, caused when limestone caverns collapse. The geology here is all wrong for that. This is a cistern. A man-made reservoir. The Maya of the Petén region didn't have lakes or rivers, so they collected rainwater in enormous cisterns called *chultuns*."

Bones regarded the pool with uncustomary apprehension. "Do we dive it?"

"We're the first to find this," Miranda said. "It's probably full of sacrificial offerings. Dad, this is exactly what you've been looking for."

Bell gave a patient smile. "There may be some trinkets in there, but unlike the cenotes, the chultuns were primarily utilitarian."

"So this isn't an entrance to the Underworld," Maddock said. "Symbolic or otherwise."

"Correct. And if this is indeed the City of Shadow, dedicated to worshipping the Lords of Death, then we may actually be looking for a temple."

Maddock, who normally would have jumped at a chance to dive, felt an unexpected measure of relief at the reprieve.

They cleared a path around the chultun and kept going. Their trailblazing uncovered more artifacts— stone benches and carved blocks that might once have been stelae. Thirty feet or so beyond the cistern, Angel uncovered another stelae, still standing but considerably more weathered than the first.

Miranda moved closer to capture a video record. "Another guide dog?"

Bell reached out for the effigy, but as he did, Maddock saw something moving atop the stone marker. Bones shouted a warning, but before he could do anything else, there was a flash of movement. It looked like a vine—emerald green, flecked with gold—but it was moving, springing toward Bell's outstretched hand.

And then something else moved, striking even faster. The blade of Angel's machete slashed through the air between Bell and the stelae, slicing the vine-thing in two. One piece dropped at Bell's feet, while the rest of it began coiling and writhing atop the standing stone before falling away into the jungle beyond.

For a moment, no one else moved. Bell looked like he might pass out. Then Miranda let out her breath in a long sigh of relief. "That was too close."

Bones bent down and looked at the severed end of the creature. "It's a palm pit viper."

"Poisonous?" Angel asked.

"Venomous," Bones corrected. "Poison refers to something you eat. Venom comes from something that wants to eat you. And yeah, their venom usually won't kill you, but since we can't exactly head to the ER, it's probably best not to test that theory." He pushed into underbrush beside the stela, evidently looking for the rest of the snake. "It's a shame you had to kill it," he went on. "These things are..."

There was a sudden noise of branches breaking and then Bones was gone, swallowed by the jungle.

CHAPTER 15

"Bones!" **Maddock and** Angel shouted, moving toward the spot where Bones had disappeared, heedless of whatever danger lay concealed in the undergrowth.

Bones was shouting too, though the noise of branches rustling and snapping partially drowned him out. The tumult subsided and for a moment there was only an ominous silence.

"Ow," Bones muttered.

Maddock bent back some of the foliage, searching for his friend. "Bones? You okay?"

"It's cool," Bones called out. His voice seemed to be coming from ground level. "Watch your step. There's a hell of a drop off there."

Maddock let out a relieved sigh, then took the machete from Angel and began clearing the foliage away to reveal an almost sheer cliff-face just beyond the weathered stelae. Bones was standing about ten yards away, the top of his head level with Maddock's feet.

"It usually takes a bottle of Wild Turkey to make me fall like that," he said, gingerly rubbing a knee. "I enjoy rolling down a hill as much as the next kid, but there's a lot of rocks poking out of this one."

"This isn't a cliff," Bell said, standing at the edge of the drop-off. "Not a natural one, at any rate. This is a ball court."

Maddock peered out across the verdant landscape. Despite the thick jungle cover, he could just make out the undulations of the terrain. The long I-shaped depression like a perfectly straight river valley where Bones was standing, and beyond it, maybe fifty yards, another steep slope rising up. It wasn't hard to imagine the area cleared of vegetation.

There had been a large ball court at Chichén Itzá — over five hundred feet long, half as wide, with thirty-foot high vertical walls. This court wasn't quite that big, and the walls had more of a slope, but Maddock could see the similarity.

"The ball game held enormous spiritual significance to the Maya," Bell went on. "It was an intrinsic part of their religion."

"So you're saying they'd be okay with Tebow taking a knee to pray," Bones quipped.

"Oh, most assuredly," Bell said, not catching Bones' mischievous tone. "The ballgame was invented over three thousand years ago by the Olmecs, but it was just a game for them. For the Maya, it was a sort of passion play. The ball represented the sun and the changing seasons, and the players were gods, battling each other to control the heavens. The ball game was a central aspect of the Hero Twins legend, and of particular significance to the Lords of Xibalba. The pyramid will be close."

He turned toward the north end of the long depression. "It will probably be that direction."

"Shouldn't we be able to see it from here?" Angel asked.

"I could climb a tree and take a look," Bones suggested.

"None of the trees around here will hold your fat ass up," she retorted. "But it's an idea."

Maddock shook his head. "If there's a pyramid here, I doubt you'll be able to see it unless you're standing on it. We'll just follow the ball court to the end."

He tied a safety line around the stelae overlooking the ball court, mostly for Bell's benefit, and then they made the descent, one at a time, to join Bones at the bottom of the depression. The jungle had reclaimed the ball court along with the rest of the city, so forward progress continued at a glacial pace, and before long, Maddock noticed the shadows deepening as the sun sank into the western sky. He knew that base camp was only a short trek away, but making that trip in the dark was patently foolish. They had already had one close encounter with the local wildlife, and snakes were only one of the many creatures that could inflict anything from a painful bite or sting, to a fatal wound. Most of the creatures preferred to avoid encounters with humans, but in the dark, a single misstep could prove disastrous. But of even greater concern to Maddock were the jaguars which roamed the forest; the big cats with their notoriously strong jaws—capable of crushing turtle shells and caiman skulls in a single bite—might not shy away from them but actually stalk them as prey in the darkness. He was about to call for a turnaround when they hit what appeared to be a dead end. Directly in front of them was a solid vertical wall, rising higher than Bones could reach. Maddock scraped away the vegetation to reveal blocks of cut stone.

"This is a structure," Bell said, stating the obvious. "A courtyard wall, or possibly the base of a pyramid. We have to explore it. There will either be a gate or steps leading up to the next level."

Maddock checked his watch. The smart play was to head back and pick up again in the morning, but if they were able to actually find the city before dusk, they could continue exploring it by flashlight and, if they located any structures still standing, utilize them for additional cover and protection from jungle predators.

"Keep looking," he said, handing Miranda his machete. "Bones and I will head back to the LZ and break camp."

No one registered an objection to the decision, but as he and Bones hiked back down the trail they had cut along the floor of the ball court, Bones voiced a concern Maddock had not previously considered. "Are you sure you want to spend the night in a place called City of Shadow?"

Maddock looked at him sidelong, trying to decide if his friend was seriously spooked or just teasing. "I know. It sounds like the set up for a found footage movie."

"Dude, you think I'm kidding? City of Shadow? Lords of Death? The Maya who built this place vanished without a trace. Like…" He made a little explosion with his fingers. "Poof. Whisked away. What if the Lords of

Death were aliens? Or trans-dimensional beings? This could have been their…I don't know, spaceport or portal to the home dimension."

"You're just bringing this up now? If Bell is right, we've been in the city for the last few hours."

"Daytime is fine. Bad stuff only happens at night."

"Who'd have thought you'd be scared of the dark?" Maddock said. "Frankly, I'm more worried about ordinary terrestrial creatures."

"You mean the Serpent Brothers? You think they know about this place?"

Maddock had not meant that at all, but decided to address the question. "I don't think anyone's been here in at least five hundred years. If they know about it, they don't visit. It's more likely that they're just protecting the legend. I think they're looking for it, too."

"Which means they could show up anytime."

Maddock shrugged. Kasey had supplied them with two SIG Sauer P226 TacOps semi-automatic 9-mm pistols, six twenty-round magazines, and a box of spare ammunition. It was more than enough to handle a jungle predator—provided they had sufficient warning—but far from ideal for repelling an assault by a team of gunmen armed with assault weapons. But like it or not, that was the situation. They would deal with whatever happened because that was what they did.

And if they did have to fight, the stone walls of the lost city would offer a lot more protection than the thin nylon panels of their tents.

They packed up the equipment and started the trek, acutely aware of the fact that the sun was now below the treetops. Down in the trough-like ball court, the darkness deepened to the point that Maddock and Bones had to break out their LED flashlights, though this decision had more to do with keeping nocturnal predators at bay than actually illuminating their way. It also served to alert the others to their approach. An answering light from further up the trail guided them in. When they reached the wall, they found Angel and

Miranda grinning in triumph,

"The girls look way too happy, Maddock," Bones said in a stage whisper. "Maybe we should have split them up."

If either woman heard, they chose to ignore the none-too-subtle jab.

"It is a pyramid," Angel said, unable to contain her excitement. "And we found a way inside."

CHAPTER 16

Maria stared at the opaque plastic wall, wondering if she should try to smash through it. She desperately needed to get past the obstacle, to get moving, even though she had no idea where she needed to go or why.

Except that wasn't actually true. She did know why.

First, they wander.

She had known this was coming, even before realizing that the old woman she had met on the mountain road was infected. When she had gone into the house to assess the four critically ill patients, she had done so with the full knowledge that, no matter how careful she was, she might also contract the illness, but that was a risk she had willingly undertaken. She saw herself as a soldier, fighting microscopic enemies rather than human ones, but no less willing to sacrifice herself to save others.

And sacrifice herself, she had.

She felt chilled, a sure sign of the fever rising in her blood, but the tell-tale symptom was the perverse compulsion to move. Not aimless wandering as the villagers had suggested, but an overpowering urge to walk in a specific direction, like the homing instinct of a migrating bird.

But overpowering urge or no, three steps was as far as she got. That was where she encountered the sterile polycarbonate walls of her prison cell. Although she had never actually seen a room like it outside of the movies, she recognized the small enclosure for what it was: a Bio-Safety Level IV isolation room.

The soldiers—she assumed they were soldiers—had taken her along with the other visibly infected patients, about a dozen people including the three Maria had been monitoring. They had all been put in a makeshift isolation ward, nothing more than plastic sheeting held together with strong tape, aboard one of the helicopters.

Maria guessed that about a full day had passed, but it was impossible to say with certainty. She had not seen the sun since taking off in the helicopter. After a short flight, they had disembarked in a closed hangar. She didn't think they could have gone very far. No more than a few hundred kilometers, but aside from knowing that she was in a BSL-IV facility, she had no idea where she was now.

Yet somehow, she knew which direction she need to go.

And she knew how it would end.

A buzzing sound distracted her, breaking the strange spell, momentarily at least. She turned and saw the light above the sealed door blinking on and off. This, she knew, was the signal that someone was about to come through the door, and that she was to lay down on the bed in a non-threatening manner. Failure to comply, she had been told, would result in her being placed in five-point restraints.

She turned away from the wall and stretched out in a supine position, but almost immediately felt herself sitting up again, swinging her feet off the hospital-style bed, turning in the direction of the wall.

"No," she whispered, gripping the side rails forcefully to hold herself back.

The door opened with a hiss and someone entered. She didn't immediately see the person's face, not until he finished connecting the air hose from his environment suit to the supply valve near the door. It was the young man who had come in earlier to draw blood and check her vitals. Then he had spoken only a few words to her in halting Spanish—probably not his native tongue—and refused to look her in the eye or answer her questions.

That had been several hours earlier, before the urge to walk had come over her.

"Are you American?" she asked in English.

The young man stiffened a little at the question. "You speak English?"

"*Sí.* I mean, yes. My name is Maria."

"Please stay on the bed. I need to check your vitals and take more blood."

"I have it," she blurted. "The sickness. I am showing first stage symptoms."

The young man in the space-suit did not appear surprised by this news, but he kept his head tilted down, hiding his face as he began wrapping a blood pressure cuff around her right bicep.

"I can help you," she went on.

He secured the cuff and activated the stand-mounted electronic sphygmomanometer. For a few seconds, the only noise in the room was the low hum of the device cycling. Maria did not move or speak, knowing that doing so might affect the accuracy of the readings. When the machine finished, she took note of the results.

Her systolic was slightly higher than normal. So was her heart rate.

The young man began loosening the cuff.

"Let me help you," she said again. "I am a physician. I can tell you what's happening to me. I know it's too late for me, but I can still help you find a cure. Please let me help you."

The man still refused to look, but his subsequent movements were hesitant, as if he were fighting his own inner irresistible compulsion.

"It's a fungal infection of some kind, isn't it?" She kept talking, hoping that her display of cooperation might somehow reach through the barriers that separated them. "That fits most of the symptoms, but it's unbelievably aggressive. It seems to be spread by skin-to-skin contact, but airborne transmission is also possible. I don't think it's contagious in the early stages. The first symptom…"

She faltered here, knowing that she was diagnosing her own terminal condition.

"The first symptom is an urge to start walking. I don't know how else to describe it. I'm fighting it right now. It's like my brain is telling me that I really want to do it. I think the infection is interfering with dopamine receptors. That makes sense, doesn't it?"

The young man placed a thermometer in her mouth, silencing her, and once again she did not resist. After a few seconds, the device beeped, signaling that it had finished measuring her body temperature.

"I have a fever, don't I?"

No response.

"It feels mild right now, maybe 37 degrees... About 100 degrees Fahrenheit," she amended. If he was American, he probably wouldn't know Celsius temperatures. "Are my eyes bloodshot? I think capillary leakage is an early symptom, too. In a few hours, I'll develop petechiae. It spreads through contact with infected blood, and maybe other bodily fluids. Aerosolized blood from coughing. After a while, I won't be lucid anymore."

The young man put away the diagnostic machine and turned to leave.

"Please," she said again. "Let me help."

The man disconnected his air supply and reached for the door, but before he hit the button to open it, he turned and faced her. His lips moved but she heard no sounds at first. Then he took a breath, and spoke again more forcefully. "Doug. My name is Doug. I'm so sorry, Maria."

Then, he turned away quickly, opened the door and left without looking back.

Doug Simpson lingered under the disinfectant shower, as if the harsh chemicals might somehow burn away the guilt he felt. The suit kept the solution from making contact with his skin, just as it kept the microbes in the patient rooms at bay, but it offered scant protection from the pain of watching another person die.

The shower was part of the multi-layered Bio-Safety protocol designed to keep infectious agents from escaping the lab and spreading to the outside world, yet despite such precautions, on more than one occasion, deadly pathogens had made it out of even the most capable BSL IV facilities. Because this was a privately operated lab, operating without oversight from any government, additional layers of protection had been put in place, including a fail-safe that would sanitize the entire facility in the event of a containment breach—something as simple as attempting to leave the airlock before the disinfectant shower finished its cycle.

After five minutes, the flow of chemicals switched to pure distilled water, which sluiced away all traces of the caustic disinfectants. The pressure of the shower pushed his clammy skin against the inside of the suit, chilling him.

What am I even doing here? he thought. *I'm not going to be able to help Maria or any of them.*

Several more patients had died, and those few from the village who had been exposed but were asymptomatic—like Maria—were now exhibiting the first signs of infection. Bloodshot eyes, fever, and that weird compulsion to move.

Maria had been partially right about that. Somehow, the disease hijacked the central nervous system, making infected victims start walking. It was probably some evolutionary adaptation to spread the pathogen. He knew of a similar example in nature—*Ophiocordyceps unilateralis*—the so-called "zombie fungus" which caused infected ants to immediately climb up the nearest tree and bite down on a leaf with a death-grip until actual death occurred, whereupon the fungus would reach maturity inside the ant's carcass and scatter spores on the forest floor below.

The thought of what would soon happen to Maria made him want to throw up. She was in the control group, which meant that, even if, through some miracle, they found the right combination of therapies to cure the afflicted patients, Maria would not be spared. When—if—such a cure was found, she would be too far gone to save.

The patients belonged in a real hospital, USAMRIID in Reston, Virginia, or maybe a CDC facility, not here, in a privately operated facility owned by a biotech outfit. What Alex had him doing was insane. It was profoundly unethical.

Worse, it was probably criminal.

He knew his boss's reputation for putting profits ahead of everything else, even basic humanity. Alex was impetuous, hot-tempered, vindictive, like his legendary father in many ways, and utterly without compassion. He had rushed into the hot zone and brought the infected patients here to this mobile BSL IV facility, not so that he could save their lives, but so that, when a treatment was finally discovered, he and he alone would control it. If the contagion ever got out into the open, the governments of the world would be forced to pay whatever exorbitant price he set for that cure.

Alex called it capitalism in action, and Simpson had tried to convince himself that he was right, but no amount of money would take away the shame he now felt.

He marched back to his office, wondering who to call first. The CDC? Or the FBI?

Who even has jurisdiction out here?

The light in the airlock went from red to ordinary white, signaling that it was safe to exit, but as he opened the door, a chill shot through him. Alex was there, sitting behind a disused desk across from the suit storage area, with his feet propped up on the desktop.

"Doug. Took your sweet time."

Simpson gaped for a moment, then finally nodded. "I was just…with the patients. Er…subjects."

"I figured as much. I took the liberty of reviewing the data you've collected so far. I have to say, I'm not altogether happy with the results. This should have been a cakewalk."

Simpson sucked in a breath. "Mister…Alex…I think we're going about this the wrong way."

Alex's eyes narrowed into cold reptilian slits. "Is that what you think?"

"I just mean…we…there are other agencies, with

resources we don't have. We should turn this over to someone else. I know what you're going to say. That there's no profit in doing things that way, but…" Simpson shook his head miserably. "Some things are more important than money."

Alex brought his feet off the desk, planting them on the ground with the suddenness of a gunshot. He pointed a finger at Simpson. "Exactly. I can see you're a man after my own heart, Doug. Maybe it's time I let you in on a little project I've been working on. I call it 'Shadow and Light.' And it's going to change the world."

CHAPTER 17

Maddock shone his light into the dark recess. The stone blocks framing the opening had been partially forced out of place by plant roots, but in an ironic twist the vegetation seemed to be the only thing preventing the structure from crumbling completely into ruin. Beyond the opening, he could see irregular stone steps descending into inky darkness.

"I thought the steps on pyramids were supposed to go up," Bones observed.

"It's the City of Shadow," Bell said, as if that ought to explain everything. "The Underworld lies below."

"Normal rules don't apply," added Angel.

Bones just grunted.

"You really think this is the entrance to Xibalba?" Maddock asked.

"That's what my research indicates, though you must bear in mind that the legends are not to be taken literally. 'Xibalba' may be nothing more than a sacred crypt or a tomb containing the men who were revered as the Lords of Xibalba." Bell was downplaying the find, but Maddock guessed he was hoping for a lot more than just an old crypt.

"Odds are," Maddock said, "all we're going to find is a flooded passage. If we're lucky."

"And if we're not?"

"A cave in." He shrugged. "Only one way to know for sure, though. I don't suppose I'll be able to convince all of you to stay up here while Bones and I check it out."

He half-hoped that Angel would take him up on the offer. Surely, tagging along with him in dark musty caves had lost any appeal it might once have held for her. And if Angel stayed back, maybe Miranda would be persuaded as well. But he knew Bell would not be left behind, not while the exploration required no technical expertise, and where Bell went, his daughter would surely follow.

"No? Okay, then. Ground rules. Don't follow too close. Watch your step but be observant at all times. If I tell you to freeze, or to turn around and run for the top, do it, no questions."

After receiving a round of nods, he started forward, sweeping back and forth with his light as he stepped beneath the misshaped lintel.

The air inside the descending shaft was markedly cooler, and the air did not smell quite as bad as the conditions would have led Maddock to expect. There was only a faint earthy aroma, not the expected reek of decay. He took that as a hopeful sign that the shaft was neither flooded nor a den for bats or other jungle creatures. After just a few steps, the intrusion of roots and other plant life abated, revealing solid uncracked masonry with no deformity. The shaft was wide enough for them to walk two abreast, so Maddock brought Bell forward to walk beside him, letting Angel and Miranda follow, with Bones bringing up the rear. The flashlights reliably illuminated an area about ten yards ahead of them, revealing damp stone steps, but nothing else noteworthy.

Maddock knew they had to be well below the level of the local water table, which meant the builders of the pyramid had engineered some method to keep the subterranean chamber more or less dry. He was about to ask Bell about this when he realized the archaeologist was softly counting the steps.

He distinctly heard the other man say, "Forty-seven."

Forty-seven steps, each one about eight inches high. That rounded to about thirty-two feet.

"No creepy-crawlies yet," Bones said. "That's a good sign."

"If you jinx us," Angel warned. "I'll toss you down these steps. Swear to God."

"Hmm. You could turn it into a game. Bowling for Maddock."

"Guys," Maddock murmured. "Trying to work here."

Bell ticked through the fifties, then the sixties. Below step sixty-five, the walls simply ended, and where they had been, there was only open space—and impenetrable blackness. Maddock sensed they were approaching the end of the descent, and sure enough, by the time they got to step number eighty, he could just make out the flat bottom of the shaft about a dozen steps away.

"Ninety-one steps," Bell said. "Just like at Chichén Itzá . There are probably three more staircases just like this one, each from a different cardinal direction, all meeting here. Counting the floor, three hundred and sixty-five, just like the days of the year."

Maddock aimed his light to the side but it was too dark to confirm the hypothesis. He could however make out the floor, which consisted of elaborately decorated stone blocks, each one a good six feet across. It took him a moment to register that the shadowy lines in the blocks were not merely relief carvings but deep holes cut completely through the stone.

"That explains where all the water goes," Bell said, shining his own light down at the block directly before them. "The entire floor of this chamber is an enormous drain, conducting seepage and rainwater away."

"One mystery solved," Maddock agreed, though that explanation seemed incomplete. "But where does the water go after that?"

"Maybe this isn't actually the bottom," Miranda suggested. "Maybe we have to keep going."

Maddock played his light on the floor at the base of the stairs, paying particular attention to where the blocks joined together. "Think it's safe to walk on?"

"Better have Bones go first," Angel said.

"Fine by me," Bones said, pushing past his sister. "I'm sick of looking at your fat behind anyway."

"Right," Miranda said with undisguised sarcasm. "Like it's *her* you've been checking out."

Bones grinned at her. "You just might fit in here."

He stepped off the staircase without hesitation, solidly planting one foot, then the other, on the elaborately decorated floor.

Maddock cringed, half-expecting the floor to collapse or spikes to shoot up through the holes in the blocks, but nothing of the sort happened. "Looks safe enough," he said, advancing tentatively to stand beside Bones. "But watch your step all the same."

"Look," Bell said, venturing out across the floor, seemingly heedless of the warning. He was shining his light on an enormous stone sculpture occupying the exact center of the chamber.

Maddock aimed his own light at the carving, a familiar reptilian head, its jaws agape, facing the staircase to their right. "It looks just like the statue at Chichén Itzá . The one at the base of El Castillo." He checked his orientation and then turned so he was facing the same direction as the carving. "We came in from the west, which means the statue is facing south."

"Interesting," Bell said. "The figure at El Castillo faces west, but thus far, south has consistently been the dominant cardinal direction." He clapped his hands together. "The guidestone indicated we would find the entrance to the Underworld at the Serpent's Maw. It would appear that was to be taken quite literally."

Maddock approached the statue for a closer look. The space between the jaws was easily large enough for him to stand inside it, which was almost certainly intentional. At the back of the carved mouth was a shadowy opening, about two feet in diameter. The hole angled downward and appeared to keep going, beyond the reach of Maddock's light. "I guess that means we have to go through there."

Bones put his hands on his hips. "Look, I'm all for sticking my big nose where it doesn't belong, but I feel like someone needs to point out the obvious. The Underworld is the afterlife—the place you go *after life*. The Maya practiced human sacrifice. So...and bear with me here... maybe we should think this through. You know, before we let ourselves be swallowed by the Hellmouth."

"He's right," Miranda said.

Maddock stared at her, waiting for the other shoe to drop, for Miranda to somehow twist Bones' wariness into a mean-spirited jab, but to his astonishment, she did not. "Dad, we've found the City of Shadow. You were right and everyone else was wrong. The discovery is the important thing. So, let's head back to civilization, and let the world know what you've found. We don't need to take any more risks."

Bell shook his head. "I can't leave without knowing what's down there."

"I agree," Maddock said before Miranda could argue. "Kasey's not going to be back until tomorrow morning. And I think I know a way for us to look before we leap."

Five minutes later, they were gathered around Bell's tablet computer, watching the live video feed from Miranda's GoPro. The camera was no longer strapped to her forehead, but was instead sliding down the carved serpent's throat, taped to the end of one of the climbing ropes, along with one of their flashlights. Bones was paying out the line slowly.

The shaft turned vertical after just a few feet, then without warning, the screen went black.

"Lost the wi-fi signal," Miranda said.

"I don't think so," Maddock said, pointing at the signal strength indicator. "The reason we can't see anything is that there isn't anything to see. There's another open chamber underneath us, but the light isn't powerful enough. Bones, how far in are we?"

"About ten feet."

Bones continued feeding the rope into the serpent's maw, measuring progress in one-foot increments. Maddock kept his eye on the wi-fi signal indicator. The deeper the camera went, the fainter the signal became until, at about twenty feet, it failed altogether.

"Keep going," Maddock said.

Bones nodded, but after just a few seconds, he

stopped. "Feels like we just hit bottom. Twenty-four feet."

He reeled in the line without difficulty. Both camera and light were functioning normally and showed no signs of damage, but the playback revealed little that they had not already seen. The only difference was at the end of the camera's downward journey when the flashlight shone upon the floor of the hidden chamber. The beam was reflected back in dozens of tiny pinpoints, as if the floor was covered with broken glass.

"There's something down there," Miranda said, running the feed back for another look. "Can't tell what it is though."

"It looks safe enough," Maddock said. "I'll go down for a better look."

With the rope secured to his field-expedient Swiss seat climbing harness, Maddock lowered himself into the serpent's throat feet first while Bones anchored the line from above.

"Oof," Bones grunted, exaggerating his effort. "I don't want to hear any more crap about my weight."

"Muscle weighs more than fat," Maddock said, playing along, but his voice sounded weird in the close confines of the passage, ruining his attempt to keep the mood light.

After a few seconds of descending, he dropped out of the shaft and found himself dangling in mid-air, about twenty feet above the floor of the lower chamber. The room was at least as big as the upper chamber, the walls beyond the reach of his light, but he could easily make out the floor below. It was decorated with elaborate carved patterns, just like the holes cut in the stone floor above except these holes were not empty, but filled with something that reflected back the flashlight beam in a weird interplay of light and shadow, like asphalt encrusted with diamonds. The only undecorated area was a four-foot square directly below him.

He rappelled down until his feet were just barely touching the floor, and then relaxed his grip on the rope, transferring his full weight onto the balls of his feet.

Suddenly the floor wasn't there anymore.

He lurched, clutching at the rope as he pitched forward toward the glittering floor. The flashlight tumbled from his grasp, and as it landed it revealed movement.

Something was coming out of the floor... No, not something but somethings. A thousand somethings, with gleaming black carapaces and pincers and hook-tipped tails, rushing up at him as he fell.

The floor of the chamber was covered in scorpions.

CHAPTER 18

The first thousand *lempira* worth of *guaro* provided Rodrigo with all the liquid reassurance he needed to justify his refusal to show Hector where Diego had probably hidden *el Cadejo Negro*. But as he drank away the rest of his windfall, he had cause to regret that decision. He couldn't remember the reason for his reticence, but he was sure of one thing; if Hector was willing to give him 2,000 lempira just to talk about it, he surely had a lot more to offer.

And it wasn't as if he had to actually take him to Diego's stash. There were lots of other old ruins he could take him to instead. Hector wouldn't know the difference, and if he complained…well, the jungle was a dangerous place. Anything could happen.

Rodrigo rose from his stool, leaving the currency notes with the empty bottle, and heaved himself at the door. He couldn't remember if Hector had mentioned where he would be staying, but it didn't matter. Palacios was tiny, with just a few hotels. He would find the wealthy stranger.

He staggered outside into the twilight of approaching dusk, bellowing at the top of his lungs. "Hector! You son of a whore. I will take you to *el Cadejo.*"

The only answer he received was silence. The streets were empty of both vehicle and pedestrian traffic.

Rodrigo turned to the right and lurched into motion, careering back and forth across the sidewalk. Somehow, he managed to stay on his feet, but the motion set his guts to churning. As soon as he rounded the corner into the dark alley behind the cantina, he bent over and vomited out a torrent of sour bilious fluid.

Relief was almost instantaneous. His head felt clearer, the nausea now just a dim memory. He coughed, spat out a gob of bitter phlegm, and then filled his lungs and tilted his head back.

"Hect—"

Someone or something seized his arm, yanking him off his feet. His teeth slammed together in his mouth and he tasted blood; he had bitten his tongue. He struggled, trying to wrestle free of his captor, but the grip was too strong and he couldn't get his feet under him for leverage. The alley was cloaked in shadow and he could barely make out the silhouette of his captor, but then a faint glow appeared in the distance. It was, Rodrigo realized, the interior light of a car, but in its scant illumination, he caught a glimpse of his assailant.

It walked like a man, but instead of skin, it had green and black scales like a lizard or a jungle viper.

There were two more snake-men waiting at the car.

Rodrigo opened his mouth to scream again, but before he could, there was an explosion of light and pain in his head and then he was falling into oblivion.

The respite of unconsciousness was short-lived, or at least it seemed that way. He awoke to the sound of drums, beating out a dull rhythm, accompanied by shrill flutes. The tumult tightened the vise squeezing his skull, a pain that was in equal parts the consequence of too much *guaro* and a mild concussion from a club wielded by one of the snake-men.

He knew that they were just men, the scales merely painted on their naked bodies, but the realization brought no comfort at all.

He opened his eyes and saw them again, dancing around him now in the ruddy glow of torchlight, chanting in a language that sounded similar to the old Ch'orti' tongue still used in some of the rural villages.

The snake-men leaned in close, shaking rattles over him, then drew back as another figure—this one wearing an elaborate mask plumed with bright feathers—came into view above him.

The voice that issued from the mask was harsh, but decidedly feminine. The words sounded like an ancient invocation, summoning a devil from hell.

Then the masked figure threw up her arms and barked out a command, and instantly the noise ceased.

For a moment, she stood like that, statue still, painted skin seeming to crawl in the flickering light. In her right hand, she held a black dagger that looked like a long shard of broken glass. But then she brought her hands together on either side of the masked visage, and lifted it away, revealing her true face.

She was beautiful in an exotic and slightly terrifying way, with a splash of freckles on her dark skin and long red hair pulled back away from her face. There was a snake draped around her neck. Its arrow-shaped head seemed to be moving, but he knew that had to be a trick of the light. The woman was breathing heavily, as if winded from the exertion of the ritual dance, but after regarding him for just a few seconds, she spoke.

"You spoke with a man today, in the cantina. What did you tell him?"

The question surprised Rodrigo almost as much as the fact that this woman masquerading as an ancient demon was speaking perfectly comprehensible Spanish.

"I...he wanted to buy relics from me. I told him nothing."

"Why did he think you would be able to show him relics?"

"That is what I do. I look for things in the jungle."

"What did you tell him?"

Rodrigo held nothing back. The story poured from his lips like another vomitous eruption—Diego's discovery, the curse, the arrival of the soldiers in space suits, the death of the village and the fire that followed.

The woman listened intently for a while, but then silenced him with a slash of her hand. "Did you tell the man where to find *el Guia*?"

"I don't understand—"

"The thing you call *el Cadejo Negro.*"

"No. I do not know where Diego hid it."

Her eyes narrowed, as if stripping bare his soul. "You are lying."

"No. I swear."

She leaned closer until her face was just a few inches away. At the corner of his eye, he saw something moving.

The snake. It is alive after all.

The viper's arrow-shaped head appeared between them, its forked tongue darting in and out of its mouth, probing the air.

"Tell me everything."

"I did," Rodrigo cried, tears streaming from his face.

"Then tell me again."

At the dawn of the twentieth century," Alex began, "The world population was 1.6 billion. From 1800 to 1900, the increase was only about half a billion. One hundred years later, it was six billion. In 2011, we hit seven billion, and today, we're over seven and a half. Developed nations have aging populations and low fertility rates, but the developing nations, the poorest countries where poverty is endemic and health care is virtually non-existent, have astronomically high birth rates. Conservative estimates predict that we will hit 10 billion before the end of the century.

"Ten billion people, Doug. Another three billion souls, fighting over resources that are already too scarce to meet our needs. It's not sustainable."

Simpson swallowed nervously. A sick feeling had taken root in his gut as Alex had ticked off the numbers. The conclusion he was driving at seemed inescapable. "Are you talking about…culling?"

Alex's answer came a little too quickly. "Doug, we're in the pharma business. That's a decision for the politicians to make. But that's not what I'm getting at.

"You're a biologist, Doug. What happens when a species exceeds carrying capacity?"

"Uh, usually there's a die-off. Too many consumers, not enough food. The population crashes."

"Exactly. But something else can trigger a die-off, particularly when a species—like ours—becomes adept at altering its behavior in order to expand its food supply. It's happened before. In the 14th Century, the Black Death wiped out sixty percent of the population in Europe. The disease spread quickly because populations were clustered together in cities and were interdependent because of trade and commercial specialization. Just like we are, only the population is larger by an order of magnitude. A pandemic disease agent like the Black Death would flash across the globe like wildfire today."

"Except we can treat the plague."

Alex nodded. "Yes. For now. But the increase in population brings with it an increasing chance of new drug-resistant strains of bacteria. Viruses, like influenza, mutate faster than our ability to develop vaccines. And fungal infections like the one we're researching here may be the worst of all. Viruses and bacterial agents can be contained with quarantine management and sterilization, but fungal spores can be carried on the wind, or lie dormant for centuries. They're like snakes sleeping in the grass.

"Are you familiar with chytridiomycosis? It's a fungal disease that's wreaking havoc in the global amphibian population. One hundred percent fatal in some species of frogs. Imagine if something like that becomes transmissible among human populations, and gets loose in Beijing or Mexico City. And fungal diseases often occur as secondary infections among people whose immune systems are compromised by AIDS or malnutrition."

He waved a hand, dismissively. "I'm not telling you anything you don't already know, of course. Finding the treatment for diseases that don't yet exist is pretty much our mission statement. We're heroes, fighting microbial monsters."

Simpson swallowed again. "You said 'Light *and* Shadow.' That makes it sound like there's a dark side."

Alex returned a cold smile. "Actually, I said 'Shadow and Light.' You can't have one without the other."

He paused, as if to emphasize the point. "Shadow is what the ancient Maya called the fungal agent you are now researching. *Maldición de la sombra*—the Shadow Curse. At least that's what Carina tells me." He cocked his head sideways. "Did I introduce you to Carina? Fascinating woman.

"The Shadow all but wiped out the ancient Maya empire in the 10th Century. According to legend, two brave warriors found the cure in a cave somewhere. I believe that, if that cure had not been found, the Shadow would have consumed the world."

"And you've got me messing around with it?" Simpson blurted. "A disease that could kill everyone? Do you even hear what you're saying?"

Alex shook his head. "You're missing the point, Doug. The important thing is that a cure can be found. Carina is off trying to find the cave with the cure, but we're men of science. I have faith that you will beat her to it. Then, we will control both the Shadow and the cure—the Light."

"Control?" Simpson said, incredulous.

"It's just good business, Doug. When those Maya warriors returned with the cure, they were revered as gods. Why shouldn't we at least see a little profit?"

"And that stuff about population? Why did you tell me that?"

"It's like the old saying, 'the cure may be worse than the disease.' The Shadow has a role to play in the future of our species. It's nature's way of restoring the balance. If that balance isn't restored, something much worse than the Shadow may be in the offing. Something we don't have a cure for."

"You said 'control.' The Shadow and the Light. You're planning to unleash this disease on the world." As soon as the words were out, Simpson regretted having spoken it aloud. If Alex was willing to decimate the world population, he surely would not hesitate to make one contrary scientist disappear.

But Alex merely shook his head. "What's the profit

in that? Besides, who am I to decide who lives or dies? No, I'll probably put the Shadow on the open market. Someone will pay. Probably some lunatic tin pot dictator, like that tub of lard in North Korea. And once someone like that has it, everyone will want it. And they'll want the cure, and we'll be able to charge as much as we like."

"Someone will use it," Simpson said. "It will get out in the open, and people will die. Millions of people who can't afford the cure."

Alex shrugged. "Everybody dies eventually anyway. This way, there's a chance to save the planet." He paused a beat. "Don't worry, Doug. Those loyal to me will of course be the first to be inoculated against the infection."

He let the implications of that hang in the air between them. "I trust you will find the cure soon, but even if you don't, Carina is close to finding the source. And I have another agent working on the problem as well. All the bases are covered. So I guess you have a choice to make, Doug. Shadow and Light? Or the darkness?"

CHAPTER 19

The rope went taut, halting Maddock's fall mere inches above the sea of scorpions, but he had to throw his arms out wide in order to keep from spinning and face-planting into their midst. One glistening black stinger filled his vision, so close that he had to go cross-eyed to bring it into focus.

"Bones," he said, his voice barely louder than a whisper. "Pull me up. Very. Slowly."

Nothing happened. Bones and the others were too far away to hear him.

Yet, in the moment or two it took him to figure this out, he realized something else as well. The scorpions weren't moving.

"Not real," he breathed, letting out a sigh of relief.

That wasn't entirely accurate though. The arachnid bodies covering the floor beneath him weren't actual scorpions, but they weren't the product of his imagination, either. They were amazingly life-like reproductions, each one the size of his hand, and carved out of a glossy black substance that reflected the light and revealed edges sharper than the blade of a razor.

Obsidian.

When he had settled his weight on the stone square at the center, it had triggered some kind of pressure-sensitive mechanism, which had in turn caused the carved scorpions to spring up out of the recessed area in the floor, creating the illusion of a living swarm. The little statues were everywhere, covering the floor so densely that there did not appear to be any space large enough to step, let alone ease himself down gently.

But he couldn't stay like this for much longer.

Moving slowly so as not to become unbalanced, he twisted his body sideways and caught the rope. From this vantage, he could make out the square of bare stone—his original intended landing area—just below his outstretched legs. The block had sunk into the floor, but only to a depth of about six inches. Just enough to throw him off balance at that crucial instant. Gripping the rope, he lifted his upper torso, tilting his legs back until his feet finally made contact.

He braced himself in anticipation of some other elaborate booby-trap, but nothing else happened. The stone floor remained solid beneath him as he brought himself to an upright position. He pulled the rope free of the carabiner he had been using as a rappelling device and shouted up to the others, "I'm down!"

The chamber was filled with echoes.

"You okay?" came the slightly muffled reply—Bones, shouting into the serpent's mouth.

"Yeah. Triggered some kind of booby-trap. About a million carved scorpions just popped out of the floor."

There was a pause, and then a fainter voice—Charles Bell—floated down to him. "Did you say 'scorpions'?"

"Yes. Why? Is that important?"

"In the *Popol Vuh*, the road to Xibalba crosses three rivers. The first is filled with scorpions."

"Great," Maddock replied. "What's in the other two?"

"Blood and pus."

Maddock gave an involuntary shudder. "I'm sorry I asked."

"Be very careful where you step," Bell went on. "They may only be carvings, but I would hazard a guess that their stingers are tipped in poison."

Maddock nodded, probing the forest of poised stingers with his light. Now that he wasn't dangling scant inches above them, he could see gaps in their ranks, large enough to step in if he moved with painstaking caution, but he hesitated.

There were several options for the first step, but he had no idea which direction to go. And he had already tripped one booby-trap; there were almost certainly more.

Then he noticed a mark carved into the stone. It

looked like a paw print—a large triangular pad with four evenly spaced oblong toes, all pointing forward. He was no expert, but it looked a lot like a dog paw.

"The lightning dog guides the souls to the Underworld," he muttered. "All right. Let's do this."

He extended a leg out over the frozen swarm and eased his foot down with all the care of someone trying to cross a minefield. The sole of his hiking boot made contact, and then he transferred his weight onto it.

The floor remained solid beneath him, and as he advanced, he saw another paw print a couple feet further ahead. Beyond it was another, set slightly to the left of the others.

"There's a path through them," he shouted. "Marked with paw prints. I'm going to follow it."

"I'm coming down," Bell replied.

Maddock could hear low voices, Miranda and Bones trying to talk the elderly archaeologist out of his stated decision. He knew they wouldn't succeed, and even though he agreed with them, he also understood where Bell was coming from.

The argument was eventually resolved, and as Maddock took his fifth step, following a path that seemed to be spiraling out from the center, he glimpsed someone starting down the rope. Not Charles Bell, but Miranda, no doubt going ahead of her father to set a belay for him from below.

Maddock could now see the far edge of the chamber, a stone wall about thirty yards past his present position—fifty or so yards from the center. He kept going, picking his way forward one paw print at a time, curling around the center as Miranda finished her descent.

The path turned him again. Instead of a wall, the beam of his flashlight revealed only deep shadow, and the paw prints were taking him directly toward it, and away from the center. He kept his focus on what lay directly ahead. The paw prints had not led him to a dead end yet, but if Bell was right, a single scratch from one of the obsidian scorpions might prove fatal.

A few more steps and he could just make out the shore—the end of the river of scorpions—a line of undecorated stone tiles. Beyond it, a smaller chamber still cloaked in shadow.

He was sweating now. The air was cool, if slightly humid, and he was barely moving faster than a crawl, but the intense concentration was as exhausting as a marathon run.

Now he could see past the dividing line, though there was not much to see. There was a gap, about six feet across, transecting the chamber, and beyond it, another line of stone blocks, parallel to the first. The gap reminded him of a man-made drainage channel, a more literal river. He wondered if he would find it filled with blood, pus, water, or nothing at all.

A few more steps, and he got his answer. The stone blocks were now only about ten feet away, and beyond them, the dark trough was bristling with sharp spikes.

"Maddock!"

Miranda's shout came just as he was about to take another step, startling him. He froze, his heart pounding, his foot hovering above the last row of carved scorpions. He forced himself to unclench and took several deep breaths.

"Yeah?"

"We're starting out."

Another breath and then he stretched his foot out and took the final step. He felt like collapsing right there, but instead he turned around and shone his light out across the obsidian deathtrap. "Watch your step!"

Miranda located the first paw print and shone her light on it. "You see it?"

Bell was hunched over, hands on his knees, trying to catch his breath after the rappel, but he nodded. "The tracks of Xlotl, the Lightning Dog, showing us the way across the river of scorpions. We've done it, Miranda. We've found the entrance to Xibalba."

Miranda was less sanguine about the discovery. "I still think we're going too fast. Finding it doesn't mean a thing if we don't make it back to tell the story." She looked up the length of the rope to where Angel was just beginning her descent. "Getting back up that rope won't be a picnic."

"The path to the Underworld is a symbolic journey," Bell said. "A spiritual pilgrimage, not a literal journey into hell. We probably won't be leaving by the same path."

"If you say so. You sure you're okay to make it across?"

"I'll do what I have to do." He straightened, took another shallow, halting breath, and then took his first step.

She stayed as close as she dared, but as they ventured deeper into the maze-like path, it was all she could do to stay focused on her own footing. The immediacy of the peril presented by the gleaming black scorpions felt like a physical assault. One slip, one misstep, one minor miscalculation and…

"Oh!" Bell gasped.

Miranda snapped her gaze forward. Charles Bell was bent over, one hand clutching an ankle. "Dad?"

"I'm okay," he said, though the quaver in his voice indicated he was anything but. "It's just a scratch."

Miranda felt her own pulse quickening. "Dad. You have to keep going. Get to Maddock. He'll be able to help. He can…" She had no idea what Maddock would be able to do for her father.

"I know," Bell said after a moment, sounding a little calmer. "You know what, I think it *is* just a scratch. I don't feel anything out of the ordinary. Maybe they didn't use poison after all. Or maybe it's lost its potency."

Miranda hoped he was right. Only time would tell. "Just keep going, Dad. And for God's sake, be careful."

Maddock shared Miranda's horror at Bell's misstep, as well as her utter helplessness. But the archaeologist completed the rest of the journey with no further difficulty. The wound, a two-inch long slice just above Bell's ankle, was weeping blood, but the surrounding skin was not inflamed, suggesting the cut was clean. Maddock rinsed the wound and bound it with gauze and an elastic bandage, finishing up just as Angel arrived. Bones was still making his way through the maze, but Maddock could see that the big man was carrying one of their SCUBA rigs on his shoulder.

"Show-off," Maddock said as Bones got within shouting distance.

"Hey, I don't mind humping in the gear, but if it comes to swimming through rivers of blood and pus, this stuff's all yours." The big Indian was grinning, but the beads of perspiration bore testimony to the difficulty of the effort. As he took the final step, he shrugged the bag with the diving gear off his shoulder and tossed it to Maddock.

At that very instant, a low rumbling rose up through the stone floor, and with a faint *snick*, the obsidian scorpions retreated back into the floor of the chamber behind them.

Bones looked over his shoulder. "Huh. If I'd known that was going to happen, I'd have waited a few more minutes."

"I think the floor's weight sensitive," Maddock said.

"Still trying to convince me that I'm fat," Bones said, shaking his head sadly. "You're just revealing your own insecurities."

Maddock ignored him. "Once you stepped off and there wasn't any pressure on it, the mechanism reset. I don't know if it's safe to walk on now or not."

"It doesn't matter now," Bell said. "Our path lies forward."

Maddock shone his light down across the trough, illuminating the nest of sharp wooden stakes protruding out from the walls on either side. Some of the spikes held onto skeletal human remains. Others were crusted with a dark flaky-looking substance,

"Looks like a BYOB river of blood," Bones observed. He paused for a second, then added, "You know, 'bring your—'"

"Your own blood," Maddock finished. "Yeah, got it. Dr. Bell, do you agree?"

Bell was nodding his head. "I would concur. Fail to make the crossing, and your blood is added to the river. Just like that poor soul." He pointed to a nearby skull, impaled on a stake through the eye socket.

"How do we get across?" Angel said. "Jump?"

"It's not that far," Bones said, "But that platform is only about a meter wide. You'd have to be a cat to stick that landing."

"There's got to be another way," Miranda said. "There's no way my dad can make that jump."

Maddock leaned forward a little, playing the light down into the depths of the chasm. It was deep, at least fifteen or twenty feet down, but something was reflecting the light back from the bottom, glittering like a pinpoint of starlight. "There's something down there," he said. "It looks like gold."

"Maya bling," Bones surmised. "Maybe skelly there was wearing a gold chain around his neck."

Maddock turned to Bell. "Didn't the Maya adorn their sacrificial victims in gold?"

Bell's eyes widened in comprehension. "Of course. The skeletons aren't from people who failed to make the jump. They're sacrificial offerings, brought along by pilgrims making the journey to Xibalba. Blood for the river." He turned to Bones. "Just like you said. BYOB."

"You mean we have to make a human sacrifice before we can go across?" Bones shook his head. "Not it."

Maddock brought his light back to the protruding spikes. "I wonder…" He straightened. "Maybe it's not about the blood. We just need something that weighs enough."

"Enough to what?"

Maddock turned to him, then picked up the bag Bones had humped through the scorpion maze. With two full SCUBA bottles, and sundry other pieces of equipment, it weighed a good sixty pounds. "It's a bit light, but hopefully it's enough."

He took out a coil of rope and tied one end around the carrying straps. As soon as he was finished, he measured off several arm-lengths of rope, passing the remainder to Bones. "Hang onto it," he said, and then heaved the heavy parcel out over the edge.

The bag crashed into the nearest spike which, brittle with age, snapped off with a sound like breaking bones and an explosion of dust. The bag continued to fall, the rope snaking into the chasm, but at almost the same instant that the spike broke off, there was another sound, a deep rumbling that vibrated in the stone underfoot. And then the floor upon which they were standing began to move, sliding forward, partially covering the trough. The stone platform on the far side of the chasm was also moving, sliding out from the opposite direction to completely bridge the gap.

The shift was abrupt, almost unbalancing them. Maddock and Angel reacted by instinctively widening their stances to stay on their feet, as did Bones and Miranda, with the latter gripping her father's arm, helping him stay on his feet. Bones then went into motion, furiously pulling up the bag with their gear lest it become permanently lost, but his haste was mostly unnecessary. When the leading edges of the two platforms were just six inches apart, they stopped moving. Maddock could now see faint paw prints etched in the stone on the far side.

"There," he said, pointing to the mark. "Step there. Move it."

With Angel's hand in his, he hopped over the narrow gap onto the far platform. Miranda and Bell quickly followed, and Bones, still trailing the rope attached to their substitute "human" sacrifice, brought up the rear. As soon as he was across, the two platforms began moving again, sliding back to their original configuration before grinding to a halt. The only difference was that now the five explorers were stranded in the middle of the chamber.

There was another channel on the other side of the platform, but instead of a deep chasm like the one they had just crossed over, this was a comparatively shallow trough—only about six feet deep—accessible by a steep flight of stone steps that descended down to the bottom of the trough, but at either end of the trough, another flight of steps rose to a third platform on the far side. There were no spikes and no sign of skeletal remains, but the bottom of the channel, however, was far from empty.

Maddock shone his light down revealing what looked like a long bramble of dried thorn bushes, covered in a fine powdery black substance, like velvet on a buck's antlers.

Bones, who was looking over his shoulder as he reeled in the rope tied to the gear bag, said, "Maybe 'pus' meant something else to the Maya?"

"You think so?" Miranda said. "Ever heard of a little thing called a staph infection? Or *candida* or *aspergillus*? That black dust is on everything. I'll bet you fifty bucks it's some kind of fungus. Even if we could get through that without a scratch, we'd probably breathe in the spores. Dad is especially vulnerable because of his COPD."

"Could a fungus even survive down here?" Angel asked. "I mean, it's been hundreds of years, right?"

"There's evidence that some fungal spores can remain dormant for at least a quarter century. And even if they're dead, they may have produced toxic or carcinogenic chemical compounds. Not many people realize it, but fungal diseases kill more people every year than malaria, and they're extremely hard to treat." She realized they were all staring at her and shrugged. "I had to take a course in infectious disease. Work related."

"So what are we looking for here?" Bones asked. "Do we need to make another sacrificial offering? Trip some switch and make a bridge across this sucker?"

Maddock shook his head. "I don't think so. I think

this was meant to be another test of faith for the pilgrims. To get to Xibalba, you had to be willing to walk through that stuff, risk getting infected by…whatever that is." He glanced at Bell for confirmation, and got a nod.

"That's not an option for us," Miranda said. "There has to be another way."

"Maybe we could get a gigantic can of athlete's foot spray?" Bones suggested.

"We'll burn it out," Maddock said. "Remember how those spikes broke off? Even though the air is damp down here, the wood is old and brittle. Those thorn bushes down there will probably go up like matchsticks."

Bell grinned. "A solution worthy of the Hero Twins."

"Whose?" Bones said. "His or mine?"

"Because hot smoke is so much easier to breathe than fungal spores," Miranda said, her tone thick with sarcasm.

"We won't be breathing smoke. We've got a SCUBA rig with a couple hours' worth of air. With the main line and the octopus, we can buddy breathe until the air clears, which probably won't take that long."

Miranda offered no further protest, but her disapproving frown remained fixed in place as Maddock began talking them through buddy breathing procedures and other precautions to safeguard them from the heat and smoke. While Bones and Angel worked to fashion a fire shelter from a reflective space blanket, Maddock created a tinder pile from pocket lint and bits of shredded paper, and when everyone was set, he used a fire-piston to set it alight. He could have just used one of the waterproof matches included in the survival kit in the gear bag, but he'd been looking for a chance to try out the fire-starting device, which used compressed air to ignite the tinder. As soon as he coaxed a small flame to life, he tossed the tinder out into the thorn-filled channel and then ducked under the shelter with the others while the fire did its work.

CHAPTER 20

Aside from a layer of gray ash and the lingering smell of smoke, nothing remained of the obstacle described in Maya lore as the River of Pus. Nevertheless, Maddock instructed the others to breathe through damp cloths and kept Bell on the SCUBA regulator as they ventured down the steps into the trough. The fire had burned quickly, consuming the dry fuel in a flash, without raising the temperature of the stone beneath, and what little heat it had created was already dissipating.

Maddock swept his boot across the ash layer at the base of the steps, revealing the first of several paw prints carved in the stone. The prints took a left turn at the base of the stairs and headed down the channel to the stairs leading up the other side. Those stairs brought them to a third stone platform, this one bordered with a row of elaborately carved columns, which unlike the ruins at Copán and Chichén Itzá , were in pristine condition, untouched by wind and weather. A line of paw prints, spaced just a few feet apart, led them between the columns and onto a balcony overlooking another vast subterranean chamber.

Bones shone his light down a wide staircase that descended into the dark unknown. "What's next? River of Crap? Hey, why can't there ever be something like a River of Dos Equis?"

Bell shook his head. "Your guess is as good as mine, but if we're descending again, I suspect it means that we've completed the preliminary tests."

"So this is it?" Miranda said. "We're entering Xibalba?"

Bell spread his hands in a gesture of ignorance, but his giddy expression told a different tale. But as they made their way down the steps, his enthusiasm ebbed.

"I'm not really sure what I was expecting," Bones said as he swept his light across the floor of the chamber, "but I'm sure it was more…" He shrugged. "Hellish?"

Instead of the Maya version of Dante's Inferno, the only thing waiting for them at the bottom of the steps was a large courtyard. There were devils—or more precisely, demonic-looking Maya deities, but they too were carved of stone. Ten elaborately carved stelae, of a style even more dramatic than what Maddock had seen at Copán, each one at least ten feet tall, stood in pairs in a loose ring at the center of the courtyard.

"Watch where you step," Maddock advised, searching the elaborately carved stone floor tiles for more paw prints, but finding none.

"The stelae," Bell gasped, shuffling out across the plaza, seemingly heedless of Maddock's warning. "They're the Lords of Xibalba. Miranda, come here. You need to record all this."

He moved around the circle stopping in front of a pair of twisted figures. "The Lords of Xibalba are always described in pairs. This is Xiquiripat—Flying Scab—and Cuchumaquic—Gathered Blood."

Bones stared at the archaeologist in disbelief for a moment then shook his head. "And people make fun of American Indian names."

"Most Maya deities are similar to those of other ancient people," Bell went on. "Natural forces, storms, heavenly bodies, war and fertility and so forth, but the Lords of Xibalba seem to have been inspired by a different sort of deadly force: Disease." He pointed to the other stelae couplings. "Ahalpuh—Pus Demon—and Ahalgana—Jaundice Demon—who cause people's bodies to swell up. There's Chamiabac—Bone Staff—and Chamiaholom—Skull Staff—who turn dead bodies into skeletons. Ahalmez—Sweepings Demon—and Ahaltocob—Stabbing Demon—who hide in the unswept areas of people's houses and stab them to death. And Xic—Wing—and Patan—Packstrap—who cause people to die coughing up blood while out walking on a road."

"Those are oddly specific descriptions," Maddock observed.

Bell nodded. "It has been suggested that perhaps these deity-pairs represent the very disease outbreaks that decimated the Maya at the end of the Classical period."

"But this place predates that cataclysm, right?"

"By at least a couple centuries, I should think."

"So the Maya knew about these diseases *before* they were wiped out. They even built this temple."

Bell inclined his head, confirming Maddock's train of thought.

Bones, who had been following the exchange, spoke. "You're on to something, Maddock. Spit it out."

Maddock took a moment to organize his thoughts. "The ancients built temples and made sacrifices to their gods as a way of trying to control the natural world. What if the Maya were trying to control this disease?"

"You mean like a…" Miranda shook her head as if the very thought was troubling. "A bio-weapon?"

"Exactly. And maybe it got away from them."

Bell nodded again. "I think that's exactly what happened."

"The guy we caught at Chichén Itzá said that the Serpent Brothers were trying to protect the world from the Shadow. 'The Shadow must remain hidden or the world will die.' That's what he said." Maddock was thinking out loud, but the pieces were falling into place faster than he could speak. "What if these Serpent Brothers aren't the bad guys? What if they're trying to stop this disease—the Shadow—from getting out again?"

Bones snapped his fingers. "The Maya apocalypse! Maybe the prophecy was a warning about another outbreak. Or a timeline. And the Serpent Brothers decided to call it off."

Maddock shook his head. "I don't know if I'd go that far, but…" He turned to Bell again. "You suspected this all along, didn't you? That's why Tam sent us in."

Bell frowned as if this line of thinking disturbed him, but then returned a hesitant nod.

Angel now spoke up. "Do you think that

fungus…the River of Pus…*was* the Shadow?"

Maddock had no answer. Neither did Bell.

"That's good, right?" Angel went on. "It means we destroyed it."

"Something tells me if it was that easy," Maddock replied, "the Serpent Brothers would have already done it. There's probably a lot more of that fungus around."

"The Lords of Xibalba have always been associated with a literal Underworld," Bell said. "The fungus probably came out of a cavern system somewhere near here. Maybe even under this temple."

"We've already tempted fate once," Maddock said. "Right now, we need to focus on finding a way out of here."

"It may be too late for that," Bell said. "I told you, we're on a pilgrimage."

Bones gave a snort of disgust. "So we have to go through hell to get out of here? Outstanding. You don't think maybe you could have mentioned Rivers of Pus and Jaundice demons before we started this one-way trip?"

Bell gave a helpless shrug.

"I'm sure there's a way out of here that doesn't involve going deeper," Maddock said. "Start looking around."

He was trying to remain optimistic despite sharing Bones' grim assessment, but it nevertheless came as a real surprise when, after just a few minutes, they found another staircase on the far side of the chamber, leading up, not down.

Maddock remained wary, half-expecting another trial or for the steps to reverse direction, but the stairs kept rising until, some fifteen minutes after departing the chamber with the statues of the Lords of Xibalba, Maddock felt fresh air on his face. Not long after that, they came to a partially overgrown opening, and emerged into the relatively open air of a Guatemalan jungle night.

Only Charles Bell seemed disappointed.

CHAPTER 21

For a long time after giving Alex his answer, Simpson sat alone in the lab office, wondering what to do.

He didn't know if his employer believed the lie. His voice had quavered a little when giving his desultory reply, "I'm with you," but surely that was to be expected when the topic under discussion was engineering life and death on a global scale.

What other answer could he have given? The subtext had been anything but subtle; play along or else a lot more than just his job would be in jeopardy. If Alex was willing to turn an unstoppable pathogenic fungal agent with the potential to destroy all life on earth over to the highest bidder, it was unlikely that he would hesitate to end the life of one reluctant researcher.

Which was why his actual answer probably didn't matter. Alex would be monitoring him closely now, watching for any hint of disloyalty. A failure to produce results might be misconstrued as uncooperative foot-dragging, or even sabotage.

I can't let him do this, he thought. Yet, what could he do to oppose Alex's scheme? There was no one he could confide in. The facility operated with a skeleton crew, and there was no way of knowing if any of those who remained could be trusted.

But he needed to tell somebody.

The answer finally came to him when a notification alert popped on his computer screen, letting him know that it was time to check on the patients.

Maria!

He hastened through the corridors to the BSL IV wing where the infected patients were kept and quickly donned an environment suit. He felt such a sense of urgency that he had to fight the impulse to rush through the safety protocols. After a seeming eternity, the light in the airlock flashed red, indicating that he was now in a "hot" environment.

Instead of methodically visiting each of the infected subjects in turn, as he had done on previous visits, he went straight to Maria's room. He found her almost exactly as he had left her, facing the wall of her isolation room, as if trying to figure out how to get through it, but now there were red streaks on the walls. Maria had been finger-painting with her own blood.

She turned her head to him as he stepped through the doorway, revealing that the fungal infection had advanced to the next stage. Her face and arms were covered with tiny pinpoint-sized spots of blood—petechial hemorrhaging. As the fever intensified, her blood was thinning, losing its clotting factor, and leaking through her capillaries, and literally oozing from her pores. Even the whites of her eyes were now bright red, and tears of blood were creeping down her cheeks.

She opened her mouth and began speaking, but the words that came out were in the same dialect several of the other patients had been using. It wasn't just fever-induced gibberish. Alex recognized the strange words. All of the patients had used them, just as they had all drawn the same pictures using their own blood and bodily fluids. Both behaviors were unique symptoms of the infection that Simpson did not yet understand. There had to be some significance to it all, but right now, that was the last thing he was worried about.

Maria frowned as if sensing his inability to understand, and took a deep breath before trying again. "Mind... My mind is losing... Mental."

Her effort was heartbreaking. "I understand," he said, trying to spare her from what was clearly an exhausting effort. What he had to say to her would be just as difficult, albeit for very different reasons. "I'm not having any success finding a treatment, and...I'm starting to wonder if I should even keep looking."

The words poured from him, a repetitive and confused rant that felt more like an apology than an explanation. Maria just stared back at him impassively for a while, but then turned back to the wall to resume painting the strange symbol with her blood, as if he wasn't even there anymore. He kept talking anyway, hoping that, by putting his jumbled thoughts into words, he might somehow find clarity of purpose.

And in a strange way, he did.

"I wish I had met you sooner, Maria," he said. "I wish I was more like you. That's why I got into this. I mean, it was part of the reason, you know? The money, too, but mostly I just wanted to help people. Find some new miracle drug to cure cancer or..." He sighed and shook his head. "It's all gone sideways. Even if I do find a treatment, it's only going to make it worse. Alex will have no reason not to make his weapon...Shadow and Light. Millions will die. Billions maybe. And if I don't do it, someone else will. Alex will just..."

He trailed off as the answer came to him. He had looked at the situation every way conceivable, worked out every permutation of the problem, gamed out every possible course of action, and had kept coming back to that same realization. Alex would get his way, whether Simpson helped him or not.

Alex *was* the problem.

And just like that, he knew what he had to do.

He reached out to Maria, touching her face, caressing her. His gloved fingertips left a smear of fresh blood.

"I'm sorry," he whispered again. "This is the only way."

He turned away, unhooked his air hose from the room supply, and headed for the airlock. Before he went in however, he called Alex on the intercom. "I've made a breakthrough," he said, aware that the quaver was back in his voice and hoping that his employer would chalk it up to distortion caused by the environment suit.

Alex's voice crackled from the speaker. "Excellent. I knew you just needed the right motivation. Is it a treatment? If so, I want you to move ahead with human trials."

"It's something else. I can't really explain it. I'll have to show you. Can you meet me outside the isolation ward?"

"I'll be right down."

Simpson let go of the intercom button, severing the two-way connection. His heart was pounding. He was terrified, not because of what he was about to do, but because he knew he would only get one chance to do it right.

He waited two full minutes before venturing into the airlock and shutting the inner door behind him. The light was still red, indicating that the environment was unsafe. The exterior of his suit was probably covered in invisible fungal spores.

The safety protocol dictated that he should begin the disinfectant shower immediately after entering the airlock, but instead he went to the outer door and peered through the viewport, watching for his employer's arrival.

He did not have to wait long. Alex burst into the staging area a few seconds later, an eager question already on his lips. He hesitated when he saw Simpson staring back at him from inside the airlock.

Alex shouted something, probably an exhortation to hurry up, but the thick walls of the airlock prevented Simpson from hearing him.

"I'll be right out," he said, and then threw his shoulder against the outer door.

The airlock doors were controlled by the same computerized system that operated the disinfectant shower, but the system had been built to keep microscopic life forms from accidentally escaping. The individual isolation rooms were equipped with heavy duty locks to ensure that none of the subjects escaped, but the airlock doors utilized a simple electronic lock, just sturdy enough to withstand slight pressure changes. The lock would not disengage until the sanitization cycle ran its course, but it was by no means an impregnable system. The lab's designers had rightly assumed that, knowing the consequences of such an attempt, no sane researcher would ever even think of breaking protocol.

Alex's eyes went wide in disbelief as the door shook from the impact of Simpson's full weight against it.

The lock held but it hardly mattered. The blow had been sufficient to break the seal, if only for a millisecond, and that was enough to initiate the emergency fail-safe system. Outside the airlock, the lights went red and a harsh klaxon alarm began sounding. Simpson knew that, all over the facility, electronic locks just like the one on the airlock door would be activated, sealing off every room and corridor.

That was only the first stage. Simpson knew that he now had slightly less than five minutes to live.

Following a suspected biohazard safety breach, a countdown would be immediately initiated, just enough time for the facility's safety officers—if there had actually been anyone serving in that capacity—to determine if the danger of a BSL-IV agent getting out of the lab was real, and for an evacuation of all personnel in non-affected areas to begin. If the fail-safe was not countermanded by the safety officer, at the end of the countdown, a thermobaric explosive device, located directly beneath the isolation ward, would be detonated. The resulting blast would immediately incinerate the lab, igniting all available oxygen in the process.

No trace of the fungal agent would remain. Maria and the rest of the infected patients, who were already facing a cruel death sentence, would be spared days of dehumanizing misery—at least, that was what Simpson told himself. He too would perish, but his death would save countless lives from Alex's mad scheme.

But ensuring the destruction of the Shadow fungus wasn't enough. He had to be sure that his employer would never get a second chance to destroy the world.

Simpson threw himself at the door again, harder this time.

The lock bolt snapped with a sound like a gunshot, and the door to the airlock flew open, spilling Simpson onto the floor of the changing area. As he fell, his suit snagged on the door handle, tearing a gaping hole that allowed cool and potentially microbe-infested air to rush in. Simpson didn't care. He knew he wouldn't live long enough to begin showing even the first signs of infection. He scrambled to his feet, located Alex, who was now backpedaling toward the locked door out of the room, and sprang at his employer.

But as he crossed the distance, Alex turned to meet him. There was an unexpectedly fierce gleam in the other man's eyes. As Simpson reached for Alex's throat, he glimpsed movement, and then something slammed into the side of his head and he saw nothing at all.

Alex leaped back, putting as much distance between himself and Simpson as the enclosed room would allow. His fist smarted where he'd struck the researcher and he absently rubbed his hand against his pant leg, knowing that doing so would have absolutely no effect on any microbial agents that might have been transferred.

No, he thought. *There's no way that happened. I'm clean.*

But he knew that was the least of his worries right now. Simpson had initiated the fail-safe, and the clock was ticking.

He fought back the urge to stomp the spineless researcher's skull to a bloody pulp. Alex knew he had only himself to blame for not recognizing Simpson's weak-mindedness. Simpson had already sealed his own fate, but there was still time for Alex to save himself.

He turned back to the door, trying the handle to no effect.

Get a grip, he told himself. *Think.*

The door was equipped with a seldom-used numerical keypad—it was rarely locked during normal operations—but the fail-safe automatically blocked employee access codes. Alex however was no mere employee. His executive code trumped even the immutable fail-safe. He punched in the four-digit code and heard a click as the latch disengaged.

The minor victory brought little satisfaction. There were several more locked doors in his way, and even if he got through them all, escaping the immolation of the lab would be a close thing.

How much time was left?

As he ran down the corridor, he dug out his phone and placed a call. He could barely hear the ringtone over the claxon, but after only a second or two, his pilot's voice came over the line.

"Get the bird fired up," Alex shouted.

"Already started," came the frantic reply. "It's gonna be close though."

Alex didn't reply. The pilot knew his job, and nothing Alex could say would change the fact that the minimum amount of time for an emergency helicopter start-up was about three minutes.

It took him nearly that long to clear all the doors to reach the landing pad. Along the way, he encountered a few of the small skeleton crew of researchers and technicians, all of whom greeted him like a savior. He brushed them off, urging them to remain at their stations while he headed to the operations center to override the fail-safe. It was a lie, of course. There was no saving the lab, and not nearly enough room in the helicopter for him to save everyone.

By the time he cleared the last stairwell up to the helipad, the Bell 407 was idling steadily, its rotor blades spinning in a flat disk overhead. The pilot waved to him, urging him onward.

Alex clambered aboard, shouting, "Go!" even before the door was closed.

The helicopter lurched a few feet into the air, then began moving forward, racing away from the helipad without gaining much in the way of altitude. Distance, in any direction, was the only thing that could save them now, and fighting gravity was a lot harder than simply cruising at low altitude above the dark waters of the Caribbean Sea.

Alex craned his head around, holding his breath as the lights of the floating mobile research laboratory—a converted derelict oil-drilling platform he'd picked up for a song—receded behind them.

And then, the tiny star-like pinpoints of light were consumed in a supernova of brilliance.

"Hang on!" shouted the pilot.

The overpressure wave hit a few seconds later, buffeting the helicopter like a stiff wind, but they had already put enough distance between themselves and the facility to escape certain destruction.

Alex sagged in his chair, but his relief was tempered by the enormity of the setback. Simpson, the idealistic worm, had just erased what little progress they had made toward isolating the pathogen.

Thank goodness I didn't put all my eggs in one basket, Alex thought, unconsciously flexing his fingers, working out the stiffness in his bruised knuckles. He turned to the pilot. "Take me to Palacios. I have to join Carina. Everything depends on her, now."

CHAPTER 22

Kasey returned the next morning, right on schedule, setting the ersatz Red Cross helicopter down in the clearing Maddock and Bones had hacked out shortly after arriving. Maddock was expecting another hurried take-off, so was a little surprised when Kasey cut power and hopped out before the rotors could wind down.

She held out a satellite phone. "It's for you."

Maddock took the phone and held it to his ear. "Maddock, here."

After a second or two—the time it took for the signal to bounce through the satellite network to its destination and back again—Tam Broderick's familiar voice sounded in his ear, though her tone was lacking its usual wry humor. "*Did Dr. Bell find what he was looking for?*"

Bones probably would have countered by chiding Tam for rushing past a polite greeting and an inquiry about their good health, but Maddock sensed that Tam was in no mood for jokes, much less rebukes. "More or less," he said. "We found the City of Shadow and just maybe solved the mystery of what happened to the Maya civilization."

"*Tell me exactly what you found.*"

"Evidence of a plague outbreak of some kind. Bell calls it 'the Shadow.'" He gave a quick summary of the previous day's exploration of the pyramid temple to the Lords of Xibalba. "So," he finished. "Are you ready to tell me what's really going on? What's your interest in all this? Is the Dominion trying to get their hands on a bioweapon?"

Tam's task force—the Myrmidons—had been created for the express purpose of rooting out and destroying the international quasi-religious far-right criminal organization known collectively as the Dominion. A few years earlier, Maddock and his crew of ex-military treasure hunters had joined the Myrmidons to stop a Dominion plot to launch a cataclysmic attack against the United States using a mysterious technology discovered in the ruins of ancient Atlantis.

There was another long silence, too long to be simply attributed to satellite lag, Tam spoke again. "*Not the Dominion,*" she said with a sigh. "*Another old friend. ScanoGen.*"

The name brought back a rush of bad memories.

Maddock's first meeting with Tam Broderick had been in the Amazon jungle, on the trail of missing explorer Percy Fawcett and the mythic lost city of "Z." Tam, at the time an FBI special agent, had been working undercover at a biotech company run by the brutish Salvatore Scano. Scano, who had partnered with Dominion operatives, was chasing rumors of a chemical compound that could turn men into mindless, and nearly unstoppable, killing machines, a search which had put him on a collision course with Maddock.

"I thought ScanoGen was kaput," Maddock replied after overcoming his initial shock. "Isn't Salvatore Scano in prison?"

"*He is. His psychopathic spawn, Alex, is now running the show.*"

"Ah. So the apple didn't fall far from the rotten tree."

"*Pretty much. Other than being a spoiled pharma-bro, Alex is the spitting image of his dad. He even has the same delusions of grandeur.*"

Maddock recalled that Tam's cover at ScanoGen had placed her very close to both Salvatore Scano and his son. If anyone was qualified to make that judgment, it was she.

"*Under Alex's leadership,*" she went on, "*ScanoGen has continued to pursue research into exotic organic compounds, with a particular interest in ethnopharmacology—herbal medicines and other traditional knowledge from isolated or extinct societies. That's how I learned about Dr. Bell's search for Xibalba. ScanoGen is one of his primary financial backers.*"

Maddock glanced over at Bell and Miranda, both of

whom were standing close enough to overhear his side of the conversation. He chose his words carefully. "I wasn't aware of that connection."

"*I doubt Dr. Bell realizes what Alex Scano has planned for his research. To be honest, I wasn't completely sure that Scano was up to no good, which is why I kept this on the down-low. That and the fact that, technically speaking, this is outside my jurisdiction.*"

Now Maddock understood. Tam's history with ScanoGen and her feelings about Alex Scano were a matter of record, and absent any demonstrable connection to the Dominion, an investigation into Scano's activities might easily be construed as a witch-hunt.

"Well, I'm afraid I haven't seen anything to confirm your worst suspicions," Maddock said.

He expected either relief or disappointment, but instead, Tam's tone remained grave. "*I'm afraid I have. While you've been playing Tarzan of the Jungle, I've been keeping an eye on ScanoGen, and they're definitely up to something. Under the guise of offering emergency medical support, they put a research team in Honduras ostensibly to help stop an outbreak of a disease that sounds suspiciously like Dr. Bell's Shadow.*"

"You do know that Tarzan was set in… I'm sorry, did you say Honduras?"

"*I did,*" Tam said. "*Your little jaunt to Copán put you practically on the edge of the hot zone, which is why I don't think any of this is a coincidence. I think Scano is looking for the Shadow, probably so he can turn it into a bio-weapon. Or maybe he already has it, and Honduras was just a test. Either way, we cannot let him get his hands on the source.*"

Maddock considered this for a moment. "If what you say about Honduras is true, then he's already got it."

"*Maybe not. Last night, his offshore research facility went up in smoke. And that Honduran village at the center of the outbreak is gone too. Scorched earth. Unless I miss my guess, Scano is back at square one, which means the next stop on his itinerary is the City of Shadow."*

"I told you. We destroyed what we think was the only supply of that fungus."

"Are you absolutely certain of that?"

Maddock frowned, recalling Bell's assertion that the true source of the Shadow fungus lay in some hidden cave system—the Underworld, realm of the demonic Lords of Xibalba. "Owing you a favor is one thing, but I draw the line at crawling around the jungle in search of the fungus of bloody pus and jaundiced death. If certain is what you want, I say nuke the entire site from orbit. It's the only way to be sure."

"Cute, but I'm not sure I'd get very far with that recommendation based on what little actual evidence we've got. But if you can get me something concrete, I'll send in the Marines and a great big bucket of napalm."

He sighed. "I'll talk to Bell. Maybe there's something we missed."

"I'll have Kasey stick with you for the duration. I'm sorry I can't do more."

"Right. But just so we're clear, you—"

The phone beeped in his ear, indicating that Tam had hung up.

"Owe me one," he finished, shaking his head.

Bones shook his head in mock despair. "She suckered you in again, didn't she?"

Maddock ignored him and turned to Bell.

"I heard you mention ScanoGen," Bell said. "They're one of my most generous sponsors. Is that a problem?"

"It might be," Maddock admitted. "When you wrote your grant proposal, did you share your theory about the Lords of Xibalba representing a plague?"

"It's the central thesis of my work."

"Well, that explains why you had no trouble getting them to fund your research. It sounds like Alex Scano is trying to find a way to weaponize the Shadow fungus." He threw a glance in Bones' direction. "You might get your Maya apocalypse after all. Just a few years late."

"Please, tell me you didn't just volunteer us to go looking for it," Bones replied.

"We just need a location." He turned back to Bell. "The exact location of Xibalba."

"So you can destroy it?" Bell put a hand on Maddock's forearm. "There's more to the story of Xibalba than just the plague. In the myth, the Hero Twins journeyed to the Underworld to defeat the Lords of Death. And they escaped alive."

"Defeat?"

"Xibalba isn't just the source of the Shadow. It's also where we'll find the means to stop it."

Maddock felt as if a light had just been switched on. "Now it all makes sense," he murmured. "Scano already has his bioweapon. The only thing he's missing is the cure. We have to find it first."

Angel made a face. "Does that mean we're going back in there?"

"We must have missed something yesterday," Bell said, nodding. "According to the *Popol Vuh*, after passing through the three rivers, a person seeking to enter Xibalba would reach a crossroads—four roads that would try to confuse and trick the pilgrim. And once past that, they would enter the council place of the Lords of Xibalba."

"The stelae?"

"That's what I thought at first, but maybe we made a wrong turn somewhere without realizing it. In the legend, the Lords tried to trick travelers with lifelike effigies. Maybe that's what those stelae were—false choices."

"Crossroads," Miranda murmured.

Maddock turned to her. "You got something?"

"Maybe." She knelt and took out her laptop computer. "I noticed this when I was reviewing the footage from my GoPro. It didn't seem important at the time, but…"

She trailed off as the video file began playing. She fast-forwarded to the moment where they descended the stairs into the courtyard with the ten stelae, and then slowed the replay to one-quarter speed. After a few seconds of this, she stopped and reversed back a few frames. "There."

Maddock studied the frozen image, which captured all ten of the statues representing the Lords of Xibalba. "The stelae. What am I supposed to be looking for?"

"Not the stelae," she said. "The floor. Don't you see it?"

Maddock shifted his focus to the shadowy textures of the decorated floor. At a glance, it looked identical to the repeating patterns they had seen in the other chambers of the pyramid. Bell however immediately saw what his daughter was talking about.

"It's a map!"

Maddock squinted, but it wasn't until Bell traced the image with a finger that the outline of a landmass came into focus. It was subtle, and impossible to see except at a distance, but it was there, filling up the entire vast chamber. "That's the Yucatan."

Bell nodded enthusiastically. "Not just the Yucatan. Most of Mexico and Central America is represented here. This is unprecedented. There are no known examples of cartography in pre-Columbian antiquity."

"No maps at all?" Bones said. "How did they know where to go?"

"They obviously did have maps," Bell said. "The Spanish must have destroyed them all. But as far as getting around is concerned, the Maya, like the Roman Empire, built roads. They called them *sacbeob*: 'white roads.'" He shifted his finger, tracing lines on different parts of the image. Against the backdrop of the map, the enormous stela, seemed small and insignificant. "The white roads connected the major commercial and religious centers. Here's Copán." He tapped more spots on the screen, which Maddock now recognized as distinctive glyphs like the star sign they had seen in the El Caracol observatory at Chichén Itzá .

"I've seen ancient maps," Angel said. "They don't

look anything like what we have today. How did the ancient Maya get such an accurate picture of the Yucatan?"

"Just like the Nazca lines," Bones said. "It's easy to see from up in the sky."

"The Maya were expert mathematicians and astronomers," Bell said, patiently. "They had centuries to make precise observations and calculations."

Miranda rolled her eyes. "Please don't tell me you guys buy into that ancient alien astronaut crap."

Angel's face tightened as she fought to hold back laughter. Maddock just grinned. "Do the stelae mark our present location?"

Bell ran the video forward several minutes to the point in time where they had examined the carvings up close, then froze it again and pointed to a tile near the statues. "There. That's the glyph for Serpens. The Serpents Maw."

"Also known as Ciudad de Sombre."

"If this is accurate, they're actually marking a spot a bit to the south of where we are. And there's a second road system leading directly here from each of the capitals."

"Black roads?" Maddock suggested.

Bell nodded. "It's as good a name as any. And here…" He traced another line leading into the circle of statues. "This is the route to Xibalba."

"Wait, so now you're saying the City of Shadow *isn't* the entrance to Xibalba?"

That took Bell's enthusiasm down a notch. He ducked his head in embarrassment. "Evidently, I misinterpreted the legend in that respect. Ciudad de Sombre is the gateway to the Underworld in a figurative sense, but not the literal entrance."

"Sort of like St. Louis is the gateway to the west," Bones muttered. "So where do we go next?"

"Not far, I should think." Bell tapped the image of the stelae. "This is somewhere in the Petén region, south of Tikal. A hundred miles or so. Unfortunately, this could represent an area of several hundred square miles."

"So the map really isn't going to help much."

"Unless I'm mistaken, the purpose of this map was to instruct travelers to follow the black road. I'd be willing to bet that road starts right where we came out of the temple yesterday."

"Only the road is completely overgrown now."

"The white roads were discovered and mapped by NASA, using remote sensing and GIS technology," Bell said, hopefully. "Perhaps we can do the same."

"It's gonna take more than Google Earth," Maddock said. "Looks like I'm going to owe Jimmy a whole case of Wild Turkey."

"One case?" The long distance Skype connection in no way diminished the disdain in Jimmy Letson's nasally voice. "Maddock, you're so far in debt to me that I'll die of alcohol poisoning if I let you pay me in booze."

"What if we threw in some Cheetos?" Bones said.

Maddock grinned. "Hard work is its own reward, Jimmy. You live for big challenges."

Jimmy grunted. "Well, you're not completely wrong. But as challenges go, this one barely rates."

Maddock knew Jimmy wasn't bragging, at least, not much. It had taken him less than an hour to come back with an answer—barely enough time for them to get settled into their hotel room in Belize City where Kasey had established cover for all of them as Red Cross relief workers.

"Allow me to direct your attention to exhibit one," Jimmy went on.

A browser window opened on the computer, revealing a satellite photo-map of Central America. The picture zoomed in close on the mostly green mass of land that was the Guatemalan rain forest. The image froze and then changed to what looked almost like a photographic negative of the same image, except that now a series of lines and shapes—all too regular and uniform to be naturally occurring—were visible. "That is the City of Shadow," Jimmy said.

Bell was suitably impressed. "This is remarkable. How did you obtain this imagery?"

"He hacked it," Bones said with a shrug. "It's what he does."

Maddock shot his friend an annoyed glance. While no one in the room was under any illusions about the illicit nature of Jimmy's activity, some discretion seemed advisable, particularly since both Kasey and Miranda were officers of the federal government.

Jimmy, however, didn't seem particularly concerned with being outed. "The CIA commissioned a LIDAR survey of the area a couple years back. They were looking for—"

"That's not important right now," Maddock said quickly, cutting him off. "Let's focus on finding the black road."

An arrow-shaped cursor floated over the map, settling on the largest square. "This is the pyramid you explored." A white outline appeared to highlight the temple. "And here is where you came out."

Maddock saw not one, but four distinct lines radiating out from the side of the pyramid, similarly accentuated.

"The crossroads," Bell said, as if reading his mind. "Only one of them is correct."

"True, but they all appear to go somewhere." The image zoomed out again, revealing how the roads curled around the outskirts of the city before diverging in different directions only to terminate abruptly at seemingly random intervals. Jimmy zoomed in on each of them in turn, revealing more structures—square buildings and round cisterns—all invisible to the unaided eye.

"The southern route," Bell said. "That will be the one."

The screen resolution bobbed and jumped and then settled on the terminus of a trail that followed a more or less true line to the south of the City of Shadow, but unlike the others, there appeared to be no hidden ruins at the site. It was also the only black road route that came anywhere near an inhabited area, just twenty miles or so from what appeared to be a fairly large city. The surrounding region had been mostly deforested and divided up into agricultural plots.

"I'm afraid that's the one site that's already been discovered," Jimmy said. "The Naj Tunich cave."

Bell seemed unfazed by the caveat. "Naj Tunich. Of course. That has to be it." He turned to Maddock, his enthusiasm back in full force. "Naj Tunich was only discovered about forty years ago. It's an enormous cave system, adorned with hundreds of paintings and hieroglyphic texts. It was a major pilgrimage site for the Maya, associated with the Underworld and Xibalba. In fact, one of the inner caves is called *Mictlan Ch'en*—Cave of the Underworld. There are still several unexplored passages, including a five hundred foot deep vertical shaft at the end of one passage. It's one of the deepest caves in Central America. That has got to be entrance to Xibalba."

Maddock thought it sounded like a long shot, but Bones just shrugged. "It's close to beer for a change."

"I suppose it wouldn't be the first time we found something hidden in plain sight," Maddock said with a sigh. "All right, Jimmy. Send me the GPS coordinates for the other three points, just in case."

"Will do." An electronic tone signaled the end of the Skype call, but the LIDAR image remained on the screen.

Maddock turned to Bell. "So what can we expect in Xibalba? More tests?"

Bell nodded. "Xibalba literally means 'the place of fear.' The Hero Twins had to make their way through six 'houses,' each of which seems to correspond to a primal fear. Dark House. Blade House. Shivering House, sometimes called Cold House, which is said to be full of bone-chilling cold and rattling hail. There's also Jaguar House, Bat House, and Hot House. And that's just to reach the part of Xibalba where the Lords of Death reside."

"Right. So lots of chances to get killed. And that's aside from insects and snakes and tropical parasites. And a five hundred foot long vertical descent in an unexplored cave." He cast a meaningful glance at Angel. "I don't suppose I can convince anyone to stay here where it's safe."

Bones, his expression completely deadpan, started to raise his hand, but Angel slapped it down. "Not a chance, Maddock," she said, firmly. "Besides, if experience has taught me anything, it's that I'm safer with you."

Maddock prayed she was right about that.

CHAPTER 23

Hector Canul did not slow as he passed the junction where the mountain road met the highway. The road was blocked by a Honduran police vehicle, and he had no desire to attract the attention of the officer sitting inside. Instead, he drove on for another mile before pulling off the road. The ground was still soft from the recent torrential rains and even with four-wheel drive there was a risk of getting stuck, but that was the least of his worries.

Rodrigo had disappeared. Hector had been counting on the old grave robber's greed as a more powerful incentive than his fear, but evidently he had misread the man. Now, he was going to have to do this the hard way.

He got out, taking along a small backpack with food and water, and a machete knife, and headed into the surrounding forest. There was a faint smell of smoke in the air, a reminder of the fire that had destroyed the mountain village of Opalaca—Rodrigo's home. The government was calling it an unfortunate accident, a wildfire caused by an ember from an untended cooking fire. How the flames had ignited the thoroughly drenched vegetation was not something the authorities were willing to address, but the area was nonetheless off limits pending further investigation.

The foliage was thick but pliant, allowing him to simply push through without hacking it down. Blazing a trail might have been faster, but it would also be noisy, and if the police decided to investigate the seemingly abandoned vehicle on the roadside, he didn't want them to know where he had gone. After about fifteen minutes however, he encountered what looked like a game trail winding through the jungle. He studied the faint trail carefully until discovering the distinctive hoof-shape of a boot heel. A smile of satisfaction touched his lips.

There was no guarantee that the boot print belonged

to Rodrigo, or his rival, Diego, but he felt certain that both men had probably utilized the trail at some point in their search for treasure and Maya relics to sell on the black market.

He pushed cautiously down the trail, heading deeper and deeper into the forest, exploring other trails and sidings. Here and there, he found evidence of exploratory excavations, and even weathered stones that might once have formed the walls of ancient Maya homes, yet despite these seeming successes, Hector's sense of the futility of his search grew with each new discovery.

After surfacing briefly, *el Guia* was going to disappear once more into the jungle. The curse—*maldición de la sombra*—would return to its slumber, perhaps for decades or even centuries, awaiting rediscovery by some new hapless victim who would unleash the terrible disease once more.

Hector checked his watch. It was already past noon. He sighed, stabbed the machete into the soft ground, and unslung his pack. He was hungry, but food was not the first priority. He took out his satellite phone and punched in Isabella's number. He had just hit the send button to initiate the call when he spied something just a few more steps up the trail. Still holding the phone to his ear, he started forward to investigate.

Now he could see it clearly, a tiny stone hut, just big enough to shelter one or two people from the weather. The thatched roof appeared to be in good repair, a recent addition, but the walls were ancient.

Isabella's voice sounded in his ear. "Tio?"

"Just a moment," he murmured, continuing forward. The hut had no windows, only an opening just big enough to allow a man to enter if he was bent over nearly double. The interior was dark.

Still holding the phone in one hand, he took a flashlight from the pack and shone it inside, not daring to hope that this might be the place he sought.

The hut was empty.

He sighed and was about to stand when a voice rang out from behind him.

"Looking for something, *mi padre?*"

Hector whirled, almost losing his footing on the soft loamy ground. Both phone and flashlight fell from hands that were groping for a weapon he did not have. Not that any blade or gun would have helped him. The woman who had called out to him—an exotically beautiful redhead, whose nearly naked body was covered in a tattooed pattern that resembled the scaled skin of a forest viper—was not alone. Six more men, similarly adorned with body art that almost perfectly blended in with the surrounding landscape, stood in a loose circle around him. Some had long blowguns raised to their lips, while the rest hefted traditional war clubs. A sheathed obsidian dagger hung from a string belt around the woman's waist, but she was otherwise unarmed. Two more men, wearing ordinary street clothes—gringos by the look of them—stood to either side of her. One of them was big, with a close-cropped haircut that suggested military service. The other was small, effete in appearance and bearing, but with a cruel face.

After regaining his balance with one outstretched hand, Hector rose, maintaining eye contact with the woman. "Carina. What are you doing here?"

A faint smile lifted the corners of her mouth. "Isn't it obvious? I'm doing what you ought to have done long ago."

"Searching for *el Guia?* I didn't know where to look until—"

"I'm not talking about the dog," Carina hissed. "I'm talking about your sacred duty as the high priest of the feathered serpent."

The ferocity of the accusation felt like a physical blow. "My duty?"

"As gatekeeper, you were charged with letting the Shadow go forth into the world at the dawn of Baktun thirteen as the gods willed. You failed that duty. You are weak. Not fit to lead the Brothers, much less preside over the new age of mankind."

Hector stiffened. "You are a mere acolyte. How dare you presume to dictate the will of the gods?" He turned his gaze to the other painted snake-men. He recognized every one of them, some he counted as friends. Their treachery stung like venom. "You speak of sacred duty, yet you would allow a mere acolyte to lead you in a rebellion against the anointed chosen one of Kukulkan?"

His rebuke elicited only another smile. "Kukulkan has blessed my efforts. He has led me to *el Guia.*"

"Then you have it? It's not too late for you to make the right choice, Carina. End this rebellion now, and I will forget what you have done."

"This has grown tiresome," she said with a flick of her hand. "I have tolerated your rudeness only because I need you to tell me how to reach Ciudad de Sombre."

Hector shook his head. "You have not earned that knowledge. In time, perhaps, but—"

"There are other ways of finding it."

Hector raised an eyebrow. "Do you mean to follow the path of *el Guia*, yourself then? I won't help you."

"And what of your *sacred duty*?" she sneered. "The Serpent Brothers exist for the sole purpose of guiding those who have been touched by the Shadow into the realm of the Lords of Xibalba. You taught us that. If you refuse, then you have already abjured your sacred oath, and are not fit to lead us."

Hector gritted his teeth. Carina had outmaneuvered him. Everything she had said was true. For centuries, the Serpent Brothers had kept the terrible Shadow curse at bay by guiding those who were touched by it into the Underworld where, provided they could survive the tests of the Lords of Xibalba, they would, if the legends were true, be restored to health and even imbued with god-like immortality. Some were incidental victims, but most who followed the Serpent Path did so intentionally, offering themselves as a sacrifice to the old gods. The Shadow—the strange substance that contained the very essence of the Lords of the Xibalba—not only compelled those who were afflicted to begin the journey, but revealed ancient knowledge as well, though the physical symptoms often prevented full expression of those revelations.

Of course, that had not happened in recent memory. The guidestones had fallen from memory, and the vessels that held the Shadow dust, like *el Guía*, which had once been kept in holy temples, had been scattered and lost with the arrival of the Spanish invaders with their new God.

Hector had never imagined that he would be called upon to fulfill that obligation, or that it would be used against him in a play to control the Serpent Brotherhood.

He tried a different tack. "This is the 21st Century, Carina. We may honor the traditions of our ancestors, but we must also blaze our own path into the future. The Shadow is a terrible thing. It cannot be controlled."

"Leave that to me," said the cruel-looking man.

Carina gave the man a sidelong glance but immediately returned her gaze to Hector. "Where is the City of Shadow? Tell me, and I may let you live."

"Kill me, and you will never know."

Carina narrowed her gaze at him. With her garish body art, she appeared more reptilian than human, a viper poised to strike.

And then an electronic trilling sound filled the air, breaking the spell.

Carina tried to maintain her intense stare, but the tone sounded again, and a hint of frustration crept into her expression.

"That's me," said the cruel man, taking out a satellite phone, identical to the one Hector had brought with him. He opened it and held it to his ear. "Hello?"

He listened for a moment, and then his beady black eyes lit up. "That's fantastic. Where is that?" Another pause. "We can be there in an hour."

He snapped the phone shut with a flourish. "Good news, Carina. I know where it is."

Hector's breath caught in his throat. "Ciudad de

Sombre?"

"Naw, screw that. We get to skip ahead a few steps. I know where Xibalba is. It's at a place called Naj Tunich."

Hector tried, and failed, to hide his reaction.

Carina focused her serpentine gaze on him once more. "It's true, isn't it? Too bad, Hector. Now I don't need you anymore."

She turned to the nearest of her minions and nodded.

Four hundred miles away, Isabella Beltran's knuckles went white as her fist tightened around her phone. She had to fight the urge to shout into the phone, to demand that her uncle's tormentors stand down or face her wrath.

Her wrath.

She had never felt more helpless in her entire life.

She had, almost single-handedly, wrestled control of the Gulf Cartel from men whose reputation for cruelty would have made the Lords of Xibalba quake. She commanded a veritable army of lieutenants and foot soldiers, and what she could not take by force, she could always buy. But there was not a single thing she could do to help her uncle.

Carina!

Isabella recognized the name immediately. Carina Rivera, a few years her junior, was one of Hector's acolytes. Isabella recalled how, as a young girl, Carina had been singled out for persecution because of her red hair—a visible sign of mixed blood—but once she had embraced the ancient religion of her ancestors, joining the Serpent Brotherhood, that had all changed. She had become part of an honored tradition among the people of Maya heritage, even those like Isabella who mostly only paid lip service to the old ways.

Evidently, the prestige of being part of the Serpent Brotherhood was not enough for Carina. She wanted more. Power. Revenge, perhaps against the world that had tormented her.

Her motives did not matter to Isabella. The bitch would pay for what she was doing.

After Carina's cold declaration, there was silence for a few seconds, and then the sickening crunch of someone—Isabella's beloved uncle—being beaten to death. The sound of blows falling went on for a while, and she again heard the male voice—almost certainly an American—shouting, "Seriously? What's with you people? He's dead, and we've got places to go."

"*Bastante!*" Carina shouted in Spanish.

The blows ceased immediately. For a few seconds, Isabella heard muffled voices, then all was silent.

Isabella's eyes clouded over with tears as she stared at the screen of her phone. It displayed the elapsed time of the call, ticking forward relentlessly, one second at a time. She kept expecting the call to drop, but after a full minute, she realized that Carina and the others had gone, evidently unaware of the open phone line. Now there was nobody left to hang up.

It occurred to Isabella that, she would have to be the one to end the call, but she couldn't bring herself to sever that final connection to her father's brother.

Then she heard something. A rustling sound, movement, and then, a rasping voice. "Bella."

The word sent a chill down her spine. "Uncle!" she sobbed. He was still alive!

"Bella. Shadow." The words trickled out, separated by agonizingly long gaps as Hector fought to draw the breath to keep talking.

"Hang on, Uncle," she cried out. "I'm going to call for help."

"Too late. Stop her. Only you can. Priestess."

"No, Uncle. Don't say that." She listened as he struggled to breathe, waiting for him to tell her something more, to assure her that everything would be all right, but then he gave a long sigh and the silence returned.

CHAPTER 24

As Kasey set the helicopter down near the gravel runway of the Poptun Airport, Maddock spied a beat-up Toyota Land Cruiser emblazoned with the logo of a regional adventure-tour company. The vehicle would normally have been driven by a guide in the employ of the company, but it seemed wise to keep involvement with the locals to a minimum. Naj Tunich was a tour destination, but the cave itself was off limits to the public. Trying to arrange for permission to explore the cave would have been time-consuming and expensive, not to mention very public, so the best option was sneaking in. Not surprisingly, for the right price the tour company operator had been willing to negotiate a "self-guided tour" option. As long as Kasey and the CIA were picking up the tab, Maddock wasn't going to complain.

Kasey stayed behind with the helicopter, standing by in the event that Maddock and the others needed a quick extraction. The cave was only about ten miles away—on the map at least—but it still took more than an hour of navigating rugged dirt roads up into the Maya Mountains to reach their destination, which was marked with a blue sign that read "*Bienvenido. Sita Arqueologico: Cuevas Naj Tunich*." Because the site was relatively close to a populated area, flying directly there would have attracted unwanted attention, so driving in seemed a prudent decision, especially since their cover as Red Cross aid workers wouldn't stand up to rigorous scrutiny. The wisdom of this decision was manifest when, as they were making the short hike into the forest to the cave entrance, Maddock heard the distinctive thump of helicopter rotors beating the sky overhead. The jungle canopy blocked his view of the sky, but he paused to listen as the sound grew louder and then gradually diminished as the aircraft passed by and continued on its way.

"That sounded close," Angel said.

"And big," Bones added. "Like a Chinook."

Maddock had been thinking the same thing. Chinook was the NATO designation for the Boeing CH-47 military cargo helicopter. The two former SEALs had taken more than a few rides in the back of Chinook helicopters which were frequently used to ferry troops to and from their mission objective. With a fuselage that looked a little like a city bus under its tandem rotors, the bird had enough room for fifty passengers, and could even transport vehicles if the situation demanded.

"There's a Guatemalan special forces training facility near Poptun. That's probably all it is."

Yet, despite this seeming dismissal, Maddock's thoughts kept going back to Copán, and the red-haired woman who had somehow arrived there ahead of them. It seemed likely that she was working for Alex Scano, and Tam's revelation that ScanoGen was operating in Honduras, at least partially explained her presence at the site, but it still seemed a little *too* coincidental.

The entrance appeared abruptly, rising out of the forest floor with almost no warning, a gaping shadowy fissure in the limestone, a hundred feet high and about five times as wide. Millennia of tropical rain had eroded the stone into freestanding pillars that seemed to erupt from the ground, and the hanging wall above was studded with thousands of dangling stalactites, all of which gave the impression of teeth in the gaping jaws of an enormous leviathan.

This similarity was not lost on any of them.

"The Serpent's Maw," Bell murmured.

Bones just shook his head. "Here we go again."

The helicopter that had passed overhead was not technically a Chinook, but a civilian variant—with the rather prosaic designation of Model 414—one of several leased to ScanoGen Pharmaceuticals for use in their "humanitarian" mission to Honduras. The 414 was a workhorse, with none of the luxury that Alex Scano was accustomed to, but there wasn't enough room in the executive helicopter for everyone, so just this once, Alex was riding coach. It wasn't an experience he wanted to repeat.

The security contractors were okay, if a bit intense. Carina's men, with their teeth filed to points and their tattoos gave him the heebie-jeebies, but what was really going to give him nightmares was the way they had tenderized that old Maya dude in the jungle.

Carina had the tattoos as well, though they were mostly covered by her blouse and military-style cargo pants, but at least she hadn't filed her teeth down. He kind of dug chicks with ink and piercings, but a mouthful of shark teeth would have been a bridge too far.

The rear cargo ramp was down, which not only allowed air to circulate through the cabin, keeping them relatively cool, but also gave the passengers a panoramic view of the landscape as it passed beneath them. For the most part, it had been an unbroken sea of green, but as they approached their destination, Alex noted a patchwork of fields and roads, and then as the helicopter made its approach to the airport, the neighborhoods of Poptun.

As the airstrip came into view, Carina jumped up and ran to open door. She lingered there for only a moment, then ran over to one of the crewmen, shouting something. Alex was content to let her take charge until, without any warning, the helicopter banked and began rapidly moving away from the airfield.

"What's going on?" he demanded.

"They're already here," Carina replied, her eyes flashing dangerously.

"They who?"

"Maddock's group. The people traveling with your contact."

Alex glanced out the open back end of the transport aircraft and saw the smaller helicopter parked at the airport, shrinking into the distance. He knew all about

Dane Maddock, the man that helped the treacherous Tam Broderick take down his father, nearly destroying ScanoGen in the process. So far, Dane Maddock's activities hadn't posed a real threat to the endeavor. In fact, the treasure hunters helping Charles Bell had unknowingly blazed the trail for ScanoGen, but with the goal in sight, they might prove more of a hindrance.

So?" he asked, returning his gaze to Carina. "All the more reason for us to set down now."

Carina shook her head. "What was it you said before? We're going to skip a few steps."

The mouth of the Naj Tunich cave was a vast open area, mostly flat, except where archaeologists had dug exploratory trenches. Bell explained that, in the heyday of the Maya Empire, thousands of worshippers would have gathered on the floor of the cave while the priests performed rituals on a terrace above them. The excavations supported this hypothesis; the floor was actually composed of artifacts, pottery and other litter, cemented into place by subsequent centuries of mineralized water dripping down from above.

"Some of the local Maya still worship here," Bell said, pointing to the remnants of a stone fire circle.

"They still worship the old gods?" Maddock said. "I thought the native religions were mostly extinct."

"The arrival of the Christian conquistadors forced practitioners of the old faith underground," Bell said with a wry smile. "If you'll pardon the obvious pun. But those traditions are deeply rooted in their culture."

At the back of the cathedral-like mouth of the cave, the explorers had to climb a steep retaining wall, built by the Maya to preserve the passage into the deeper reaches of the cave. Maddock and Bones took the lead in order to help Bell up the incline. As Angel scrambled up to join them, Bones used a pry bar to pop the lock on the gate erected by the Guatemalan government.

As they stood there, poised to begin the descent into the confines of the cave, Maddock could feel a breeze on his face, rising out of the cave, as if it were breathing. "This place really is alive," he mused.

"It was to the Maya," Bell said, wheezing a little as he struggled to catch his breath after the climb.

If the entrance to the cave was the breathing maw of a living beast, then what lay beyond was the throat—a cramped, hundred-yard long passage, sloping down into the depths. Although there were adequate handholds and steps cut into the limestone, the rock was slick with moisture. Fortunately, previous expeditions had left behind a fixed safety line which Bell clung to as he made his way down.

The initial descent ended at a chilly pool where mineralized water flowing down the far wall had created lobes of glass-like flowstone that glittered in the beams of their lights. The effect was spectacular, but there was little time to stop and appreciate it. The vertical shaft, which Bell believed would lead them to the realm of Xibalba, lay at the end of a long arterial passage, more than two miles beyond.

As they splashed through the pool, Bones shouted over his shoulder, "Hey, Miranda, be sure to keep your phone dry."

Angel moved closer to Maddock, embracing him in a seemingly spontaneous display of affection, but as she brought her face close to his, she whispered, "Bones is really giving her a hard time about the phone. I can tell when he's busting chops. This is something else. What's up?"

Maddock shook his head. "Maybe nothing."

"Dane. Come on. No secrets between us."

He glanced over at Miranda who was helping Bell across the pool. "She's always on that phone. That's a bad habit for an intelligence officer. Unless it's something else. ScanoGen got to Copán ahead of us. I gave Miranda the wrong coordinates to the City of Shadow, and nobody bothered us."

"That doesn't prove anything."

"No, it doesn't. That's why I'm going to keep right

on being careful around her."

Angel drew back a little, one eyebrow raised accusingly. "I don't buy it. This is her father's expedition. Why would she risk it…risk his life? Are you sure this isn't just because she likes girls?"

"I'm sure." He was certain of that much, but he wasn't as certain about his suspicions. All he really had was a lot of assumptions. The near-encounter at Copán might have been a mere coincidence, just like the Chinook fly-by was probably nothing.

In any event, it didn't matter now. They were well outside the mobile coverage area, and even if Miranda had possessed a satellite phone—which she did not—the signal wouldn't get through the tons of rock surrounding them.

They continued through passages adorned with Mayan glyphs and paintings that depicted human sacrifices and bloodletting rituals, as well as graphic sexual images. Bones could not resist commenting on one painting that depicted a naked Maya couple embracing in preparation for intercourse. The male figure sported an enormous phallus which was thrusting toward the belly of the female figure. The detail of the stylized image left little to the imagination.

"I'll bet that guy was a god," he remarked.

"You'll like this one, Mr. Bonebrake," Bell said, pointing to another painting of a squatting man.

"A guy taking a crap?" Bones said, raising a dubious eyebrow.

"Not exactly. This is a depiction of a bloodletting ritual. The Maya believed that there was great power in blood, so when a king wanted the fertility gods to bless him with a child, he would drive a bone needle or a stingray spine through his penis as an offering."

If Bones was shocked by this, he didn't let on. Instead, he just grinned. "Hey Maddock, sounds like Kyle Olsen?" Even though he had pitched the question to Maddock, he turned so that he was facing Miranda. "This guy in our platoon had a Prince Albert piercing.

When he got drunk, he'd whip it out and put a carabiner through it, then hang heavy stuff from it."

"That's hot," Miranda replied, deadpan but with a wicked gleam in her eye. "You should get one."

"As much as I love a trip down memory lane," Maddock said, "we should probably keep moving."

"Dane," Angel called out. "Everyone. Look at this."

She was pointing to another glyph further down the wall and apparently all by itself. The image was more weathered than the explicit sex scene, but was nonetheless instantly recognizable.

It was the same canine figure depicted on the golden guidestone they had found in the cenote in Mexico, except this dog was facing to the side, in profile, with one paw extended as if to point the way, pointing deeper into the cave.

"I guess we're in the right place," Maddock said.

They continued down the winding passage, finding more of the guide glyphs wherever the passage branched off in more than one direction. At a few points, the passage narrowed to the point where they were forced to move single file. Bones had to unsling his pack just to scrape through.

A short almost vertical descent dropped them down into a cavern with adjoining passages to the left and right. Directly ahead was a ledge that overlooked a seemingly bottomless abyss. The shaft was not very wide, in fact, it was barely larger than the diameter of a chimney, but was so deep that their lights could not reach the bottom. On the back wall of the shaft was another guide glyph, this one pointing straight down.

"I suspected the guide glyphs were leading us here," Bell said. "We're in the section called the Cave of the Underworld. The Naj Tunnel leads out of here and back to a cavern called 'the Quiet Way.' But this…" He gestured to the vertical shaft. "This was the sacrificial well. A cenote of sorts. A passage into the Underworld."

"A regular highway to Hell," Bones muttered.

"I suppose if you were at the bottom of it, you'd call

it a stairway to Heaven. The Maya thought of caves as both. They believed that at night, the sun descended into a cave in the west, traveled underground and then emerged from another in the east at dawn. As you can imagine, it's not a place where mortals are exactly welcome. To the best of my knowledge, only one expedition has reached the bottom, and they were only able to spend a few minutes down there."

"Why?" Angel asked.

"I believe one of their team members was injured, forcing them to hasten their exit. There was also a problem with the air. High carbon dioxide levels, possibly from some decaying organic matter."

Maddock had anticipated this problem when Bell had first mentioned the five hundred foot deep shaft earlier in the day. In addition to all their other gear, he had brought along a low-tech CO_2 detector—a cheap disposable cigarette lighter he'd picked up in Belize City. He took it out and spun the wheel with his thumb, producing a bright yellow flame. "Old caver trick," he said. "As long as it's burning yellow, there's enough oxygen in the air. If the flame burns blue, we might have to turn back."

Angel leaned out over the shaft and made a face. "You know, we probably shouldn't have left poor Kasey all by herself at the airport. Is it too late to change my mind about this?"

Maddock just blew her a kiss.

They had brought along two SCUBA rigs and a single bottle of compressed air, just in case it proved necessary to swim through flooded passages. In a pinch, they could buddy breathe, just as they had done in the City of Shadow, but the supply wouldn't last long enough for a prolonged excursion. If they ran into befouled air, they would probably have to cut their investigations short. Maddock doubted it would be a problem as long as the was air moving up from the depths.

With help from Miranda, who had almost as much

rope training as a SEAL, Maddock and Bones rigged up a fixed line—the first of several pitches that would be required to reach the bottom. There was a reason the passage had confounded earlier expeditions. They would be descending about forty-five stories—half the height of the Eiffel Tower—and getting down would be the easy part. They had brought along over a thousand feet of rope, which when combined with the rest of the climbing equipment and the SCUBA gear, represented a lot of weight. Fortunately, they wouldn't have to pack it any further.

He just hoped Bell's remark about mortals not being welcome in the Underworld would not prove too prophetic. Descending the shaft might well prove to be the easiest part of the day.

CHAPTER 25

If Angel had chosen to rejoin Kasey Kim, she would not have had to go very far. Kasey was still by herself, but she was not at the airport. She was, in fact, racing up the mountain road toward Naj Tunich.

Just thirty minutes after Maddock and the others had set out for the remote archaeological site, a twin-engine Beechcraft Baron had touched down at the airstrip. Kasey had watched with only mild curiosity as the plane taxied down the gravel runway, but decided it might be worthwhile to call Tam with the plane's tail numbers, just in case. While she was waiting for the ID, an SUV drove out to meet the plane's lone occupant, an attractive dark-haired woman that kind of looked like Penelope Cruz. What piqued Kasey's interest however was the woman's attire; she wore tigerstripe pattern camouflage fatigues. So did the men who got out of the SUV to meet her.

To the best of Kasey's knowledge, no army or law enforcement group in Central America was using tigerstripe camo, but it was readily available on the civilian market, and sometimes used by agencies and organizations with the freedom to pick their own gear—the CIA for example.

The plane belonged to a shell company with an address in Wilmington, Delaware, which Tam informed her was believed to be a front for the Yucatan-Gulf Cartel, and the woman who looked like Penelope Cruz was none other than the Cartel's current leader, Isabella Beltran. She was definitely not one of the good guys, but as far as Tam knew, she had no connection to ScanoGen.

Nevertheless, Kasey's curiosity was growing. All were dressed up for action and in a hurry, and that was enough to make her want to know more. She took the parabolic microphone from her surveillance kit and decided to listen in on their conversation. The portable eavesdropping device had a range of up to three hundred feet, but she only managed to catch a few words before they all got in the SUV and took off.

One word had stood out from the rest.

Cueva.

Cave.

The descent was tedious, but not as difficult as Maddock had anticipated. He let Miranda play mother hen to her father, and focused on making sure the pitches were securely anchored to the limestone. This far from the surface, they couldn't afford any mistakes.

The last hundred feet or so were the hardest, with the shaft narrowing to an uncomfortably tight squeeze between walls slick with mud, but at the bottom, the cavern opened into a bulb-shaped chamber. The floor was covered with an ankle-deep layer of thick mud. If, as Bell had suggested, the Maya had thrown sacrifices into the shaft, then there were probably hundreds of shattered skeletons compressed into the sediment beneath him, not to mention a fortune in gold jewelry. Maddock however was more interested in the opening at the back of the cavern, and the barely discernible guide glyph etched into the damp stone.

After everyone was down, and Bones had made the obligatory joke about naked mud wrestling, they headed into the passage, which meandered up at a gentle incline for about a hundred feet before emptying into a round chamber, and an apparent dead end.

There were no visible exits, but a quick look around suggested there was a lot more to the room than was evident at first glance. The chamber was almost perfectly circular, and the circumference was adorned with several high relief carvings of very familiar looking figures seated on thrones.

"The Lords of Xibalba," Bell said, confirming what Maddock had already deduced.

"There were ten Lords in the City of Shadow." Maddock swept the room, performing a quick head count. "I count twenty here."

"This is the Council of the Death Lords. It was a test for travelers wanting to enter the Houses of Xibalba. The Lords sat alongside mannequins designed to confuse the arriving supplicants. The only way to gain entry to the Houses was to greet the Lords by name. They also tried to trick the travelers into sitting on a bench that was actually a hot cooking stone."

"Nice," Bones remarked. "And why exactly did the Maya worship these guys?"

"To get the cure to the Shadow disease," snapped Miranda. "I guess you haven't been paying attention."

Bones tilted his head. "I ask a lot of rhetorical questions. I guess *you* haven't been paying attention."

Maddock ignored their exchange and brought both his flashlight and his attention back to the recess with the low shelf, directly opposite the passage through which they had entered. "That kind of looks like a bench."

He squatted down and shone the light into the space beneath it. The beam revealed a small round pit. A teepee of wood had been erected in the center, atop a bed of gray ash and black charcoal. He picked up one of the pieces of wood, half-expecting it to crumble to dust. It didn't, but it was as light as balsa in his hand. Still, it was hard to believe that the wood had been there for hundreds of years. Maybe they weren't the first ones to make it this far after all.

"It's a fire pit all right." He looked up at Bell. "So what now? Does the legend say how to pass the test?"

"You mean besides not getting punked?" Bones said.

Bell shook his head. "In the *Popol Vuh*, Hun Hunahpú and Vucub Hunahpú, the father and uncle of the Hero Twins, journey into Xibalba and basically fail all the Council's tests. They even sit on the cooking stone and get burned, but the Lords allow them to enter the Houses of Xibalba anyway because their plan all along was to sacrifice them later. The Court tests were just a joke to them. Later, when the Hero Twins arrive, they trick the Lords into revealing their names, and then when the Lords tell them to sit down on the bench, they simply refuse."

"Isn't it obvious?" Miranda said. "There's probably a secret door here somewhere. To unlock it, we have to figure out which of these statues are the real Lords of Xibalba."

Maddock considered this for a moment. "I think you're right about there being a secret door, but I don't know if there's a trick to opening it."

"What do you mean?"

"Remember those three rivers in the City of Shadow? The only way to get past them was with sacrifice. And the paw prints lead right to the cooking stone."

"What are you saying? That we have to sit on the stone?"

Maddock shrugged and then without waiting for further prompting, lowered his backside onto the shelf.

Nothing happened.

"Maybe you have to preheat," Bones said.

Knowing Bones, it was meant as a joke, but Maddock knew his friend had hit the nail on the head. "That's exactly what we have to do."

"You're not serious," Miranda said.

But Maddock was serious. If there was one thing he had learned from his previous encounters with the ancient architects of Xibalba, it was that they were sadistic sons of bitches. He took the lighter he'd brought along as a CO_2 detector, crouched down to the firepit and struck a light, holding it to the dry wood until yellow flames began rising. The smell of woodsmoke soon filled the air, but there must have been a chimney at the back of the recess, because the chamber remained relatively clear. After a few minutes. Maddock could feel a change in ambient temperature. The room was heating up. The mud on his clothes and skin was rapidly drying out, forming an itchy crust. As he stared at the stone shelf, his enthusiasm for meeting the test head-on began to wane.

"Stone takes a while to heat up," Bones observed. "But once it does, it stays hot." He grinned at Maddock.

"Having second thoughts?"

"Second, third and fourth," Maddock admitted. He touched a forefinger to the stone shelf. It was warm but not enough to burn him. Not yet.

Instead of sitting, he stepped up onto the shelf, reasoning that his boot soles would afford an additional layer of protection, provided they didn't melt down. As soon as he transferred his weight onto his leading foot, the shelf shifted beneath him, dropping an inch or so. A low rumble shuddered through the stone and the back of the recess abruptly slid aside, revealing a dark passage behind the cooking stone.

"Open Sesame," Maddock said, trying to sound triumphant, but mostly just feeling relieved.

"Awesome," Bones said disingenuously. "We're all going to hell."

"Not if you don't get moving," Maddock said. He could feel the heat in his boots now and knew it would only get worse. "It might close if I step off, so go past me, one at a time. Bones, take point."

For once, the big Cherokee did as instructed without comment, stepping up onto the shelf and pushing past Maddock toward the opening. He stopped at the back, shining his flashlight in to get the lay of the land, then stepped off the cooking stone and into the darkness. Maddock peered into the revealed passage, but aside from Bones' silhouette, there was nothing to see.

Miranda went next, but lingered on the shelf to help her father move forward. She winced as the heat got to her, and began hopping from one foot to the other as Bell struggled to catch up. Maddock was sorely tempted to imitate her fire dance. The heat was well past the point of merely being uncomfortable, and he knew that soon it would actually do physical injury, but he was worried that too much movement on the stone slab might inadvertently cause the secret door to slam shut.

As soon as the Bells were past, it was Angel's turn. As she brushed by him, she gave him a quick kiss. "Hey, hot stuff."

"Hey, yourself." Maddock tried to smile, but with his teeth clenched against the pain, it was more of a grimace.

He was about to follow when he saw something moving in the chamber they had just vacated. For a fleeting instant, he assumed it was just a trick of the light, that the flickering of the flames under the cooking stone was making the carved statues of the Death Lords appear to move, but it was spooky enough to prompt him to shine his light into the gloom.

It wasn't a trick of the light.

Standing in the center of the chamber was a man, at least Maddock assumed it was a man. It was hard to know for sure, since his first impression was of reptilian scales. The figure threw a hand up to shield his eyes from the intensity of the light, giving Maddock another second or two to process what he was seeing.

It was a man all right. Beneath a layer of streaky mud, his nearly naked body was painted or tattooed with a pattern of scales. His black hair was pulled up in a top-knot, similar to what was portrayed in Mayan glyphs.

Maddock recalled what Bell had said about modern Maya carrying on the old traditions and wondered if this man was the local shaman who had seen them sneaking into the cave.

Busted.

Despite the heat that was starting to cook the soles of his feet, Maddock raised a hand. "Sorry. I can explain."

By way of an answer, the main raised a long reed to his lips, pointed the other end of it at Maddock and then puffed up his chest in preparation to blow.

Maddock ducked instinctively as a tiny projectile shot toward him, missing his cheek by scant inches.

The attack galvanized Maddock into action. He turned his back on the Maya warrior and bounded into the passage where the others were waiting. Even as he did, something clicked and he realized the significance of his assailant's appearance.

"The Serpent Brothers!" he shouted. "They found us."

CHAPTER 26

Maddock whirled around again, hoping to see the stone door sliding back into place, but the passage back to the council chamber remained open. The snake-warrior stood at the far end, carefully sliding another dart into his blowgun. Maddock's warning however had not gone unheeded. Bones reacted instantly, drawing his pistol and firing down the passage before the man could shoot his dart. The multiple reports were painfully loud and set Maddock's ears ringing, but through the haze of gunsmoke, he saw the Serpent Brother go down.

"You think he was alone?" Bones shouted.

"I wouldn't bet on it," Maddock replied. He kicked himself for having pushed the mysterious brotherhood down the list of possible enemies. Tam's revelation about ScanoGen had distracted him from other threats. "Hopefully, that cooking stone is hot enough to keep anyone else from trying to get through, so maybe we've got a few minutes. In any case, I don't think we're leaving that way."

He turned slowly, sweeping his light around to survey their new surroundings. After making their way through so many extravagantly painted chambers, culminating with the elaborately carved Council of the Death Lords, this new cavern felt like a bit of a letdown. It was essentially just a big natural cavern. The ceiling was studded with stalactites, and the uneven floor was a maze of stalagmites and other mineral formations, but there was nothing to indicate it had ever been used for ceremonial purposes, much less that it served as the Maya equivalent of the first level of hell.

"What did you call this place?" Maddock said, speaking to Bell. "Dark House?"

Bell nodded. "A place of total darkness. A traveler would have to feel their way through, or be lost forever."

"Good thing we brought flashlights," Bones said,

sweeping his across the floor and revealing several shadowy voids that looked like fissures and crevasses in the floor. "I can see how it might be a bit of challenge without them."

"They might not have had flashlights," Angel countered, "but they could have brought torches, right?"

"There were probably priests in the Council chamber who confiscated their torches before allowing anyone to begin the ritual journey."

Maddock however thought Angel had a valid point. "Without some kind of light source, we wouldn't have gotten this far. That would have been just as true for the ancients. The Death Lords were all about making people suffer. There's got to be more to this challenge than just finding our way through a dark cave."

Bell spread his hands helplessly.

"All right," Maddock said. "Let's fan out. Search every corner of this place. Watch for traps and remember, just because something looks like a way out, doesn't mean you should rush through."

"Typical Maddock," Bones said with a snort of laughter. "Armed snake-men out there and he wants to work a grid."

"It's not a grid," Maddock said. "Or maybe it is, but you know there's a reason why we do things that way sometimes."

Bones raised his hands in a show of surrender, but couldn't resist getting in a final dig. "Must be that time of the month," he said in a stage whisper.

He paid for the comment as Angel and Miranda took turns slugging him in the biceps, each blow landing hard enough to make the big man wince. When they were done, Bones shook his head and rubbed his arm. "Forgot I was outnumbered," he mumbled. "Next time, Maddock, let's stick with the regular crew. Those guys at least have a sense of—ow! Ow!"

Maddock turned away, shining his light out across the cavern. "Okay, let's work a grid."

Carina froze, raising her hand and cocking her head sideways. "Did you hear that? That was gunfire."

They were about halfway down on the third pitch, dangling from the ropes left by the rival party.

Not the best place to stop, Alex thought.

But he had heard the noise too, though he wasn't as certain about the source. "It sounded more like someone beating a rug to me." He shrugged. "I didn't think your warriors were packing heat."

Carina and her men had taken to the ropes like spider monkeys. Alex didn't share their boldness, which was why they were only partway down the four hundred foot shaft. Carina had sent two men ahead to scout the bottom of the passage. Presumably, they were the cause of the noise.

"They aren't," Carina said through clenched teeth. "That was someone shooting *at* them. Maddock's people." She kept her head turned, listening for more reports.

"Sound can do funny things down here," Alex said. "Are you sure it wasn't coming from the surface? My guys *do* have guns. Maybe they were shooting at a monkey or something."

On Carina's advice, he had left his contracted security men topside—a couple to guard the helicopter, the rest watching the entrance to make sure nobody got too curious about their excursion. Carina had explained that the cave was sacred ground, and while Alex was under her protection, the Lords of Death would not look kindly on the presence of so many outsiders.

The mumbo-jumbo surprised Alex. His initial impression of Carina was of someone who had outgrown the primitive traditions of her forefathers, recognizing the old myths about gods and demons as allegories, concealing a truth better explained by science, but evidently playacting as the would-be high priestess of the Serpent Brothers had triggered some kind of spiritual relapse. He really didn't have a problem with that, provided of course she was still able to produce a cure for the Shadow, but his willingness to indulge her superstitious beliefs ended when there was a threat of getting shot.

"It wasn't from the surface," Carina insisted.

"Then maybe we should have brought my men instead. No, scratch that. No maybe about it. This is what I pay them for. Let's head back up and get them."

Carina ignored him. The noises had not repeated, but after a moment of consideration, she started down again, rappelling faster, practically at a freefall. Alex was sorely tempted to start back for the top, but climbing up was going to be a lot of work and he doubted he could convince Carina's men to go back up the shaft in order to pull him up.

Gritting his teeth in frustration, he started down, pushing the limits of his comfort zone. The rope burned across his palm, but he pushed on to the next ledge, unclipped and started down the last pitch. A few minutes later, he splashed down in the mud pit.

"Ugh," he groaned. "Disgusting."

There was nobody there to hear him complain, but streaks of mud on the far wall revealed where the others had gone.

He slogged across the mud, cursing every step, and climbed up into the passage where he found Carina and the others bent over two prone figures.

One of them was clutching one shoulder, trying to stanch the flow of blood from a wound there. His tattooed skin was covered in mud and blood, and his filed teeth were bared in a rictus of pain, but he was gasping out some of that strange gibberish language he had heard them using. Carina was replying in the same dialect.

This irked Alex. He had instructed Carina to always speak English in his presence, and while he was willing to tolerate the odd exchange in Spanish—he spoke enough to get by—he was pretty sure that wasn't the language they were using. Carina looked up to acknowledge his arrival. Her expression was fierce with anticipation. "They found the Council chamber. We must hurry."

"Carina! Wait."

But she paid no heed, starting down the passage at a near run, with the wounded scout and the rest of the snake warriors following close on her heels. Alex growled in irritation, but his curiosity was a stronger motivating force than his wariness.

He finally caught up to them in a room adorned with several elaborately carved images and, stranger still, a fireplace with an actual fire burning in it. The heat in the small chamber was stifling, but Carina and her warriors were crowding around the fire as if desperate for even more warmth.

"What the hell are you doing?" he growled.

Carina cast an impatient glance back at him. "We are in the Council chamber of the Lords of Xibalba. The entrance to their realm is there." She pointed to a shadowy void behind the low fireplace.

"Well, what are we waiting for?"

Carina frowned at him. "You forget. Maddock's people have guns. They may be waiting to ambush us as we go through."

Alex frowned. He had not expected timidity from someone as fierce and aggressive as Carina. Maybe he had misjudged her. "Fine. I'll go first."

"You think they'll spare your life?"

"My contact won't let them kill me." He couldn't be 100% certain of this, but it was a risk worth taking, particularly in contrast to Carina's hesitancy. He pushed through the group of warriors, but the heat radiating from the fireplace stopped him in his tracks. He reached out a hand, but just six inches above the flat stone surface, he thought he could feel his skin starting to blister.

"Is this the only way in?" Without waiting for an answer, he knelt down and then thrust his hand into the flames.

"Stop!" Carina shrieked, though her reaction had

come a fraction of a second too late to matter. Alex's open palm had already struck the flaming ember pile, swatting at it. The orange flames disappeared as the coals were scattered across the bottom of the fire pit. Although they continued to glow a dull red, the chamber was plunged into near total darkness.

"Don't worry," Alex said. "I did a hot coal walk at Lighthouse seminar. It's possible to touch hot coals without getting burned as long as you don't maintain contact for very long. It's called the Leidenfrost Effect. As soon as that stone cools down a little, I'll—"

Before he could finish the statement, a low rumbling sound vibrated through the stone beneath him, punctuated by a loud final thump.

"What the hell was that?" he asked, groping for his flashlight.

"That was the door closing," Carina said, irritably. "You can't fool the Lords of Death with mind games you picked up at a self-improvement seminar. The only way to reach the Underworld is by going through the fire."

"Well, that's a stupid idea."

"This is why I wanted your men to stay behind. They aren't prepared to make the journey into the Underworld." She sighed. "We'll need to gather some more firewood."

"Screw that. My men have explosives. We'll just blast our way through." He sensed another objection coming and raised a hand. "We're doing this my way, now."

He stood and was about to start back down the passage when he saw a light coming toward them. He couldn't make out any other details, but assumed it had to be one of his men. That assumption was proved correct when a male voice called out. "Mr. Scano?"

"Alex," he growled under his breath. "Why can't anyone get that right?" Then, loud enough to be heard by the approaching group, he said, "Right here. What took you so long?"

The guy clearly had no sense of humor. "Uh, I know you told us to stay topside," he said as he closed the remaining distance. "But we thought you would want to know about this."

There were four more figures making their way down the passage, but one of them was not a member of the security team. It was a woman, and she was being dragged along between two of the armed men. Alex shone his light into the woman's face.

The woman was average height and slender, with a lean physique that suggested she spent at least part of every day exercising. She had porcelain pale skin and jet black hair pulled back in a severe ponytail that didn't suit her at all, but was consistent with the tiger stripe pattern camouflage uniform she wore. She was beautiful, Alex thought, despite—or maybe because of—the bruises on her cheek and the blood streaming from a gash on her left temple. Like everyone else, she was liberally frosted with mud.

"Who's this?" he asked.

"We were attacked," the security leader said. He sounded angry. "No warning. A bunch of guys with assault weapons came out of the jungle. We kicked their asses, but we lost a couple guys in the process. It looked like she was the leader, so we let her live."

Alex stalked forward until he was almost nose to nose with the captive. "I paid a lot of money to keep the Guatemalan government off our backs. You better believe I'll be getting a refund."

"She's not Guatemalan," Carina said from beside him, her voice low and dangerous. "I know this woman."

Alex glanced sidelong at the redhead, one inquisitive eyebrow raised, but before he could frame a question, the prisoner straightened and spat a gobbet of blood on the floor in front of Carina. "And I know you," she hissed. "*Puta*. You killed the only man who was ever kind to you."

"She is Isabella Beltran," Carina said, ignoring the insult.

"Beltran?" Alex knew this name. "The Queen of the Yucatan-Gulf Cartel? I've heard about you. You're one tough *chica*. I didn't know you were mixed up in this Maya voodoo garbage, though."

Isabella's gaze flashed toward him. "Mixed up like you, *pendejo*?"

Her black eyes seemed to drip with venom for a moment, but then she recoiled from him as if he were a leper.

"She is the niece of Hector Canul," Carina went on. "The former high priest of the Serpent Brothers." She stressed the word *former*, twisting the knife in what was clearly an open wound of grief. "She thinks she came here to avenge him."

"Ah. The plot thickens. I guess you girls have some catching up to do."

"Hector raised her in the traditions of our people. He meant for her to be his heir."

Carina's triumphant tone did not escape Alex's notice, but the reason for it was lost on him. "And that's important why?"

"She knows the innermost secrets of the Brotherhood. She can lead us through the Houses of the Dead."

CHAPTER 27

After several minutes of fruitless searching, Maddock was ready to admit defeat. Despite the obvious wisdom of his preferred course of action, the cautious approach had not paid off. About the only thing he could take comfort in was the fact that none of them had fallen into one of the many seemingly bottomless pits that riddled the cavern floor like holes in a block of Swiss cheese.

Those chasms seemed to be the only way out of Dark House, especially since the passage to the Council had abruptly closed, sealing them in. He assumed that was the handiwork of the Serpent Brothers who had elected to trap them inside rather than pursuing them into Xibalba. There was no point in trying to get the door open again since the snake warriors were lying in wait on the other side, ready to turn them into blow-dart pincushions. Aside from the round stone covering that passage, there was nothing manmade in the chamber; no paintings or carvings that might have concealed a hidden door, and worse, no paw prints. No, the only way out, Maddock knew, was down.

Each of the fissures seemed like a portal to a different level of hell. Some were venting heat and reeked of sulfur, while others were blowing positively frigid air, as if they were connected to an industrial air conditioning unit. None of the holes seemed particularly welcoming, but that was probably the point.

Maddock joined Miranda and her father near the center of the cavern. "I think we're going to have to climb down into one of these pits," he said. "We've got enough rope for a single pitch, but I don't think we've got the time for a trial and error approach. Any suggestions?"

Bell's forehead drew into a frown of concern. "My apologies, Mr. Maddock. I really didn't expect it to be quite so challenging."

"Just imagine what it must have been like doing this in pitch darkness," Angel put in as she joined them.

Maddock looked at her sideways. "Yeah," he said slowly, trying to do exactly that. "I wonder…"

"Uh, oh," Bones warned. "He's thinking again. Stand back. Don't get any on you."

"What if we're supposed to be doing this in total darkness?"

"Right," Bones said slowly, the sarcasm unmistakable. "That's a really good idea."

"No, he's right," Miranda said. "Back in the cenote in Tulum, I got confused and didn't know which passage to take. I was out of air and I knew I had to get it right on the first try, so I shut off my dive light. There was just enough daylight getting through to show me the way forward."

"The operative word there being 'daylight,'" Bones countered. "I don't think there's any of that where we need to go."

"You're missing the point," Maddock said quickly. "These tests, the rivers, the cooking stone… We keep thinking we need to find a way to avoid them, but every time, the only solution is to play along."

Bell nodded slowly. "In the *Popol Vuh*, the Hero Twins had to spend the night in the Dark House. They were given a torch but they knew it was a test, so they refused to use it."

"That's it then. It's something we can test at least." He switched his headlamp off, though there wasn't a noticeable difference in the light level. "Turn off your lights. We'll see what happens."

Angel and Miranda immediately did, but Bones hesitated, giving Maddock a chagrined look before finally complying. When the last LED light winked out, darkness fell over them like a heavy, stifling blanket.

"This sucks," Bones mumbled.

"Afraid of the dark, big bro?" Angel said.

"Give it a second," Maddock said. "Our eyes haven't adjusted to the dark yet."

"They're not going to adjust to this, Maddock. To see in the dark, you have to have at least a little bit of light."

"Maybe we're supposed to use sonar," Angel suggested. "Echolocation. Like bats."

"Shh," Maddock hissed, trying to concentrate on piercing the veil of night with his eyes. He knew Bones was right. Night vision was one thing, but without some faint source of illumination, the pupils of their eyes would never dilate wide enough to let them see in absolute darkness. If he saw anything at all, it probably was just his eyes playing tricks on him.

"Okay," he said after a moment, "It was worth a—"

"Does anyone else see that?" Miranda said, cutting him off. "On the ceiling? It looks like stars."

Maddock had seen them, faint points of gleaming pale blue, but had assumed they were just an optical illusion.

"I see them," Angel chimed in.

"That's Serpens," Bell exclaimed.

"You're not actually suggesting that we can see the stars through solid stone," Bones said.

"It must be some kind of phosphorescent lichen," Maddock said. "There's no way we would have ever seen that with our lights on."

"It's showing us the path," Bell continued. "If we follow the Serpent Route, we'll find the way out."

"Wait!" Maddock shouted, quickly before the archaeologist could act on this revelation. "Nobody move. I'll do this. Once I figure out where we need to go, we can turn on our lights again."

"Why you?" Miranda asked. "You're not Superman, you know."

Maddock had to fight the urge to snap back at her. "You can go first next time, okay? For now, just keep it down and let me concentrate."

Without waiting for her consent, he dropped to his knees and placed his palms flat on the rough stone floor. Raising his eyes toward the ceiling, he located the nearest "star" and began crawling toward it, testing the ground ahead of him as he went. He was doing fine, making good time, right up to the moment when he put his right hand out and, instead of finding solid stone, it just kept going. Unbalanced, he tilted forward suddenly, his chest slamming down against the edge of the chasm he had nearly plunged into.

Angel and Bones cried out to him almost simultaneously; she used his first name, and Bones used his last.

"I'm good," he shouted, regaining his four points of contact and backing slowly away from the pit. Despite that assurance, the near miss left him a little shaken and the unrelenting darkness wasn't making it any easier. Nevertheless, he eased forward, probing the floor to locate the rim of the hole so he could find a way around it.

After what seemed an eternity—probably a good thirty seconds or so—he was moving again, albeit a little more cautiously. He had to navigate around two more fissures, though finding them was a lot easier since both were venting hot fumes. The third hole he encountered was directly under the point of light that corresponded to the star in the Serpens constellation they had begun calling "the Serpent's Maw." Maddock thought he could feel a cool breeze rising from the chasm, but there was nothing else remarkable about it.

"I think this is the one," he called out. "Turning on my light now."

He shielded his eyes against the expected shock of brightness and hit the switch. Even with that precaution, the brilliance stung his eyes. Blinking away tears, he shone the light down into the hole.

The fissure was small by comparison to most of the others, more a jagged crack in the floor than a gaping hole. The sides were not sheer opposing faces, but undulated in and out, forming a series of easily discernible handholds and steps. Climbing down it would be a piece of cake, at least for everyone but Bell, and even he would probably be okay as long as there was someone to belay him.

The only real danger was the uncertainty of what lay below.

The cavern lit up again as the rest of the group switched on their lights and came to join him.

"Should we send the camera down?" Angel asked.

Maddock shook his head. "No time. Bones, rig up a hasty belay. I'm going to climb down and check it out."

"Aren't you forgetting something?" Miranda said. When Maddock returned a blank look, she added. "You said I could go first."

"I did?" Maddock shook his head, more in exasperation than anything else. Maybe Bones was right. This was definitely a lot easier with his regular crew backing him up. "Fine. Knock yourself out."

"I think what he meant to say," Angel said, "is 'be careful.'"

Miranda gave her a big smile, and then promptly sat down on the cavern floor, her legs dangling out over the edge. With no apparent hesitation, she lowered herself into the fissure, and began climbing down as if descending a ladder.

Maddock leaned close to Angel and whispered in her ear. "She's just doing this to impress you, you know."

"You've got nothing to worry about," Angel whispered back. "But you know, you don't always have to be the first one through the door."

"I let Bones go first sometimes."

She touched a finger to his lips, shushing him.

Miranda's head and shoulders emerged from the fissure a few seconds later. "I don't know if this is the right one after all. The climb down is easy, but the bottom is a death trap."

Bell knelt beside. "Describe it."

"It's like the River of Scorpions, only a lot worse. The floor is covered with shards of obsidian, sticking straight up. They're everywhere. If we try to go down, we'll get sliced to ribbons."

"So much for that idea," Bones said. "Back to the

drawing board?"

Bell shook his head grimly. "This is the correct passage," he said. "The chamber below us is another test. The House of Blades."

"How did the Hero Twins beat that one?" Maddock asked.

"Uh, they told the blades not to hurt them. The blade points lowered and they were unharmed."

"Maybe there's a specific phrase in the Mayan language that will make the blades retract into the floor," Bones suggested. "How do you say, 'Hey Siri, lower the knives,' in ancient Mayan?"

"I doubt they had the technology to pull that off," Miranda said, rolling her eyes. "Or maybe you believe in magic?"

Maddock stared down into the fissure. "Did you actually step on any of the blades?"

Miranda stared at him like he had two heads. "Are you kidding?"

"It might be a test of courage. Your boot soles will provide some protection. And if the points are close enough, it will distribute your weight, just like a swami on a bed of nails." He grinned. "Want me to go first?"

She shot him a withering look, and started down again. A few seconds later, her voice welled up from below. "I'm about to step onto them."

Maddock braced himself for a cry of pain or a stream of curse words. Instead, there was just a loud *snick.*

CHAPTER 28

Isabella Beltran glowered at Carina. "You killed my uncle. What makes you think I would ever help you?"

The red-haired woman stared back implacably for several seconds. "I regret what happened to Hector, but he betrayed our gods. You must realize this."

"You're one to talk about betrayal."

Carina ignored the accusation. "Hector failed his most sacred duty to usher in the new age. But it's not too late to correct his mistake."

"The Shadow?" Despite everything Hector had taught her about the Shadow and the role of the Serpent Brotherhood in keeping it a secret, she had always wondered if any of it was really true. Now she knew the terrible truth. "You actually *want* to start a pandemic?"

"Such was always the will of the gods. At the end of every age, they have swept away the failures and started anew."

Isabella looked past the other woman, studying the other faces in the chamber. She didn't recognize the gringos, but she knew the others—acolytes of the Brotherhood, just like Carina.

Traitors.

"Don't tell me you agree with her? Did Hector teach you nothing? Our traditions are there to anchor us to our ancestors. They were never meant to be taken literally."

None of the warriors would meet her gaze, but the gringo who had recognized her spoke up. "Miss Beltran, I can see why you might not want to see the world cleansed. You are criminal. A drug dealer. Your wealth and power were built on a foundation of undesirable people and anti-social cravings. But surely you must see that it's not sustainable in the long term. There are just too many of them."

"Them? You mean human beings?"

"Oh, please. They're miserable cockroaches. That's why they turn to your drugs. They know they're miserable."

Isabella stared at him for a moment. "Who the hell are you?"

"Call me Alex."

She remembered that one of the gunmen had earlier called out another name. "Alex Scano. I've heard of you. How dare you call me a drug dealer? You've made more money selling pills to those 'miserable cockroaches' than I could dream of."

"Ah, but the difference is that I'm ready to stomp them out. You'd rather keep them as pets. They're parasites, Miss Beltran. An infestation that needs to be wiped out."

"If you really feel that way," Isabella said, holding his gaze, "then what are you waiting for? You have the Shadow already, don't you? I know you found *el Guia* in Honduras." She paused, setting the hook. "But you're afraid to die like a cockroach, aren't you? You're here because you think you can find a cure to keep you safe."

Alex turned to Carina. "This is a waste of time. Let's just blow the wall."

"Wait!" Isabella cried out. Although it had perhaps not been Scano's intention, that was the one attack against which she had no defenses. "You don't need to do that. There's a way into the Houses of Xibalba."

"And you will show us?" Carina said, her voice edged with suspicion. "Why the change of heart?"

"You said it yourself. Hector made me his heir. I am the high priestess of the Serpent Brotherhood, not you. I cannot let you destroy this sacred place. If you truly honored our traditions, you would feel the same way."

Carina's only answer was to gesture toward the still hot cooking stone. "Do it."

Isabella shook loose of the grip of her captors, but instead of approaching the passage, she went to the stone figures at the periphery of the chamber. She chose one, placed her hands against it and spoke in the ancient tongue. "Morning, Hun-Came."

She then moved to the statue beside it, and greeted it as well. "Morning, Vucub-Came."

"Of course," Carina whispered. "The test of recognition. I should have seen it."

Isabella looked over her shoulder at the other woman. "Yes, you should have."

Although she had never been in the chamber, Isabella knew this was the correct solution. Hector had told her this story when she was just a little girl, the story of how the Hero Twins sent Mosquito to bite the Death Lords in their Council chamber. The first two were revealed to be effigies of carved wood, but the third one cried out when bitten, which caused the fourth one to ask his brother what was wrong, not only identifying them as the real Death Lords, but naming his brother as well. In this fashion, Mosquito had learned the names of the Death Lords and reported back to the Twins, which allowed them to bypass the test.

Allowing the intruders free passage into the Houses of Xibalba might have seemed almost as sacrilegious as letting them blast their way in, but she knew that this was the simplest trial they would face.

The Lords of Xibalba might not have been real, but they were by no means defenseless.

"It worked!" Miranda called out. "You were right!"

Maddock let out the breath he had been holding with a relieved sigh, and climbed into the fissure. As Miranda had indicated, the way down was much easier than some of their earlier descents, with a veritable ladder of holds turning into an actual staircase down to the cavern where Miranda was waiting.

The beam of his light was reflected back in hundreds on glittering pinpoints, like sunlight dancing on a wind-rippled sea, only this sea was made entirely of glossy black obsidian shards, each one as long as Maddock's arm from elbow to fingertip.

An area of a several square feet around Miranda was

clear, revealing a flat floor perforated by hundreds of little holes, from which gleamed more shiny black points. It was all eerily reminiscent of the river of scorpions. Scattered amidst the thin razors of volcanic glass were no less than three human skeletons. There was a clear section about ten yards long off to the left, like the start of a path, but Miranda wisely had not started down it yet.

"As soon as I put my foot on the blades, they dropped into the floor. That way looks clear. But look at that."

She indicated the wall about fifty yards beyond the clear path. The chamber was not a natural cavern, but more closely resembled the interior of the pyramid in the City of Shadow, with walls of stacked stone. There were rectangular doorways in each wall—Maddock counted ten in all, including the one through which they had entered—but that was not what Miranda was pointing to. One section of the wall was reflecting their lights back with a warm golden hue which Maddock instantly recognized.

"That's another guidestone."

"But are we supposed to walk toward it, or in the direction it's looking?"

The latter choice would mean intentionally stepping onto more of the obsidian blades, but there was no guarantee that the cleared section would stay that way.

"Whatever we do, we should stay together," Maddock said. He ducked back into the stairwell. "Come on down. It's safe."

"Ha!" Bones' disbelieving laughter echoed down at him. "Sure it is."

Nevertheless, in a matter of just a few minutes, they were all gathered on the floor of the Blade House. Bell studied the alignment of the guidestone on the wall for a few seconds before giving his opinion. "It's just a guess, but if this is a test of courage as you suggest, then taking the easy way is probably not the right answer."

"That's my feeling as well," Maddock said. He turned

to Miranda. "Is it my turn again?"

She scowled at him, and then answered with action rather than words, raising her foot above the obsidian blades.

As soon as she transferred her weight onto that foot, there was another loud click, and another section of blades, about five yards long, retreated into the floor. Simultaneously, the blades in the cleared section they had not chosen, shot out of the floor. There was one other change, which Angel noticed first. "The guidestone is gone."

Maddock turned his head to look and saw that the golden plate had indeed disappeared, but even as he was processing this news, Bones called out. "Found it. Right there."

The guidestone—or more likely a second one exactly like the first—now shone out from a different wall, almost perpendicular to the newly cleared section.

"There's our answer," Maddock said. "Go where the guide dog is looking."

"Unless it's some kind of trick," Bones said. "What if they change the rules halfway through the game?"

"The Death Lords were cruel," Bell said, "but not particularly devious. The tests described in the *Popol Vuh* were rather simplistic. Of course," he finished, "Anything is possible."

"Way to inspire confidence, doc," Bones grumbled, but he pushed past Maddock and Miranda, oriented himself away from the newly revealed guidestone, and stepped out onto the blades....

Which promptly vanished, along with the golden plate that had shown the way.

They proceeded cautiously, following the gaze of each new guidestone as it was revealed. As they moved through the maze of blades, the temperature dropped noticeably until it was chilly enough to raise gooseflesh on their arms. The frigid air was issuing from one of the doors, which not surprisingly, was exactly where the guidestones seemed to be leading them.

"This must be Shivering House," Bell said as they reached the doorway. His speech was abrupt, clipped, as if he was having trouble breathing again. "Also called Cold House."

"You think?" Bones said, grimacing. "Feels like being in a meat locker."

"What did you expect from something called 'Cold House'?" Miranda said.

"I figured it would just be chilly and damp. You know, like a cave."

"As much as I hate to admit it," Angel began, "my brother's got a point. That's not a natural cave-y cold in there. If feels like…well, a meat locker."

Maddock sniffed the air. He earlier noticed a faint chemical odor, like cleaning fluid. It was stronger now; strong enough that even a mere whiff of it made him cringe. "That smell. Ammonia. It's a natural refrigerant."

"Natural?" Angel sniffed and then winced. "You're kidding, right?"

"It's true," Miranda said. "Ammonia is a naturally occurring organic nitrogen-hydrogen compound. It was a very low boiling point, several degrees below zero, but at certain pressures it stays in a liquid state, acting as a very efficient refrigerant."

"You're a chemistry expert now?" Bones remarked.

"I know a lot about explosives," she replied, for once without a trace of sarcasm in her voice. "Especially ammonium nitrate, which is made from, among other things, guano. Like you find in caves sometimes. But figuring out how to use it to chill the air…" She shook her head. "We didn't figure that out until the 19th century."

"You were saying something about ancient technology?" Bones said. "I keep hearing about how advanced the Maya were. They could have come up with something like this. Especially if they had help from—"

"Don't say it," Angel pleaded. She hugged her arms to her chest. "There's a Hot House, too, right? Sooner we get through this, the sooner we can warm up. Let's save the wild speculation for later, okay?"

"Sounds good to me," Maddock said. He turned to Bell. "Any helpful hints from the *Popol Vuh*?"

"The Cold House is described as a place of unimaginable cold, with rattling hail. As far as how to survive it goes, I'm afraid all it says is that the Twins dissipated the cold. It doesn't say how."

Maddock took a cautious step through the doorway and onto a ledge about four feet wide that ran parallel to the wall behind him. Directly ahead, the floor fell away at a forty-five-degree angle, sloping down into a hazy fog that completely shrouded the lower reaches of the cavern. The ceiling overhead was thick with a forest of dangling protrusions—icicles of frozen water that had formed atop mineral stalactites. The ledge, like the stalactites, was covered in a thin layer of ice.

"Well, I don't know about hail," Maddock said as the others filed in behind him, "but it's definitely going to be cold. There's nowhere to go but down, into that."

He pointed down the slope and immediately felt his foot start to slide. He threw his hands out, flailing to arrest his fall. Bones' caught him before he could hit the icy floor or pitch headlong down the slope, but not quite soon enough to preserve his dignity.

"Slippery," was all he could think to say.

Angel edged close to the precipice and shone her light down, sweeping it back and forth across the slope. She trained the beam on one spot about ten yards to their right and few feet down. "That looks like a paw print. Maybe that's the direction we should go."

"Once we start down that slope, there's no stopping," Bones said. "How are we supposed to get down there without getting ourselves killed?"

Maddock straightened. "I'd say, very carefully."

CHAPTER 29

Crossing the still warm cooking stone reminded Alex of the firewalk he had done, except this time, the potential reward wasn't just some abstract sense of accomplishment or empowerment. When this was done, he was going to literally change the world.

He felt an almost overpowering urge to keep moving.

"This is Dark House," Carina said as he stepped down onto the floor of the cavern.

"Well, that's a clever name," he retorted. He played his light across the pitted floor of the chamber. "Who would have expected a cave to be dark? Oh, wait. We did. That's why we brought flashlights."

"Your lights won't help you find a way through the darkness," Isabella said. There was still a hint of contempt in her tone, but Alex thought she mostly just sounded beaten.

"I suppose you're the only one who can guide us?"

Carina spoke quickly. "We don't need her. I learned the same stories she did. I know what we have to do. We must trust the darkness." She stared at Isabella, as if looking for confirmation. The latter raised an eyebrow but said nothing. "Turn off your lights. All of you. In a few minutes, the path will be revealed."

"That sounds like a really lame idea," Alex replied. He turned to Isabella. "If she's right about that, then we probably don't need you anymore."

Isabella shrugged. "Do as you will."

Alex laughed. "All right, then. Lights out, everyone."

He maintained his confident façade right up until the moment the last light winked out. The darkness was like nothing he had ever experienced before, a void so ominous that he almost dropped to his knees to avoid falling.

This was much, much worse than dancing across hot

coals.

"Carina," he sang out, unable to completely mask the quaver in his voice. "How are we coming on that path?"

"Patience," came the hissed reply.

"Not my strongest personality trait." As he said it, he thought he heard a muffled grunt in the darkness. Cold adrenaline dumped into his veins, and for an instant, he could see monstrous shapes emerging from the absolute darkness.

"I'm turning on my light," he said, frantically trying to find the switch.

"No! We will never find our way through if we give into our fears."

Alex growled in frustration and kept his hand poised above the switch. "You'd better hurry. We need to keep moving."

As the seconds ticked by, his other senses became hyper-aware. The sounds of the men around him breathing, sniffing the air, coughing, passing gas. He could definitely smell that, too. The air was a rank mixture of sewage and something like cat piss.

"Enough!" he shouted. "You had your chance, Carina."

"No, wait. I see something—"

Alex ignored her plea and hit the switch, unleashing a focused but nonetheless blinding shaft of light into the cave depths. He winced, squinting against the painful but welcome brilliance, and brought light around toward their captive.

Except Isabella wasn't there anymore, and the two men who had been holding her between them lay motionless on the cavern floor, with blood streaming from slashed throats. The other men from the security team immediately went to work trying to assist their fallen comrades, but it was plainly evident that the men were already beyond help.

Alex could barely form words through his rage. "Where is she? Find her."

"Forget her," Carina snapped. "You'll never find her

in here. You'll only get more of your men killed."

Alex rounded on her. "And I suppose you've got a better idea?"

"I do. There's a map on the ceiling. It's phosphorescent, so you can't see it with the lights on, but I saw where it was leading." She took a few confident steps forward, then shone her own flashlight down onto the floor. "I didn't notice this earlier, but look. These marks on the floor here…"

She shifted the light, following a series of smudges on the rough limestone. "That's mud, left behind by someone crawling on hands and knees. It perfectly follows the map on the ceiling."

"Who? Isabella?"

"No. There wouldn't have been enough time for her to kill your men and crawl out. More likely, it was Maddock's team. They're helping us and they don't even know it." She knelt and dragged a fingertip across one of the smudges. "It's still wet. We're close. We can catch them."

Alex stared at her for a moment, then looked back at the two dead men. His private army was dwindling fast. Part of him couldn't help but wonder if that had been Carina's intention all along.

With the last of the rope, Bones anchored Maddock for an exploration of the fog-shrouded bottom of the hill. The vapor was like evaporating dry ice, and as he slid down the frozen slope, Maddock had a feeling the air inside would be just about as cold, too.

Up close, he had a couple feet of visibility, just enough to see what looked like a narrow protrusion—barely wider than his hand—extending horizontally from the slope. To either side of it, there was an abrupt vertical drop into the impenetrable cloud.

"Hold up!" he shouted, barely able to get the words out through chattering teeth.

Bones immediately locked down the rope which kept him more or less at the edge of the freezing cloud.

"Gi…Give me…a foot."

Bones played out a few inches of rope, just enough for Maddock to plant his feet on the protrusion, which he now saw continued out across the gap, like a bridge.

A very narrow bridge.

Covered in an inch of solid ice.

With painstaking care, he eased himself down until he was straddling the span. The cold knifed up through his body. The ice stuck to the fabric of his clothes, and the exposed skin of his palms as he began shuffling himself forward.

"More!"

The rope slackened, allowing him to scoot out a little further. Now he could see all the way across the gap to the hidden ledge at the end of the bridge. There was another doorway there.

He slid the rest of the way across, frantic for any respite from the bone-chilling cold. The ledge, as expected, was thick with ice, but the doorway was close enough to give him something to hold onto as he got back to his feet. Even better, he could feel warm air—relatively speaking at least—flowing through the opening.

He turned and looked back but couldn't see anything except white mist.

"Made it across," he shouted, finally able to catch his breath.

"Cool," Bones shouted back.

Maddock tried to think of a suitable rejoinder, but his brain was still partly frozen. "Yeah. There's a really narrow bridge down here, and door on this side of it. But the bridge is slippery and it's really cold. I think we might be better off to rig a Tyrolean traverse."

"I'll take care of things on this end," Bones replied. "Let me know where you're ready to start catching."

It took only a few minutes for the two to anchor the line at both ends, forming a zip-line across the chasm. Once the line was secure, the others began sliding down, one at a time. Bones slid the pack with the SCUBA gear along, and then followed.

When he was finally across, he hugged his arms across his chest. "Man, I'm glad there are no babes around to see my package right now."

"Don't use shrinkage as an excuse," Angel quipped. "I've talked to enough of your exes."

"Let's focus." Maddock nodded to the open doorway. "Any idea what we're going to find in there?"

"We've made it past Dark House, Blade House, and Cold House," Bell said. "If I had to hazard a guess, I'd say we've reached the House of Jaguars."

"Literal actual jaguars?" Bones shook his head. "That makes no sense. How could a population of big cats survive down here, closed off from the outside world? What would they even eat?"

"Hopefully not us," Maddock said, and stepped through the doorway.

The jaguars that waited for them were not literal flesh and blood animals, but rather larger-than-life carved stelae, dozens of them, arranged in haphazard rows on the floor of a large natural cavern. The layout was somewhat reminiscent of Dark House, only with statues instead of stalactites and pitfalls.

"That's a jaguar?" Bones remarked, shining his light on the nearest stylized image. "How can you tell?"

"Easy," Angel said. "It's got spots."

"So does a Dalmatian."

"When you've studied the Maya as long as I have, it's obvious," Bell replied. "But these aren't all jaguars." He shone his light onto one of the other figures. "That's a monkey. And there's a rabbit."

"If you say so. They remind me of the terra cotta warriors in the Emperor's Tomb in China."

"Or the chess game in that Harry Potter movie," Angel added.

"Obviously we don't have to worry about them eating us," Maddock said. "But must be some other kind of threat here. A booby trap, maybe."

"That would seem a logical assumption. I would

recommend giving them a wide berth."

"I'm not sure that's going to be possible. Any hints in the *Popol Vuh*?"

"The Hero Twins kept the jaguars at bay by giving them bones to chew on instead. I'm not sure how that helps us."

"Could be a weight activated trap," Bones suggested. "Like the River of Blood."

"We'll go with that for now," Maddock said. "Dr. Bell, keep calling out the animals as we get close. Everyone else keep a look out for the trigger mechanisms."

They moved out single-file, heading toward the stelae that Bell identified as a monkey. As soon as they were past it, Bell excitedly pointed to another stelae. "There. Those two. They're dogs. And they're facing each other. That's the way we should go." Before anyone could respond, the archaeologist pushed past Maddock and strode out to prove his theory.

"Dad!" Miranda shouted, but Bell was almost to his goal.

Maddock held his breath as Bell reached the narrow gap between the two carvings, but nothing happened. Bell shone his light into the next row. "There are two more dogs here. This is the way. Follow me."

Maddock exchanged a glance with Bones.

"Guess it was his turn to go first," Bones said with a shrug.

Bell led them from row to row, finding the paired dogs that, evidently, indicated safe passage through the death trap. As they progressed, Maddock felt the pins and needles of sensation returning to his frost-numbed fingertips and extremities.

"Thawing out is worse than getting frozen in the first place," he remarked to Angel.

"I know, right? I take back what I said about wanting to get to Hot House."

Maddock looked out at her sideways. "What do you mean?"

"It's like a sauna in here. And getting worse."

"So it's not just me."

Miranda, walking alongside her father, looked back. "Definitely not just you."

The passage at the far end of Jaguar House was like the open door of a blast furnace, glowing red with radiant energy, and even Bell seemed reluctant to approach it.

"Hot House," he announced. "Also called the House of Fire. It is said to be filled with fire. The Twins passed through unhurt, but there's no explanation given as to how they were able to do so. But the lightning dog hasn't led us astray yet."

"It's got to be close to 200 degrees in there," Angel said.

"Yeah, but it's a dry heat," Bones remarked.

He probably meant it as a joke, but Maddock knew that humidity made a big difference as the temperatures increased. During the course of their search for Atlantean technology a few years earlier, he and Bones had rescued their teammate Matt Barnaby from the Cave of Crystal Giants in Mexico. The cavern was filled with enormous gypsum crystals, and situated above a magma plume. The temperature in that cave was only about 150 degrees Fahrenheit, but because the humidity was nearly 99%, even with protective equipment, the safe limit of exposure was only about half an hour.

Unfortunately, they didn't have any protective gear now.

"You know," Bones went on, looking right at Angel. "It just might be hot enough in there to burn all that nasty hair off of your back."

He quickly retreated a few steps before she could slug him.

Maddock turned to Miranda. "You want this one?"

Miranda stepped back and made a sweeping gesture. "After you, hero."

I guess she's done trying to impress Angel, Maddock thought, and then stepped through into the passage.

The cavern was smaller than the last, or at least it seemed that way because the neon red glow emanating from cracks that crisscrossed the floor lit it from end to end. The limestone walls and floor were a uniform white under the beam of his headlamp, which had the effect of distributing the magma-like glow, and presumably the heat as well. There were no shadowy corners or blind spots, but at the opposite end of the chamber, maybe fifty yards away, he could see the dark outline of another doorway. The floor, which appeared to be covered in fine white dust, was mostly flat, except where it was cracked, but scattered randomly throughout were little statues that gleamed a metallic orange in the dull light. He couldn't tell which if any were dogs, but he was pretty sure that they were all made of the same fire-resistant material.

Gold.

His original plan was to step into Hot House just far enough to identify the specific dangers they would face and, if he was lucky, spot a guidestone or some other relevant marker, but that plan quickly went out the window.

As he took his third step, he heard a sound like an eggshell being crushed. He drew back, but the crunching sound was now coming from his back foot. He moved again, sideways this time, but no matter where he stepped, the floor crunched like thin ice.

It wasn't ice of course, but rather a thin layer of limestone, baked brittle by the persistent heat of a partially exposed magma pocket.

A line from an old poem flashed through his head. *In skating over thin ice, our safety is in speed.* Instead of retreating, he started forward, almost running.

The crackling sound followed ominously, and each step seemed to release a fresh wave of heat.

He doubted that the original architects of Xibalba had done anything to make this room more dangerous. Nature had done all the work for them, but the floor was now almost certainly more fragile than it had been centuries earlier, during the time of the Maya. Still, it seemed logical that the cracks marked the places where the crust was weakest, so he avoided these. The golden statues might have been placed as guidestones or as bait to lure the greedy to their doom; there was no way to know for sure, so he avoided these as well.

The floor held up. He reached the other side in mere seconds, savoring the relative cool of the dark passage beyond, despite the overwhelming stench in the air. The odor stung his nose and brought tears to his eyes.

"I'm across," he shouted back into the cave. "The floor is thin. I don't know how much weight it can hold, and I don't think we want to test it. There's no trick really, except haul ass and watch your step."

Behind him, in the darkness, there was a strange chattering sound, and despite the heat, Maddock felt a chill shoot down his spine.

He turned away from the passage and slowly turned his head to illuminate the cavern he had just entered.

Just past the entrance, a flight of irregularly carved steps descended down into a vast, stadium-sized chamber. The floor of the cavern was covered in a substance that looked like dark mud. To get through, they would have to wade through a sea of the stuff, but that was the least of their problems.

He tilted his head back, shining the light up at an angle. Wherever the light touched, the ceiling rippled like a field of wheat being stirred by a stiff breeze.

Bones' voice echoed across the glowing chamber behind him. "Looks like I'm going last again."

The chattering got louder and the rustling grew more feverish, as if the ceiling were alive...which in fact, it was.

He had come to the sixth and last house of Xibalba.

CHAPTER 30

After hundreds of years of silence, the Lords of Death were again playing deadly tricks on those foolish enough to enter their dark realm.

Alex had lost two more of his security men. One had fallen victim to a trap in the room Carina had called Blade House. Razor sharp obsidian blades had sprung out of the floor, slicing up through the unlucky man's boots, turning everything below his knees into bloody chunks. Without legs to stand on, he had promptly fallen over and been impaled on the blade points. The second man had slipped on the icy threshold of Cold House and disappeared into the freezing mist at the bottom of the chasm.

That was when Alex had decided to let Carina's men take point.

The Serpent priestess clearly wasn't happy about having to risk her men's lives, but it was simple math. Alex was down to just four men now. Carina had twice that many, and if the old gods started talking to her, telling her that the gringo intruders weren't worthy to enter their sacred realm, the odds were stacked against Alex and his surviving men.

And if Carina didn't actually know how to get them safely through the subterranean death maze, what point was there in keeping her around anyway? So far, Maddock's expedition was doing a better job of showing them the way forward.

"What's this place called?" he asked, rubbing his arms to warm them up after the arctic zip-line ride.

"Jaguar House," Carina replied, not looking away from the rows of statues.

"Uh, huh. What are we supposed to do here?"

She frowned. "I'm not sure. In the old stories, the house was full of captive jaguars. But these are just statues."

"I doubt very much that they are *just* statues," Alex said.

"True." She turned to her warriors, chose one of them. "You."

Despite his fierce appearance, the man went pale. He glanced to his comrades as if looking for moral support, but none would meet his gaze.

"Go," Carina commanded. "Show us the way."

"You should be the one to go," the man hissed. "Or are you afraid to face the Lords of Xibalba? Maybe you are not fit to lead us."

He started to raise his war club, but at that instant, all four of Alex's men brought their assault rifles up, aiming them at the man's chest.

Alex laughed. "Is this going to be a problem, Carina?"

Carina moved like lightning, drawing her obsidian dagger and pressing it to the warrior's throat before he could even blink. She leaned close to him and whispered, "It is an honor to be sacrificed to the gods of heaven and earth. Or would you rather I spill your blood like this?"

"You never liked me," he spat. "That is why you are sending me to die." His eyes flicked to the side. "She will sacrifice all of us, brothers, and give the Shadow to this outsider."

"If the gods will it, you will pass safely through the jaguars of Xibalba." Carina lowered the blade and eased away from him.

The warrior bared his teeth and shook his club, but then turned away from her and started across the floor of the cavern toward the rows of stelae.

Alex pretended to follow the man's progress but he was far more interested in the silent power struggle going on between Carina and her warriors. Underneath their tattooed savagery, they were cowards. Cosplay warriors, ready to kill, but afraid to die. Carina would not be able to maintain her control of them for long if—

There was a loud *snick* and a blur of motion right in front of the advancing scout. One of the carved figures had spun completely around, and as it turned, a score of sharp, obsidian blades—each at least three feet long—had shot out from holes in its body.

A haze of red mist filled the air around the warrior, and then he collapsed onto the stone floor.

In pieces.

"Ouch," Alex said, wincing a little. He faced Carina but continued to watch the other warriors. "Next batter?"

Carina's expression was more confident now. "He was a coward and the gods demanded his blood. But his sacrifice has appeased them. I know the way, now. Follow me."

Without waiting for anyone to acknowledge, she turned on her heel and started out across the floor.

None of the warriors moved.

Alex shook his head in disbelief. This woman had more balls than any of her men, but courage alone wouldn't guarantee her safety.

She reached the bloody chunks of the fallen warrior and turned left, moving along the row of statues until she reached two that looked like mirror images facing each other. Without hesitating, she stepped between them.

Nothing happened.

"I didn't understand at first," she called out, without looking back. "But then I remembered why *el Guia* appears to us in the form of the Lightning Dog. The jaguars kill, but the dogs show the way."

"Guide dogs," Alex muttered, hurrying to be the first to follow in her footsteps. "Of course."

Bones was still twenty feet from safety when the floor under his left foot split apart with a resounding crunch. He stumbled forward, hitting the floor face down, and triggering another loud *crack.* Jagged fracture lines, like red lightning bolts, shot out from underneath him.

Maddock's breath caught in his throat and his hands curled into claws, as if he might, through sheer willpower, keep the floor from collapsing and delivering his friend into the volcanic fury below.

Willpower or not, the floor remained more or less intact.

"Don't move," Maddock hissed, mindful of what might happen if he raised his voice any louder.

"Easy for you to say," Bones called out. His words were fast and clipped. "Now I know why bacon makes that noise on the grill."

"Don't try to get up. Keep your weight spread out evenly."

"Can we give the fat jokes a rest?" Bones said through clenched teeth as he reached forward, placing his palms flat on the superheated surface, and began pulling himself forward. He had let Miranda take the heavy pack with the SCUBA equipment across, but even without it, he was still the heaviest of the group. Maddock wanted to crawl out and lend a hand but knew that any extra weight on the already damaged floor might cause it to fail completely.

After several excruciating minutes, his hands and legs blistered and raw, Bones reached the doorway. "Holy crap. That was—"

Angel and Miranda shushed him in harmony.

He stared at them in disbelief. "No, it's okay. I'm fine. Just second-degree burns."

"Shhh!" Angel hissed again, pointing up at the ceiling. "Bat House."

Despite the obvious pain he was in, Bones brightened. "For reals?" He looked past the others, shining his light out across the cavern floor. "This isn't at all what I expected. If I don't see Anne Hathaway in about ten seconds, I'm officially calling shenanigans." In response to Miranda's look of confusion he added, "Catwoman? Because we're in the Bat Cave? Jeez. Tough crowd, tonight."

"Sorry. She doesn't really do anything for me," Maddock kidded.

Bones' eyes went wide in shock and he clutched his chest as if having a heart attack.

Maddock grinned. Bones had to be in a lot of pain, but his sense of humor remained indomitable.

"Bats are a good sign, right?" Angel whispered. "They have to be able to get in and out, so there must be another entrance nearby."

"There better be," Bones said. "No way am I going through that again."

"We're lucky they're just ordinary bats," Bell said. "The *Popol Vuh* describes a house filled with giant Death Bats that have blades for wings."

"Lucky is one word for it," Maddock said. "But if they get spooked, it's going to get ugly in here." He shone his light down onto the cavern floor below. "We're going to have to get across that."

"Smells like the world's biggest litter box," Angel said, wrinkling her nose.

"Close," Miranda replied. "It's guano."

"Bat droppings are rich in nitrates," Maddock said. "That's got to be the source of the ammonia refrigerant. There must be channels in the floor that shunt the liquid ammonia away to another cavern under the Cold House."

"The Maya figured out how to turn bat crap into a refrigerator over a thousand years ago, but they never invented the wheel." Angel shook her head. "That's insane."

"It's batshit crazy," Bones agreed.

"Clean up your act," Angel said, "or I'll tell Grandfather."

Bones rolled his eyes.

"Getting across that guano field to the other side isn't going to be easy," Maddock said. "It's probably several feet thick. The fumes are almost certainly toxic, but if we stick to the perimeter of the room where the accumulation is thinnest, we should be able to make it through without breathing too much."

Even as he said it, he realized that what he was suggesting might be too much for Bell, but the archaeologist just nodded. "I'll manage."

"That's probably where we'll find the door to…" He looked at Bell again. "What's left?"

"I can't say for sure, but Bat House was the last of the six Houses."

"So we should be close to whatever it is we're hoping to find."

"I just hope we're close to a way out," Angel said. "What about the bats?"

"If something disturbs them, just hit the ground and let them fly on by."

"The ground that's covered in bat crap. I'm sorry I asked."

"Better that than having a rabid bat get caught in your hair."

"Rabid?"

"Kidding," Maddock said quickly. He took the heavy pack from Miranda and slung it over a shoulder. "But let's just try to avoid spooking them. It will be easier all around."

He started down the steps, walking heel to toe, moving even more quietly than their whispered conversation.

At his first tentative step, his boot sank ankle deep into the guano, which was thicker and drier than the mud at the bottom of the shaft through which they had entered, but a lot more disgusting. The accumulation probably went down several feet. He could feel it compacting underfoot with each step, like powdery snow.

He could now see another staircase rising up on the far side of the cavern, less than fifty yards away if they abandoned the original plan, but the guano was heaped higher in the center, and getting through it would be messy and dangerous.

For a few minutes, the rustling noise above continued, but as the bat colony grew less restive, Maddock became aware of a different sound that was, in its own way, even more ominous. It was the sound of bat urine and feces hitting the guano-covered floor, a veritable shower of excrement raining down all around them. And on them.

He decided to pick up the pace a little. They were just halfway across when a piercing shriek tore through the quiet.

Maddock froze. He didn't think the noise had come from any of them. It was loud and high pitched, but distant, like the whistle of an approaching train, and lasted only an instant, but that was long enough to send the bats into a frenzy.

Bestial screams, accompanied by the sound of ten thousand pairs of leathery wings unfurling, filled the cavern with noise. Motes of dust and vapor swirled in the air as those tiny wings began stirring the air.

At first, the tumult was mostly confined to the upper reaches of the cavern, but he knew that as the creatures' panic intensified, they would soon begin swooping lower, forcing the team to duck and cover.

Disregarding his own earlier advice, Maddock shouted over the din. "Run!"

He stepped to the side and began motioning for the others to go ahead. Angel sprinted ahead, looking uncharacteristically desperate. Miranda came next, holding her father's hand, urging him to move faster, but Bell was clearly struggling even at a jog.

"I got this!" Bones roared, scooping Bell off his feet and throwing him over one shoulder. The archaeologist choked out a curse but there was little else he could do as Bones charged forward, outpacing even Angel. Miranda stared after them, frozen in disbelief, so Maddock grabbed her hand and pulled her along.

Something flashed in front of his face. He made a reflexive swipe at it with his free hand. The bat veered off at the last instant, but two more took its place, and then the air in front of them was filled with the rustling of wings. The weird clicking chirp of echolocation, multiplied a thousand times over, was an assault on the senses, vibrating through every nerve of Maddock's body.

Miranda stumbled, her hand wrenching free of Maddock's grasp, and went down, plowing a furrow in the guano as she skidded forward. Maddock leaped after her, looped a hand under her arm and dragged her to her feet as small furry bodies began slamming into both of them.

On a rational level, Maddock knew there was little risk of injury. With rare exceptions, most bats weighed less than an ounce, had very small teeth and zero interest in attacking a human or anything else larger than a mosquito. That was little comfort in the midst of the storm, however.

There was also a very real danger of getting lost and stumbling into some ever greater peril. He was already disoriented. With an opaque cloud swarming around them, it was impossible to tell which way to go. He couldn't see the far stairwell or the lights of the rest of the group.

He turned in the direction he thought would take him to the cave wall and, still holding Miranda's arm, started toward it. The carpet of guano seemed to grow thicker underfoot, so after five steps, he turned to the left and tried again.

This time he found the wall.

The swarm was a little less intense near the edge of the cave, where the bats had less room to maneuver, allowing him and Miranda to move at a near run. He kept his free hand in contact with the wall at all times, while maintaining his grip on Miranda's hand so they would not become separated. After a few minutes, or maybe it was only seconds, he saw flashes of light directly ahead through the haze and heard a familiar voice calling out to him.

"Dane!"

He veered toward the light. "Angel. I'm here."

Suddenly she was there, throwing her arms around him. She was streaked with filth and clearly terrified, but seemed otherwise unhurt.

Now he could see more lights, Bones and Bell,

climbing the steps to safety. The swarm was thinning, the majority of the bats probably fleeing the cavern by whatever hidden route they used to reach the outside world.

"We're almost there," he promised, taking Angel's hand. Now that he could see the way to safety, there was no need to grope along the wall.

A few hundred bats were still flitting about overhead, but Maddock ignored them as he cut the last corner and kicked through the guano pile to reach the stairs. He let go of Miranda there, letting her charge ahead, but kept his grip on Angel. He gave her hand a reassuring squeeze as they mounted the steps.

As soon as they cleared the passage, the first thing Maddock did was take several deep breaths. The stink of guano still clung to him, but the air seemed a little clearer here, the ammonia fumes slightly less overpowering.

Then the rest of his senses caught up.

This new cavern was magnificent, easily twice the size of the cathedral-like entrance at the surface, but its size was only the beginning.

In the distance, along the far edge of the cavern, water spewed from the rock wall, an underground river spilling out in a waterfall hundreds of feet high. The water splashed down into a large round pool, and then ran away in several directions down what seemed like perfectly straight canals. There was little question that the canals were man-made since they ran parallel to paved streets, lined with structures—pyramids and temples like those he had seen only as ruins in Chichén Itzá, Copán, and the City of Shadow.

That he could see any of this was the most remarkable thing about the cavern. The sheer size of the place should have left most of it hidden in shadow, but he could make out the distinctive outlines of the buildings and the spray of the waterfall because the cavern was aglow with pale blue phosphorescence, most of which seemed to be concentrated in the sprawling city complex.

Much closer, he saw Miranda walking down a broad staircase that descended toward the hidden city. The steps ended in a long box-like courtyard that looked eerily familiar. At the far end of the courtyard, dominating the center of the cavern, stood an enormous pyramid, easily as big as El Castillo.

Bones and Bell were descending the stairs, just a few steps past Miranda.

And then Maddock realized that there were two more people on the steps, coming up as if to greet them all.

His first impulse was to go for his gun, but even as he did, his brain caught up. He didn't know the dark-haired beauty on the left, but the other woman was instantly recognizable. He just couldn't figure out what she was doing here, deep underground.

"Hey Maddock," Kasey Kim shouted. "What took you so long?"

CHAPTER 31

Alex Scano screamed again as a glowing red spider-web pattern of fractures appeared in the blistering hot floor of the room Carina had called Hot House. He was going to die, just like the two men from his security team who had broken through the white crust and plummeted into the superheated magma below, and there wasn't anything he could do about it.

Now he regretted having Carina and her men take the lead. The red-haired priestess and her barefoot warriors had practically floated across the fragile floor, but he knew now that they had simply been lulling Alex and his men into a false sense of safety while further weakening the thin limestone crust.

The bitch had betrayed him, just as he feared she would.

There was a loud crackling sound behind him and a short cry of terror as one of his two remaining men broke through and joined his comrades in the inferno below.

Am I next?

He gritted his teeth against the heat rising up through the floor on which he lay. Even if he didn't fall through, he wasn't going to last long. Maybe a quick death in the magma pit was the better option….

And then, as if things weren't bad enough already, the air in the super-heated room was suddenly full of bats.

Great. As if I didn't have enough to worry about.

"Alex," Carina called out. "Don't move."

"Right," he spat back at her. "You'd like that."

But to his astonishment, she was moving toward him, crawling on her belly to distribute her weight across the crumbling floor.

"Your guns," she shouted. "They're too heavy. You have to get rid of them."

He realized that she wasn't calling out to him, but to the remaining man from Alex's security detail a few steps behind him. The soldier-for-hire was still on his feet, but trapped on an isolated section of the floor that, seemingly in defiance of gravity, was still intact. There was a two-foot wide gap separating him from the part of the floor where Alex was slowly being cooked alive. The man stared back at her uncertainly, unwilling to part with his guns and tactical gear, even though he probably knew she was right.

"Drop your gear," she repeated. "You're going to have to jump when I tell you to."

"No!" Alex shouted. "If he tries to jump, this whole place will collapse. We'll both die."

"I know," she hissed, scooting closer to him, close enough to extend a hand. "Take it."

He glared at her, wondering what sort of trick this was.

No trick. Maybe I was wrong about her.

He caught her hand, felt her firm grip.

"Now, crawl toward me." She began scooting backward, pulling him along as she went.

Alex didn't need convincing, but with every push forward, he heard and felt the floor giving way. More cracks appeared, shooting out ahead of him. Some of the cracks came together, opening into wider gaps as jagged chunks of limestone crumbled and fell into oblivion.

But the floor was holding together and the closer they got to the exit, the more solid it felt. After an initial flurry of activity, the bats had vanished. Evidently they didn't like the heat any more than he did.

Ten more feet. Five. Almost there.

Two of the tattooed warriors reached out, pulling Carina up, and then another one of them reached for Alex.

He regarded the hand warily for a moment, then took it, allowing himself to be pulled to safety.

There was another scream behind him. Alex didn't look back. He didn't need to. The last of his hired security team was gone. Maybe the man had tried to make a desperate leap—forward or back, it was impossible to say—or maybe the floor beneath had finally given out. Either way, he was on his own and at the mercy of the Serpent Brotherhood.

"How the hell did you get here?" Bones said, addressing Kasey. "And who's your friend?"

He grinned and thrust out a blistered hand. "These guys call me Bones, but you can just call me anytime."

"Nice," Kasey said, rolling her eyes.

"Seriously," Maddock said, descending to join them. "Those are two valid questions. If you knew about a shortcut—"

"I didn't." Kasey glanced at her companion. "But she did. This is Isabella Beltran."

"Isabella." Bones said it slowly, as if savoring every syllable.

Maddock didn't recognize the name, but Miranda evidently did. "Queen of the Yucatan Cartel?"

Isabella, who was staring intently at Charles Bell, nodded absently. "Among other things."

"Isabella also happens to be the new High Priestess of the Serpent Brotherhood," Kasey said.

"We ran into some of your friends earlier," Maddock said.

Isabella now turned to look at him. "Those men are not my friends. They are rebels. They have betrayed our faith."

"They're working with Alex Scano," Kasey added.

"Scano?" Maddock snapped his fingers. "That Chinook. That was him, wasn't it?"

"Isabella showed up at the airport a little while after you guys took off. I overheard her talking about going to a cave. It seemed suspicious, so I decided to tail her. Scano got here first though, with a bunch of these renegade Serpent Brothers and a squad of mercs. The mercs stayed behind to guard the helo and when Isabella's guys got there... Well, it was ugly. The surviving mercs grabbed her and took her into the cave. I decided to follow. Fortunately, I had an advantage over them."

She held up a black object that looked sort of like a pair of compact binoculars "PSQ-20 enhanced night vision goggles."

"Sweet," Bones said. "Don't suppose you brought enough for everyone to have one."

"Sorry. And before you ask, no you can't borrow them. Maddock doesn't pay you enough to replace them if they get broken."

"Tam won't care."

"Tam works for the federal government, just like me. And believe me, the bean counters will care." She let go of the PSQ-20, allowing it to hang by a lanyard around her neck. "Anyway, I caught up to them all in…what did you call it, Bella? Dark House?"

"Yes."

"When they turned out the lights, I took out the guys holding Bella and snuck out." The casual way Kasey said the words "took out" reminded Maddock that despite her petite size and seeming youthfulness, she was a skilled intelligence officer and a trained killer. "Once I explained what was going on, she showed me a shortcut. We figured you'd end up here eventually. If Xibalba didn't kill you first."

"She's a drug lord," Miranda said, making no attempt at tact. "Why on earth would you help her?"

"Because I am also the High Priestess of the Serpent Brothers," Isabella said. "After Scano and Carina killed my uncle Hector. We want the same thing."

"Revenge?" Maddock said.

"No. Yes, I want to make Carina pay, but there is something much more important going on."

"You're talking about the Shadow."

She nodded. "For more than a thousand years, the Serpent Brothers have guarded the secret of the Shadow as the gods commanded. But keeping the secret is only part of our sacred duty. You see, the Shadow is not just a disease.

"Long ago, my ancestors discovered it; a black mold growing in the jungle. Anyone who touched this mold or inhaled its spores became sick with a terrible fever in the blood, but something else happened too. In their fever, the gods spoke to them, revealing secrets hidden from mortals including, it is said, the secret of how to defeat death."

"How do you know that isn't just feverish delirium?" Maddock asked.

"The first sign of infection comes before the fever. You know that the Shadow has touched someone when they begin the journey."

"Journey? To where?"

Isabella fixed him with a patient stare. "Here. To Xibalba."

"That doesn't make any sense," Bones said. "Nobody even knows how to get here. We had to figure it out the hard way."

"The priests of the Serpent know. But it is said that the Lords of Xibalba reveal the way to the City of Shadow where they may begin the test of the Black Road and the Houses of Xibalba. The Serpent Brothers existed only to protect them on the journey. And to keep others from being touched."

"Xic and Patan!" Bell exclaimed. "Wing and Packstrap—the first two Lords of Xibalba. They bring death as a fever to those *walking on the road.*"

Isabella inclined her head to him. "It is said that, when the fever sets in, the Lords reveal other secrets. Ancient wisdom. Prophecy. But at a terrible cost. A sickness in the blood. Sores that ooze blood. The organs and even the bones dissolve inside the body." She shuddered, composed herself, and continued speaking.

"The Serpent Brothers contained the Shadow in vessels shaped like the Lightning Dog—in Spanish, we call them *el Guia*, the Guide—and guarded these vessels in secret rooms in the temples to the Great Serpent God. When a priest or someone else desired the knowledge of the Lords of Death, or a sacrifice was demanded, the chosen one would open the vessel and let the Shadow touch him. If a person survived the tests of the City of Shadow, and passed through the Houses of Xibalba, it was said that he would not die, but would become as the gods."

"Then there is a cure here."

Isabella spread her hands. "These are stories that I learned from my uncle as a little girl. For more than a thousand years, no one has undertaken the journey. After the Shadow devoured the old Maya, the Serpent Brothers hid the Guides away. The City of Shadow was abandoned, and none were permitted to speak of it. Only the stories of Xibalba remained."

"But Alex Scano found one of those vessels."

"Not Scano. A relic hunter in Honduras. There was an outbreak in a rural village. My uncle went to contain it, but Scano got there first."

"He had help," Kasey added. "A traitor in the Brotherhood told Scano all about the Shadow. And where to find a cure."

"Carina is only an acolyte. She was never told where to find the City or Xibalba." Isabella narrowed her gaze at Maddock. "You led him here."

Maddock let the accusation slide. "Is there a cure?"

"Until just a few days ago, I did not believe any of this was true. But the stories say that it is possible to defeat the Lords of Death, just as the Hero Twins did."

"Sounds like a cure to me," Bones remarked.

"Scano doesn't just want a bioweapon he can sell," Kasey said. "He actually wants to turn it loose. Full apocalypse mode. He has the fungus, but no way to control it. That's why he's here. And that's why we have to blow this place."

This was evidently news to Isabella. She rounded on Kasey. "This is a holy place."

"I'm afraid I have to agree with Miss Beltran," Bell said. "Not only is the destruction of such an archaeological wonder unconscionable, but you would also be wiping out the only source of a cure to the Shadow plague."

Miranda spoke up just as quickly. "And I'm afraid I have to agree with Kasey, Dad. We can't let Scano turn the Shadow into a bioweapon. This thing wiped out the entire Maya civilization, and they had the cure. What chance do you think we'd have today? Scano is on his way here. He's probably got that vessel with him. If we destroy Xibalba, we destroy both the plague and any chance that some madman will try to weaponize it."

Maddock raised his hands, playing referee. He was a little surprised at Miranda's declaration, but wondered if it concealed an altogether different agenda. "Kasey, what's your plan, exactly? Unless you've got a pocket nuke, I don't think you're going to be able to do the kind of damage that will need to be done."

"The guano," Miranda said. "You're going to make it into a bomb."

"Even I know you need more than just bat crap to make ammonium nitrate explosives," Bones said, dismissively.

"I've got this." Kasey reached into her backpack and brought out a red cylinder, about the size of a can of shaving cream. "Incendiary grenade. Burns at 4,000 degrees Fahrenheit. That's hot enough to ignite the ammonia vapors and start a flash fire chain reaction. It should sweep through the entire cavern, sanitize the whole place. If that doesn't do the trick, I'll toss in a couple pounds of C4 as a trigger charge."

"Just for the sake of argument," Maddock said, "Let's say we do that. How do we make it out?"

Kasey nodded her head at Isabella. "Ask her."

Isabella folded her arms across her chest. "Why should I help you destroy Xibalba?"

"For what it's worth," Maddock said. "I agree with you. Destroying the Shadow is one thing, but blowing up the whole cave is overkill."

"This isn't a democracy, Maddock," Kasey snapped. "I've got orders."

"Illegal orders," Bell said. "You don't have the authority to go around blowing up historical monuments in foreign countries."

Kasey rolled her eyes again.

"Look," Maddock said with a note of finality. "Right now, all that matters is getting out of here alive. Once we're back on the surface, someone else will have to make that decision, but I guarantee that we're not going to let ScanoGen start a plague."

Kasey scowled but nodded her assent. Maddock turned back to Isabella. "So, will you help us?"

"I have never been here before. All I have are the stories my uncle told me."

"He obviously told you about the shortcut."

Isabella frowned, then sighed resignedly. "It is said that the only way to leave Xibalba is through water."

"The pool," Bell said. "It must feed an underground river. In the *Popol Vuh*, the Twins transformed themselves into fish-people to avoid destruction at the hands of the Lords of Xibalba."

Isabella nodded affirmatively. "But to reach the water, you will first have to win the ball game."

Maddock looked past her, and shone his light out across the courtyard. Below them was a balcony overlooking the ball court. More stairs at either end of the balcony led down to the floor which appeared to slope gently up toward the pyramid at the far end. Arranged throughout were several more carved stelae similar to those they had seen in the Council Chamber and Jaguar House.

"The ball court of Xibalba," Bell said, breathlessly.

"I thought it looked familiar," Bones said. "I take it that's the home team out there on the field?"

"Another test," Maddock groaned. "Obviously we're not playing against a real opponent. How do we win?"

"According to the legend, the Lords of Xibalba demanded the use of a special ball—a skull with a dagger blade that would spring out and kill anyone it touched."

"Cheating bastards," Bones muttered.

"The Twins saw through the trick and refused to play unless the Lords agreed to use a regular rubber ball. Even so, the Twins either lost or tied all their subsequent games, which eventually led to their sacrifice."

"I thought they defeated the Lords of Xibalba."

"They did ultimately, but only after coming back from the dead several times."

"I don't think that's going to be an option for us."

"The closest they came to actually beating the Lords was in the final game. They didn't exactly win, but they pulled a trick of their own. It's a long story involving a headless man, a rabbit, and a gourd."

"Sounds promising."

"Didn't Professor and Jade have to deal with something like this at Teotihuacan?" Bones said. "Too bad they aren't here."

Maddock saw Angel frown at the mention of his ex-girlfriend. *Got to love the Bonebrake family. No matter how dire the circumstances, there's nothing so small that it will escape their notice.* "I didn't hear about that," he said quickly, and started down the steps to the ball court. "But it looks like we can't win if we don't play."

"You've got that backward," Bones replied "The quote is, 'the only way to win is not to play.'"

Maddock ignored him. "Just like before. Look for serpent and dog glyphs, and keep an eye out for anything that looks like a trap or a trigger."

He stepped down onto the floor of the court and immediately heard a crack like the sound of a Louisville slugger hitting rawhide.

"You mean like that?" Bones shouted to him.

In the eerie blue light, the object sailing down the length of the court looked black, but as he tracked it with his light, Maddock saw that it was actually as white as bone. A skull bone, in fact, though judging by its momentum as it shot toward him, rotating slowly, it was probably made of something heavier, carved and painted to resemble a skull. The ball was heading right toward him, about as fast as a thrown football, giving him just enough time to ponder the appropriate response.

Dodge, catch or block?

From what little he knew about the game, the point was not to catch the ball or dodge, but to deflect it with hips or torso, but he also recalled Bell's warning about the Lords' trick ball. He didn't see a dagger blade protruding from the ball, but that didn't mean it wasn't there, waiting to spring out on contact.

He quickly shrugged the pack containing the SCUBA bottle off his shoulder, gripping its straps in both hands. When the ball got within range, he swung for the bleachers.

There was a resounding *clank* as the skull-shaped projectile made contact with the nylon fabric and the aluminum tank inside, and then the ball was winging away toward the side of the court.

From the balcony, Angel couldn't resist cheering. "Woo-hoo! Way to go, slugger."

The ball bounced once, twice, and then hit the wall.

Or more precisely, the wall hit it.

A split-second before the skull would have made contact, a ten-foot long section of the wall swung out on concealed hinges to bat it away. The bounce, combined with the boost from the wall, supplied just enough energy to send it shooting right back at Maddock.

"Oooh, no joy in Mudville," Bones chortled.

Maddock considered shooting his friend a one-fingered salute, but since he still wasn't sure what would happen if he let the ball stop rolling, he readied himself for another swing.

There was another distant thump at the far end of the court as a second ball was launched.

"Oh, you've got to be kidding," he muttered, then raised his voice to a shout. "Guys, you'd better get down here. We need to get through this fast, before it gets any worse."

And then it got worse.

From behind and above, Miranda cried out. "We've got company! The Serpent Brothers. They're here."

CHAPTER 32

Maddock batted the first ball away again, timing his strike so that it sent the skull-ball sailing back down the length of the court and hopefully out of play. He recalled that the ball game could be won by getting the ball through a hoop, a virtual impossibility given the rules which did not permit the use of hands or feet, and the fact that the ball typically weighed about eight pounds. This ball didn't seem quite that heavy which was something at least. The Lords of Death might have been cheaters, but surely the game was still winnable.

He looked around quickly, searching the walls for a hoop, and instead found a hole in the wall right behind him, just below the balcony. It was the right size for a goal, but trying to deflect the ball coming straight at him into it would require precise timing and position. He doubted he would be able to get it right on the first try, and with an unknown number of Serpent Brothers swarming down from above, he wasn't going to get too many more chances.

He knocked the second pitch back, trying for a high pop-fly, but even as he made contact, he heard a second sound, the muffled noise of the other ball being struck by something solid.

Still in play, he thought.

Angel appeared on the floor of the ball court, with Kasey and Isabella right behind her. Miranda and Bell were there a second later, and Bones brought up the rear, looking like he was contemplating giving the ailing archaeologist another ride.

"What's going to happen if we make a run for it?" he called out, hoping that either Bell or Isabella would have an answer.

There was another loud *crack* as a third ball was launched across the court to join the other two, which were careening back and forth, rebounding off of walls.

The stelae were also moving, swinging out to deflect the balls whenever they got close. Something was triggering that action, probably pressure plates in the floor. The same thing would probably happen to them if they got too close and triggered that mechanism.

"Rabbits!" Bell shouted.

"Outstanding," Bones growled. "Now we've got to worry about killer rabbits. Kasey, I hope you've got the Holy Hand Grenade in that pack of yours."

Bell shook his head and pointed to one of the nearby stelae. "That's a rabbit."

Maddock didn't ask how he could tell the difference. The carvings were stylized and grotesque; Maya artisans were not exactly known for their realism. But he thought he grasped Bell's meaning. "A rabbit helped the Hero Twins in the final game. How?"

"The rabbit distracted the Lords of Xibalba so they could switch out a gourd for the ball," Bell explained quickly. "But I think the solution is much simpler. The rabbit stelae are safe. The others aren't. If we stay close to the rabbits, we should be able to make our way across the ball court."

Maddock hoped the archaeologist was right. There wasn't time to test the hypothesis with a weighted stand-in. He charged to the towering stelae that Bell had indicated, bracing himself for the hit if he was wrong, but nothing happened. He stopped just short of actually touching the carving, and looked back. "Doc, get up here. I need you to show us the way."

Bell advanced, shuffling more than jogging. Kasey dropped back, her pistol now unholstered and at the ready. Bones had his weapon drawn as well. Behind and above them, the serpent warriors were scattered up and down the staircase, brandishing war clubs and blowguns. He counted at least six, but more were emerging from the passage to Bat House. If it came to a fight, their primitive weapons would be no match for the firepower Maddock and his friends were carrying, but the ball court was not the place to make their stand.

He turned back, keeping an eye on the skull-balls—four of them now—caroming around the ball court. "Doc!"

"There!" Bell pointed to another column, fifty feet away near the left edge of the court.

"Let's move," Maddock called.

The court was now alive with noise and movement as multiple balls were batted back and forth all around them. Maddock gave up trying to track them all, and simply kept his head on a swivel, checking in all directions for incoming projectiles that might pose a threat to himself or the others. By the time they reached the halfway point, there were at least six balls in play. He wondered if there was a limited supply of them, or if the unseen mechanisms that controlled the game would run out of steam, figuratively, if not also literally. Twice, he had to stop to deflect a ball away.

He also kept track of the serpent warriors, some of whom had already ventured out onto the ball court. He wondered if they knew about the rabbits, too.

As they neared the far end, Maddock realized that the Lords of Xibalba had one final test for them. There was a gap at the bottom of the twenty-foot high back wall where it met the sloping floor, an opening just wide enough to let the balls roll through. It reminded Maddock of the goal slot on a foosball table, and it probably served the same purpose, allowing the system to retrieve balls and put them back in play. Higher up on the wall were three openings just like the one at the far end, but unlike that hole, these were not for scoring goals. As if to confirm this supposition, a few seconds after they reached the wall, another ball shot out of the center hole and sailed out over the court.

Conspicuously absent, however, was a staircase to take them out of the arena.

Maddock intuitively realized that they were probably supposed to beat the game, maybe by scoring a goal, or maybe more than one, but he also knew that doing so wasn't really an option. There probably was a staircase there somewhere, hidden in the floor or walls, just waiting for them to pass the final test.

From further down the court he heard a truncated scream and a loud crunch, the sound of breaking bones, as one of the Serpent Brothers went down. The rest were still coming.

"Buddy system," Maddock shouted, turning to face the others and putting his back against the wall. "Human ladder."

Bones understood immediately. He stuffed his pistol into his waistband and ran forward to take a similar stance alongside Maddock. He leaned over slightly, hands coming together to form a step. "Kasey. Angel. You're next."

Kasey, who had no doubt gone through the same kind of team-building exercises as the two former SEALs, ran to them and without a moment's hesitation, planted her right foot in the cradle formed by Bones' fingers, and vaulted up onto their shoulders. She repositioned herself so that she was also facing out, one foot on Maddock's shoulder and one on Bones', and extended her hand to Angel, who was already starting up.

Angel had watched enough Spartan Races on television to grasp what was expected of her. She scrambled up Bones' chest and caught Kasey's hand. Though Angel was a little heavier, her momentum was going the right direction, and Kasey was able to launch her even higher. High enough to grasp the stone lip. She used her feet to push even higher and then, with a final heave, pulled herself to safety.

Isabella went next, a little more tentatively, but with Angel reaching down from above to catch her, the final part of the ascent was considerably easier.

Miranda also seemed to know exactly what to do. "Dad, I'm going next. When I get to the top, you go up. Kasey will boost you, and the rest of us will pull you up. Don't think about it, just do it."

She didn't wait for him to acknowledge, but ran

forward and scaled the human ladder like an old pro, joining the others at the top.

"Move it, Doc!" Maddock yelled, a lot more forcefully than was his custom, partly because he hoped to jolt Bell into motion, and partly because two Serpent Brothers were emerging from behind the last line of stelae, just fifty feet away.

As Bell closed the distance separating them, a skull-ball bounced into view and struck one of the snake warriors. The blow knocked him flat, spilling him into the path of his comrade, but when the ball struck, it ricocheted away at a right-angle that put it on a collision course with Bell.

"Kasey!" Maddock yelled. "Shift!"

As soon as he felt her weight leave his shoulder, he pushed off the wall, leaping toward the uncomprehending archaeologist.

Bell stopped in his tracks, eyes wide in disbelief as Maddock barreled toward him. It was absolutely the worst thing he could have done, but Maddock poured on the speed, reaching Bell a fraction of a second ahead of the ball. Tackling the older man to save him would probably have been just as dangerous to both of them, so instead he grabbed ahold of Bell's arm and spun around on his heel, whipping the other man around and out of the way. The ball bounced past both of them, and disappeared into the gap at the bottom of the wall, missing Bones, with Kasey standing on his shoulders, by scant inches.

Now Maddock and Bell were out in the open, with more Serpent Brothers emerging from the shadows. Maddock, still in mid-pivot, propelled the other man ahead of him, toward the wall. "Bones! Take care of him."

He kept turning until he was facing the ball court again, drawing his SIG Sauer as he moved. He dropped the nearest Serpent Brother with a controlled pair, took a step back, found another target. Fired.

The reports echoed throughout Xibalba.

The Serpent Brothers were scattering now, but behind the elaborately tattooed warriors, a pair of figures in street clothes—a dark-haired man and a woman with red hair—were urging the warriors to press their attack. The woman had to be Carina, the renegade acolyte from the Serpent Brotherhood. The man could only be Alex Scano.

If you want to kill the snake, Maddock thought, *cut off the head.*

But as he put Scano in his sights, he heard Bones call out. "Uh, Maddock, we've got a problem."

"Deal with—"

There was another report, but it hadn't come from Maddock's pistol. He ducked as a round sizzled through the air above his head.

"Drop the gun, Dane!"

A chill went through Maddock. The voice, like the shot, had come from behind him, and both had come from Charles Bell. "I'm sorry, but I can't let you kill him. Drop the gun."

CHAPTER 33

Stunned, Maddock did the only thing he could. He raised his hands, the barrel of the SIG pointed up at the ceiling, and turned around.

Charles Bell was standing a few paces away from Bones, a pistol in his shaking hands. He seemed uncertain of what to do with it, pointing it at Maddock, then at Bones, then back again. The gun was just like the one Maddock still held. Bell had probably swiped it from Bones' belt. The question of where he'd gotten the weapon was of far less importance than why, but Maddock thought he knew the answer to that question as well.

"Dad!" Miranda shouted, frantic. "What are you doing?"

"Isn't it obvious?" Maddock shouted, locking stares with Bell. "He's working for ScanoGen. Helping them find Xibalba."

"That's impossible," Miranda said.

There was a strange grinding noise in the wall, and then with another loud report, a skull ball—possibly the same one that had just rolled past—shot out of the elevated hole on the right.

Some kind of automated ball return, Maddock thought. From start to finish, the process had taken only about thirty seconds.

Bell flinched as the ball sailed over their heads, but then stabbed the pistol at Maddock. "I told you to drop it. No one else has to get hurt."

"That's right, Maddock!" called out another voice. Maddock knew it had to be Scano himself. "I don't want to hurt you or your friends."

"Dad?" Miranda said again, but this time it was a desultory question. "Why?"

"He's the mole?" Bones said, incredulous. "Not Miranda?"

"Me?" Miranda gaped at Bones. "You thought I was working for the other side?"

"You were always on your phone. And you got all pissy when you thought we were leaving you out of the loop. You were the logical choice."

"Thanks a lot."

"Sorry."

"ScanoGen got to Copán ahead of us," Maddock added, maintaining eye contact with Bell. "And they showed up here right on our tail. We knew someone was leaking information to them. Just couldn't figure out why. I know you said ScanoGen was giving you grant money, but this is something else, isn't it? Did he offer to let you and Miranda be among the chosen few to survive the apocalypse he's going to unleash?"

Bell clenched his teeth. "I said, drop it!"

Maddock inclined his head and then slowly bent his knees and lowered his arm, placing the SIG on the floor rather than actually letting it fall. He was stalling, waiting for his chance to act. He did not believe for a second that Bell really wanted to shoot anyone, and it looked like Scano and the snake warriors were adopting a wait-and-see mentality, but eventually someone would do something to escalate the situation.

For a few seconds, the only sound in Xibalba was the noise of the ball court—skull-balls bouncing, walls and stelae swatting them away. Maddock risked a glance back and saw Alex and Carina advancing, with six Serpent Brothers spread out in a half-circle behind them. Some had blowguns raised, others were hefting war clubs studded with obsidian blades. The warriors looked about uncertainly, clearly as concerned with what was going on behind them as they were with the confrontation.

"Dad," Miranda said again. Her voice sounded hollow, desolate with disbelief. "Tell me this isn't true. Tell me that you didn't know what he was planning. This is just a mistake, right?"

"Unleashing the apocalypse?" Bones said. "Yeah, definitely a mistake."

"There isn't going to be an apocalypse," Bell said. "The Shadow will be just another doomsday weapon that nobody will ever dare use. But the cure. The knowledge that studying it will reveal? That will change the world. New antibiotics. Cures for cancer, and other diseases we don't even know about yet."

Maddock nodded in understanding. "Maybe even a cure for your COPD."

"Yes. Why not?"

"Were you dropped on your head as a kid, Doc?" Bones snarled. "You can't believe anything he says."

"ScanoGen is not the same company it was under my father," Alex said, taking a step forward. "Whether you believe it or not, I just want to help people. Save the world. And men like Dr. Bell share my vision of looking to the past for the cures that will save the future."

"You're going to save the world with bioweapons." Maddock shook his head. "Sorry, I just don't buy it."

"You've been misled, I'm afraid," Alex said, smiling. Maddock guessed the man had no idea how arrogant it made him look. Or maybe he did and he just didn't care. "We're only trying to develop a cure for a terrible disease."

"Sure you are."

Another ball bounced into view, most of its energy spent. The warriors shifted a few steps out of the way, though they were never in much danger to start with, and the ball rolled past them, into the slot at the base of the wall.

As ancient stone machinery rumbled to life again, Maddock started a mental countdown. He glanced past Bell, meeting Bones' stare for a second, telegraphing his intention with his eyes. Then he looked up, ever so slightly to Kasey, still perched on Bones' shoulders, a good ten feet from the top of the wall where Angel, Isabella and Miranda waited. He flicked his eyes up, hoping she would get the message.

"You are a fool!" Isabella shouted from the wall, an accusatory finger pointing at Scano. She spat the words out with a contemptuous laugh. "You are dead already. The Shadow has touched you."

Scano stiffened at the odd accusation, and then looked at Carina. "What the hell is she talking about?"

"I know the signs," Isabella said. "Eyes as red as blood. I saw it earlier. Now I am sure. Did you do this to him, Carina? When you found *el Guia*?"

Carina looked back at her wide-eyed. "No. She's lying. Trying to divide us." But she nevertheless took a step back, as if trying to distance herself from him.

"Damn it," Alex snarled. "That worm, Doug. He did this. Don't worry. I'm probably not contagious yet."

Isabella's pointing finger now shifted to Bell. "You have also been touched."

Bell's eyes went wide, wide enough for Maddock to see that the whites of his eyes were indeed blood red. After all they had been exposed to—from smoke to ammonia fumes—that was hardly a surprise, but Bell sagged a little under the weight of the revelation.

"The scorpion sting," he whispered. "In the City of Shadow. I was infected."

Scano shook his head. "It doesn't matter. We're here now. And so it the cure."

"Fool," Isabella said again. "There is no cure."

Her revelation could not have come at a better moment.

With another loud crack, the skull-ball was launched into play, startling everyone.

Everyone except Maddock, Bones and Kasey.

"Now!" Maddock shouted.

Right on cue, Bones reached up to grab Kasey's ankles, and then thrust her straight up. She flew like a rocket, rising as high as the top of the wall, but her back was turned to it, and even though she tried to twist around to face it, there was no way she was going to be able to grab the edge.

Fortunately, Angel saw what was going on and reacted immediately. As Kasey reached the top of her vertical journey, Angel reached out with both hands and snagged the strap of Kasey's backpack. The sudden transfer of weight pulled Angel down, slamming her against the edge of the wall. Kasey swung back and hit the stone with an audible grunt, but within seconds, Miranda and Isabella joined the effort and, working together, easily hauled Kasey up.

On the floor of the ball court, Bell was slow to react. He jerked the gun around toward Bones, giving Maddock the opening he'd been waiting for. He sprang at the archaeologist, tackling him.

The gun flew from Bell's hands and went skittering across the floor. Maddock heard a faint huffing sound as some of the Serpent Brothers launched darts at them, but didn't feel any stings. Pushing away from Bell, he dove after the gun, sliding on his belly across the floor, caught it and brought it up ready to fire from a prone position, even as one of the warriors charged toward him, war club held high.

Maddock squeezed the trigger twice and the warrior went down.

The rest of the warriors, along with Scano and Carina, were scattering, but Maddock knew the pandemonium would not last. Eventually, the warriors would launch another volley of darts which were almost certainly tipped with poison. He spun around without rising, and scrambled on all fours toward the ball return gutter.

While he had been going for the gun, Bones had gone after Bell, scooping the treacherous archaeologist up, carrying him under one arm like a sack of dog food. He hesitated though as he stared into the dark gap at the bottom of the wall. "You sure about this?"

Maddock wasn't at all sure. He knew that there was room enough for the skull-balls, which were a bit larger than the size of an actual human head, and that somewhere inside, under the pyramid, there was some sort of mechanical system for lifting the balls up to the launcher, but whether there was room enough for a person was anyone's guess.

If he was wrong, instead of lifting them to safety, the stone machinery might very well grind them to hamburger.

"If you've got a better idea, let's hear it." Maddock didn't wait for an answer, but plunged headlong into the gap.

He crawled a few yards through a claustrophobic gap before falling out into a trough that looked remarkably like a gutter at a bowling alley, except for the fact that it was tilted down at sharp angle. The stone was smooth, but provided enough resistance that he did not slide down to the end of the trough where something that looked sort of like an enormous upright stone screw was slowly turning. There were two more troughs leading away from the sloping floor, and similar screw-elevators at the end of each. Maddock assumed that the screws would lift a recovered ball—or anything else they picked up—up to one of the three launchers, but there would be no need for them to follow that route because there was also a raised walkway behind the screws, and a passage leading out.

He got his feet back under him and started down the trough toward the relentlessly turning screw. A glance back revealed Bones emerging from the gap, dragging along a stunned Charles Bell. After the earlier revelations of treachery, to say nothing of the fact that Bell might be infected with a deadly and highly contagious pathogen, Maddock had no idea why Bones had elected to bring the archaeologist along, but figured his partner had his reasons and didn't question them.

"Bones. Down here."

The big man nodded in acknowledgment, and climbed out into the trough behind him.

Maddock stepped up onto the spiraling screw and was immediately lifted up and rotated around toward the walkway where he was able to easily step off. Bones, with Bell now thrown over his shoulder, followed suit.

"Go!" Maddock shouted, urging Bones on as he swept the area behind them with his light and the business end of the pistol. There was no sign of pursuit yet, but he knew it was only a matter of time. "I'll cover you."

Bones hastened into the passage, and after giving him a few seconds' lead, Maddock headed after him. The passage became a narrow staircase, sandwiched between walls of cut stone under a flat ceiling, and rising up to what he hoped would be an exit on the balcony where the others were already waiting.

He was almost right.

As he climbed the stairs, he could see a pale blue glow silhouetting Bones. The steps ended at a T-junction, with a passage where the glow was even stronger, and as he stepped out into it, he saw that the stone floor was dotted with large patches of phosphorescent blue lichen, glowing so brightly that he could see the full length of the passage.

Something about the luminous shapes nagged at Maddock, triggering a primal avoidance instinct.

"I think we're inside the pyramid," Bones said. "Which way?"

Maddock wasn't sure there was a right or wrong answer, but before he could decide, he heard an urgent voice—Angel's voice—echoing down the tunnel.

"Dane! Bones!" She was standing at the mouth of the passage to the right. "Here."

"Go! But watch your step." Maddock kept watch on the opening to the staircase, his gun at the ready, until Bones was clear. Then he turned and headed after Bones, careful not to step on the glowing blue spots.

The passage opened onto the balcony overlooking the ball court, at the base of the great pyramid at the center of Xibalba. As he neared the exit, Maddock saw that the blue light was even brighter outside. The balcony was completely covered in the blue lichen, a dense carpet upon which he would have to walk if he wanted to leave the pyramid. Bones had already stomped through it to join the others. If there was some hidden danger here, they were already deep into it, but as

Maddock took a tentative step onto the glowing substance, his feeling of dread deepened.

He forgot all about that when he realized that someone was missing.

Bones had laid Bell down on the balcony floor, just a few feet from the exit, and both he and Miranda were kneeling over her father. Angel was also kneeling, only she was next to Kasey, who sat with her back against the side of the lowest tier of the pyramid, holding a hand to her head.

"What happened?" Maddock said. "Where's Isabella?"

Kasey looked up, her face twisted in a snarl of rage. "Gone. She sucker punched me and took my backpack before I knew what was happening. She's got all my demo gear. My night vision goggles, too."

"I guess she wanted to make sure we couldn't destroy Xibalba," Angel said.

"Right now, all I care about is getting out of Xibalba."

"Dane!" Bones called out.

Maddock felt an ominous chill. Bones never called him by his first name. He turned slowly to where Bones and Miranda were tending to Bell. The archaeologist hadn't moved.

"What's wrong? Is he...?"

Bones shook his head and spoke in a low voice. "He's still breathing. Barely." He looked up, meeting Maddock's gaze. "You think Isabella was right? If he's got it... I mean, we've been with him this whole time."

Bell gave a rattling exhalation that wasn't quite a cough, and Maddock realized he was trying to say something. "Dar..."

"Dart," Bones said, sounding only slightly relieved. "He must have gotten hit by a blowgun dart. Probably tipped with curare or some kind of paralytic."

"Mira..." Bell said, "Don... Don't. Go."

Tears streamed down Miranda's face. "I won't leave you, Dad."

Bell's eyebrows came together in a frown. In the blue light, his skin had the pallor of someone already dead.

"Atropine," Miranda said, looking up at Maddock. "That might help. Do you have atropine in your first aid kit?"

Bones' diagnosis was probably right on the mark. Curare compounds had been used for centuries in Central and South America. The poison was a powerful paralytic, which strangely did not affect the heart. It did however paralyze the muscles of the diaphragm, and without treatment or artificial respiration, death by suffocation was almost a certainty, especially for someone like Bell, whose pulmonary system was already badly compromised. Maddock didn't think atropine or any other treatment would reverse what was happening. He could tell that Bell knew it, too.

"Go," Bell rasped again. "Dead... Shadow."

"No," Miranda said. She spoke with an urgency borne of desperation. "We're here. The cure is here. You just have to stay with us." She turned her gaze to Maddock again. "This lichen or whatever it is. It's the cure, isn't it?"

"No... Cure." The effort seemed to take the last of Bell's energy. His eyes rolled back and he was still.

"He's not breathing," Miranda cried.

"I got this," Bones said, as he began repositioning Bell flat on the lichen-carpeted stone. He tilted the archaeologist's head back a little, clearing his airway, pinched Bell's nose shut with one hand, and bent over to administer a rescue breath, mouth-to-mouth.

"Stop!" Maddock shouted, so loud that his voice echoed throughout the chamber. He grabbed Bones' shoulder, pulling him back.

"Maddock," Bones warned, instinctively going on the defensive and fighting against the restraining grip.

"He's infected. He's got the Shadow. You heard what Isabella said."

"Maybe he does," Bones growled, a fierceness in his eyes that Maddock rarely saw directed at him. "And maybe he doesn't. But he's going to die for sure without CPR."

"He's already gone, Bones." Angel said from behind them. She and Kasey had both moved closer, ready to interfere if the confrontation escalated.

"No," Miranda said. "Curare is a paralytic, but it's not fatal if we can keep him breathing."

"Miranda, he's infected." Maddock softened his tone, knowing how much his words would hurt, but did not let go of Bones' shoulder.

"And this is Xibalba. The cure is here."

"It's not a cure," Maddock replied.

"You son of a bitch," Miranda said, almost screaming at him. "Whatever he did, he doesn't deserve to die."

Maddock knelt beside them, drawing back Bell's pant leg to reveal the bandage covering the wound the man had sustained in the City of Shadow. He carefully peeled the gauze pad away to reveal the scabbed-over wound. "Look."

There were faint specks of blue light shining out of the scab, and a corresponding line of the same substance on the bandage.

"It's not a cure," Maddock said, again. "We have to go. Now."

CHAPTER 34

After clobbering Kasey, Isabella Beltran had run, but not very far, only a hundred yards or so down the length of the balcony and around the corner of the base of the pyramid, just enough to be sure that none of Maddock's group would pursue her. Once concealed there, she watched Maddock and the others arguing about what to do next. She couldn't hear what was going on, but she could see everything through the night vision goggles she had taken from Kasey.

It looked as though Maddock had figured it out, for all the good it would do any of them.

She swung the goggles down to the ball court. The enhanced infrared display showed the large arena in startling detail, allowing her to see not only Scano, Carina and the surviving rogue Serpent Brothers as they attempted to follow Maddock's escape route, but also the distant end of the court, and all of the skull-balls that were still bouncing wildly throughout.

She waited until they were gone, and then shouldered Kasey's backpack and darted from her hiding spot to the edge of the balcony.

She peered over the side. Through the night vision device, the floor of the ball court looked deceptively close. Stuffing the goggles in the deep cargo pocket of her trousers, she dropped onto her belly and squirmed out over the edge, lowering herself down until her arms were fully extended and her fingertips supporting her full weight.

Only now did she feel a trace of panic. A two-story drop waited below, but there was no other way to get where she needed to go, and even if she had been inclined to change her mind, getting back up the wall would have been nearly impossible, especially as the muscles in her arms were quivering from the exertion of simply holding on. Bracing herself against the expected shock of impact, she forced her fingers to uncurl.

The landing was about as bad as she expected it to be. A flash of pain shot up through her feet, all the way to her hips. She pitched sideways, landing hard on her left shoulder. Another flash of pain went through her chest, and suddenly she couldn't breathe.

Just knocked the wind out of me, she told herself, fighting back a fresh wave of panic. She lay there, waiting for her body to recover from the shock. When she finally caught her breath a moment later, she rolled over onto hands and knees, then stood, wincing as the pain returned. Her ankles and knees screamed in protest, but she didn't think anything was broken or sprained.

She took out the night vision goggles again and held them to her eyes, locating the safe path to the distant end of the ballcourt, and watching for incoming balls. Then she started moving.

After a few steps, she figured out how to mostly compensate for the constant pain in her feet and ankles, limping forward with a shambling gait that nevertheless allowed her to cover ground quickly. She only had to stop twice to avoid the hurtling skull-shaped projectiles.

The steps out of the ball court and back up to the passage into Bat House proved similarly challenging. She had to lean forward over the steps, supporting some of her weight with her hands, like a chimpanzee, in order to make the ascent, but she did so because she knew what had to be done.

Bat House was no longer a mad flurry of activity. Most of the bats, roused from their slumber, had fled, lighting out through fissures in the ceiling. The narrow crevices were a link between Xibalba and the outside world, emerging in the jungle a mile or so from the entrance to Naj Tunich, though they were much too small for any other creature to get through or even notice.

Isabella knew she would not be leaving through that route.

She unslung the backpack, and dumped its contents

out onto the stone floor. There were three large red cylinders—incendiary grenades—along with a few other similar devices in varying shapes, sizes and colors. She was familiar with most of them and quickly located what she was looking for—paper-wrapped blocks of Composition C-4 and four pencil detonators. She set the latter to their minimum time delay and pushed them one at a time into the blocks of plastic explosive compound, which had the consistency of stiff modeling clay. Only after the first fuse was activated did it occurred to her that there was no undoing this, no going back.

She armed the rest of the improvised explosive devices, shoving them all back into the pack. When she was done, she heaved the bundle out into the midst of the guano pile. Then, she pulled the safety pins on the incendiary grenades and hurled those out as well.

At first, she couldn't see where they landed, but a moment later there was a soft pop as the first of the grenades ignited, followed by a brilliant flash that lit up the whole cavern, and a harsh hissing sound as the white phosphorous inside the cylinder began to burn.

"Forgive me, *Tio,*" she whispered as the other grenades sizzled to life. She felt certain he would not only forgive, but approve. Indeed, she knew now that this had been her destiny all along.

You are dead already. *The Shadow has touched you.*

Isabella's pronouncement rang in Alex Scano's ears as he followed Carina and her warriors up the stairwell into the transverse passage beneath the pyramid.

Doug Simpson, that bleeding heart cretin, had done this to him, exposing him to the Shadow pathogen with his crazed suicide mission to destroy the lab and all traces of the fungus. Simpson probably hadn't counted on Alex being able to get away before the explosion, but in breaching the BSL-IV safety barrier, he had just as effectively doomed his employer.

"No," he muttered, clenching his teeth. "No, no. I'll beat this. I'll find the cure."

That was, after all, why he had made the journey into

Xibalba.

In his backpack, sealed inside multiple bio-hazard bags, was the little figurine of a dog—*el Guia*, was what Carina had called it—the vessel that contained the dormant fungus which, when exposed to a human host, began to multiply. Alex supposed he was also a vessel for the pathogen, but it didn't matter because soon, he would have the cure as well.

Shadow and Light.

His designation for the project wasn't just poetic; it was on-the-nose literal. He had realized that the moment he laid eyes on the glowing city. The phosphorescent blue lichen *was* the cure.

As he stepped out into the passage, he knelt at the first patch of the glowing material and began scraping some into an empty bio-hazard bag. The lichen clung to his fingers like damp soil. He held up his hand, staring at it as if hypnotized, and then touched one finger to his tongue. It didn't really taste like anything.

"What are you doing?" Carina called back to him.

"This is the cure," he said, reverently. "Light to banish the Shadow."

When she didn't reply, he looked up and found her staring down at him with a perplexed expression. "Your eyes. They're…" She shook her head. "Your man, Bell. He's dead. Maddock and the others left him behind."

"Where are they?"

"They headed out into the city."

"What are you waiting for?" He gave her a perturbed frown, and then looked down in order to begin filling another sample bag. "Kill them. We can't have them getting out with the cure, can we?"

"We don't know what they're doing," Carina said, her voice strangely uncertain. "They might be looking for a way out."

"Good point." Alex stuffed the bags into his pocket and stood, wiping his hands on his thighs, leaving traces of glowing blue on the fabric of his pants. "All right. We'll ask them about that. Then we'll kill them."

CHAPTER 35

Maddock could feel Miranda's hateful stare on the back of his neck as he ran through the streets of the dead city. One day, he knew, she would understand and realize that there had been no other choice, but right now, there wasn't time to explain.

The streets of Xibalba glowed blue beneath their feet as they ran through the ankle deep accumulation of the strange phosphorescent lichen. The stuff was everywhere. On the streets, on the tiers of the pyramids and other structures, even lining the edges of the canals that flowed from the pool at the base of the waterfall. With the exception of the ball court, every horizontal surface in the cavern seemed to be covered in the stuff.

That, too, was something Maddock tried not to think about.

They headed straight for the pool, a distance of only a couple hundred yards. He had no idea what would happen once they plunged into it. The fact that the cavern was not completely submerged suggested that the pool drained into an underground river, and both Isabella and Bell had confirmed that the only escape from Xibalba was by water. He still had the backpack with the SCUBA gear in it—hopefully none of it had been damaged when he had used the pack as a makeshift bat on the ball court—and that would give them a fighting chance, but relying on a centuries-old myth, which had already proven to be a somewhat unreliable guide, was a big gamble.

Still, it was better than the alternative.

He glanced over his shoulder, looking past the still glowering Miranda, and spotted several figures descending from the pyramid. The blue light cast an eerie glow on their tattooed bodies, making them look like phantoms as they sprinted toward the city.

He slowed, waving for the others to keep going, and

shoved the backpack into Bones' hands. "Company's coming. I'll hold them off. You get everyone out of here."

He knew Bones would understand what had to be done, but Angel stopped beside him, and so did Kasey, with her own pistol drawn, ready to make a stand with Maddock. Before either woman could speak, he stopped them. "Don't worry. I'll be right behind you."

"Better listen to him, ladies," Bones shouted back. "Unless you're half-fish like him, you need to stick with me."

As they headed out, Maddock squeezed off a couple shots in the direction of the advancing Serpent Brothers. They were barely within the effective range of the pistol and moving, which meant scoring a hit was unlikely, but hopefully the shots would slow them down long enough for Bones to organize the underwater exit.

Sure enough, the garishly decorated warriors veered off, seeking cover behind the temples and houses that lined the street.

Then a voice echoed out across the city. "Maddock!"

It was Alex Scano.

The psychopathic pharma-bro had just come down the steps of the pyramid, and was moving slowly down the street with Carina beside him. They were in the open, but well out of pistol range. Scano had his arms extended out away from his body, but it seemed more like a quasi-Messianic pose than a gesture of surrender.

"Maddock," he said again, his voice echoing weirdly in the confines of the cavern. "Be reasonable. I've got what I came for. I don't care about you. But you're going to run out of bullets eventually and then what? Let's work together."

Maddock recognized the stalling tactic for what it was. The Serpent Brothers were probably sneaking through the maze of side streets, trying to come up on his flanks.

Two could play that game.

"Sorry, Scano," he shouted. "But you're not going to be working with anyone. You're infected."

Scano laughed. "You're wrong. I was infected, but I've been cured, just like the legend says."

"There is no cure. Look around you."

Seventy-five yards away, Scano did exactly that. Maddock could see his head moving from side to side. "What exactly is it you think I should be looking at? The Light? It's the cure."

"It's not a cure," Maddock retorted. "It's what's left of everyone who made it this far."

Scano stopped in his tracks. Despite the distance separating them, Maddock could see the confusion in the other man's expression.

"This blue growth," Maddock continued. "The Light—it kills the Shadow fungus all right, but it doesn't do anything to help the infected. Sorry to break it to you, but you're a dead man walking."

"No." Scano shook his head, angrily. "No, you can't know that."

"Think about it. If the Maya had a cure, they wouldn't have been wiped out."

"You don't know that's what happened."

"I do. The proof is all around you. This place…Xibalba… was their version of an isolation ward. When the Shadow plague burned through their civilization, they did what they knew they had to do. They came here. All of them. Most probably didn't make it this far, maybe only a very small percentage—a few thousand out of hundreds of thousands. They came here, laid down and died. Just like you're going to."

"No. You're wrong."

"The Light isn't a cure. It's just another organic fungus. One that feeds off the Shadow, but it's only here, deep underground. When those Maya died, it consumed their remains." He made a sweeping gesture. "This is all that's left of them. Ask your friend. I'll bet she's already figured it out. Isabella did. She took one look and figured out the truth."

"It is true," Carina said. She spoke so softly that Maddock could barely hear her. She turned to face

Scano. "I did not understand, but now I do. This is the fate of all who are touched by the Shadow."

"That's insane. Of course there's a—"

Scano was cut off, literally, as Carina slashed her obsidian dagger across his throat. He fell back, hands clutching his throat.

Carina turned to Maddock and started toward him, her knife eager to draw blood again. "I should thank you," she called out in a tone that sounded anything but grateful. "I was led astray, but now I have returned to the true path."

Maddock kept the pistol trained on her, but he could see movement from of the corner of his eye. The serpent warriors were emerging all around him. He didn't think he was in range of their blowguns, but he would be soon if he didn't move.

Carina kept advancing, unfazed by the threat of the gun. "The Serpent Brotherhood guards the world of mankind from the Shadow, until the gods decide it is time to cleanse the world."

"Works for me," Maddock said slowly, taking a step back.

"I cannot let you leave," Carina went on. "None of you can be allowed to return to the surface world."

"That… doesn't work for me."

Carina made a slashing gesture, and suddenly Maddock was surrounded by movement as the Serpent Brothers rushed him en masse. He pivoted, squeezing off a shot that dropped one, then another, but they were coming too fast.

He turned to run, but an invisible hand knocked him off his feet, and suddenly the world was full of fire.

CHAPTER 36

The explosion rocked Xibalba to its core. Jagged cracks shot through the floor. Pyramids crumbled like Jenga blocks, and stalactites began falling down like missiles to spear the broken floor. But that was only the first taste of the destruction. Far across the cavern, the wall separating Bat House from the ball court had disintegrated, unleashing a cloud of dust and a wall of flame that was now rolling across the city faster than a freight train.

Maddock scrambled to his feet, slipping on the lichen-covered floor, almost stumbling again. The pool was close, but the fire behind him felt even closer.

There was no sign of the others. He hoped that meant Bones had gotten them out in time.

A cry tore from his lips as the heat flashed to searing intensity. The blue lichen—the Light, though its glow was now wholly overwhelmed by the brilliance of the flames rushing through Xibalba—darkened and withered to ash all around him. The fire scorched his back; he thought he could feel his skin blistering and bubbling under his shirt. But even as it burned him, the fire was also his deliverance. The superheated air pushed him from behind, a hot wind driving him forward toward the pool and salvation.

As he fell forward into the water, he sucked in a desperate breath. The air, full of smoke and dust, burned in his lungs. He knew it would be his last breath for a while…maybe the last breath he would ever take. The water however was an instant relief, cool and embracing, quenching the heat and soothing his burned skin.

The fires above lit up the depths like daylight, revealing the underwater cave at the bottom of the pool, almost directly under the crashing waterfall. Maddock dove deeper, pulling himself toward it. Then the current caught him and he was sucked into the cave, swallowed by the darkness.

He could feel the sides of the submerged passage rushing past, scraping against him, and knew the most immediate danger was of being knocked senseless by a rocky protrusion, so he curled into a fetal ball, letting the river take him wherever it chose.

Time lost all meaning. Under normal circumstances and with adequate preparation, he could hold his breath for well over two minutes without discomfort, but the miasma he had breathed last in Xibalba was an unknown quantity. He could feel the acid burn of too much carbon dioxide in his bloodstream, and the spasms of his body demanding he exhale and replace it with fresh, oxygen-rich air. He fought the urge as long as he could, tried every trick he knew to fool himself into believing that he could hold out a little longer, and then, when he could fight no longer, he opened his mouth and blew out the foul breath in a final silent shout of defiance.

"Maddock!"

The shout brought him most of the way out of the dark void of unconsciousness. The slap did the rest.

He opened his eyes and found Bones staring back at him, so close their noses were almost touching. Drops of water were falling from Bones' hair like raindrops, landing on Maddock's cheeks and running into his eyes.

"If you were your sister," Maddock mumbled, "I'd kiss you."

Bones grinned. "Angel. He's asking for you."

Maddock blinked the water away and sat up...tried to sit up. A spasm of pain gripped him like a giant's fist.

"Easy, partner," Bones said. "You've probably got some bruised ribs. I know I do. That was some ride, huh?"

Maddock took a couple breaths and then tried to sit up again. He could see rough stone overhead, the ceiling of a cave, but the air was too fresh to be the trapped atmosphere of a closed environment, and the light was too bright to be from any artificial source. When he finally managed to bring himself to an upright position, he saw that the reality was something in between. They were in a cave of sorts, an open-air grotto where the subterranean river that had carried them out of Xibalba broke from the earth and spilled out into the Guatemalan rain forest.

He found Angel, sitting with Kasey and Miranda nearby. All three were shivering, probably coming down from their adrenaline high. For a long time, no one moved or spoke.

Bones finally broke the silence. "I'm afraid we ducked out before the credits rolled. What the hell happened?"

"I'm not really sure. There was an explosion. I don't know what caused it." He glanced over at Kasey.

Kasey shook her head. "Wasn't me. I never got the chance. It must have been Isabella. I wonder why she changed her mind."

"Maybe she realized what was at stake," Maddock said. "I guess you can report back to Tam, mission accomplished. Any idea where we are?"

Bones shook his head, but the question prompted him to stand. "Wherever it is, we're gonna have to walk out of here. It's going to be dark soon, so we should get moving."

Maddock stood as well, ignoring the groans of protest from his battered body. He reached out a hand to Angel, helping her up first, then turned to Miranda.

Her blond locks were plastered to her face, giving her a haunted, desolate look, like a war refugee, but when she gazed up at him, he saw no trace of anger in her eyes.

"I'm sorry," he said, offering his hand.

"I know." She took the hand, letting him draw her up. "I heard what you said to Scano. I think my father figured it out, too. He knew he was sick and that there wasn't a cure. He was telling us to leave him." She took a deep breath, let it out in a sigh.

"He was right about everything," Maddock said, hoping she would find some comfort in that. "The City of Shadow. Xibalba. At least he got to see it before…"

She nodded and managed a wan smile. Then, she turned to Bones and with no warning whatsoever, threw her arms around him, pressing her cheek against his chest.

"Whoa!" Bones' look of surprise quickly became a grin of mischief. "Hey, I didn't think you liked me that way."

"Bones!" Angel hissed in a stage whisper. "For once in your life, shut up."

"Thank you," Miranda murmured, still holding him. "For trying to save my father. After everything. I can't excuse what he did, but I'm glad he got to see Xibalba before it was over."

Bones' grin softened. Maddock thought he actually looked a little embarrassed. "Oh, sure. I mean, he didn't really…"

"Shh," Miranda whispered. "Listen to your sister. She's a smart girl."

EPILOGUE

The rural folk lived simply, as they had for countless generations, ever since the Shadow scourge brought the great empire of their ancestors to its knees. The Spaniards had come with their steel and their new God, but the people never forgot the old ways. From time to time, they would gather in the shadow of the ancient cave, the doorway to the Underworld, and remember anew. Over the centuries, the story had grown and changed with each telling, but none doubted that something both terrible and wonderful slumbered in the depths of the earth beneath them.

So, when the ground shook and a cloud of bats rose from the smoking jungle, the people of the land knew the ancient beast was stirring.

They had all had heard the noise of the great helicopter arriving earlier, and the sound of battle, and knew that the outsiders had done something to anger the spirits of the Underworld. They quickly gathered offerings of food and trinkets, and hurried up the road to assemble in the shadow of the living cave where they lit fires and danced around them, chanting prayers to the old gods and playing flutes to lull the ancient beast back to sleep.

And then, at almost exactly the same moment that the sun descended into the Underworld, their prayers were answered.

A low murmur rose across the cavern as the word spread, and all eyes turned to the forbidden balcony at the rear of the cave—the threshold of the passage into the depths.

A figure stood there, a woman so streaked with mud that she resembled one of the gods' failed experiments from the dawn of creation.

The murmur became a jumbled cacophony of awe and confusion. Was this one of the outsiders who had blasphemed the sacred paths into the Underworld? Or was it perhaps one of the Lords of Death, come to unleash the ancient Shadow scourge, the promised cleansing at the end of days?

One old man dared to approach, bowing his head reverently, just in case the latter proved to be true.

"Have you come from the Underworld?" He spoke in the old tongue, testing her.

She stared back at him for a moment, her dark eyes full of pain and confusion, then spoke a single word. "Yes."

The old man let out a wail of dismay and dropped to his knees, terrified. The woman was no outsider. She had understood him. She knew their language.

A hush fell over the crowd.

The woman gazed out at them for a moment, then took a deep breath and spoke again, louder so that her voice filled the cavern. Her speech was different than theirs, but it was similar enough for them to understand her words.

"Yes," she said. "I am the Priestess of the Serpent. Listen, and I will tell you of the heroes who journeyed into the Underworld to defeat the Lords of Xibalba."

End

ABOUT THE AUTHOR

David Wood is the author of the popular action-adventure series, The Dane Maddock Adventures, and many other works. Under his David Debord pen name he is the author of the Absent Gods fantasy series. When not writing, he co-hosts the Authorcast podcast. David and his family live in Santa Fe, New Mexico. Visit him online at http://www.davidwoodweb.com.

74156535R00170

Made in the USA
Middletown, DE
21 May 2018